Mike Lunnon-Woo
Australia and New Ze&
ten years before movir.
acterised by the quality of research he conducted, spending time with soldiers, sailors and airman in support of each book. Mike Lunnon-Wood passed away in 2008, survived by his son, Piers.

Also by Mike Lunnon-Wood:

The British Military Quartet made up of:

Let Not the Deep
King's Shilling
Long Reach
Congo Blue (originally published as Heraklion Blue)

Other fiction titles:

Dark Rose
Angel Seven
Somewhere Out There
The Protector

A PLACE TO DIE

Mike Lunnon-Wood

SILVERTAIL BOOKS ♦ *London*

This edition published by Silvertail Books in 2023
www.silvertailbooks.com
Copyright © Mike Lunnon-Wood 2023
1
The right of Mike Lunnon-Wood to be identified as the author of this work has been asserted in accordance with the Copyright, Design and Patents Act 1988
A catalogue record of this book is available from the British Library
All rights reserved. No part of this publication may be reproduced, transmitted, or stored in a retrieval system, in any form or by any means, without permission in writing from Silvertail Books or the copyright holder
978-1-913727-26-0

All characters in this publication other than those clearly in the public domain are fictitious and any resemblance to real persons, living or dead, is purely coincidental.

Foreword

No fictional story is completely fiction. There are always facts interspersed throughout any novel. In September of 1978, and again in February of the following year, surface-to-air missiles fired by terrorists brought down civilian airliners in Rhodesia (the country which is now Zimbabwe). Both aircraft had taken off minutes earlier from Kariba, on Rhodesia's northern border. The first occasion was certainly the more horrific of the two, because some survivors of the crash – only a handful of the luckiest on board – were later killed in unparalleled savagery by the same men who had shot down the aircraft. They were all civilians. Both times people walked clear of the site, and made their way to the nearest main road and subsequent safety.

There were, in fact, only two Grand Crosses of Valour ever awarded in Rhodesia's war years, and considering the everyday tales of extraordinary courage displayed by so many people, the honour of that award, equivalent to Britain's Victoria Cross, was honour indeed. It must therefore rank as one of the world's most difficult medals to earn, and it is with no disrespect to Captain C. Schulenberg GCV, SCR (Selous Scouts) or Major Grahame Wilson GCV, SCR, BCR (Rhodesian SAS) that I have taken an author's license in creating a third recipient of that award.

The characters and story told here are the product of my imagination and other than references to real people by characters in this story no resemblance to persons living or dead is intended, and any that may exist are coincidental.

There were, however, civilian airliners shot down at this time in Africa's history, there were survivors killed, there were civilians who fought back, and there were Selous Scouts. The Selous

Scouts were a special forces unit of the Rhodesian Army that operated during the Rhodesian Bush War from 1973 until the reconstitution of the country as Zimbabwe in 1980. Formed by Lieutenant-Colonel Ron Reid-Daly at the behest of Rhodesian military leader General Peter Walls, the Selous Scouts were to write their name into the annals of military history as one of the finest counterinsurgency units of all time.

1

1981

The first shaft of sunlight left patchwork squares high up on the wall as the old man shuffled down the passage, his bare callused feet on the polished red concrete floor. Without knocking or announcing his presence in any way he let himself in, crossed to the curtains and swung them open, and, looking about, finally crossed to the bedside table and put down the coffee.

The figure in the bed stirred briefly, and the old man said, 'Boss, time to get up,' and prodded the sleeper, grinning to himself as he enjoyed these brief moments of power.

A head separated from the pillow, and said, 'Piss off, Jackson.'

'Boss, the madam, she come 7 o'clock.'

'Jackson...'

'I know. Jackson piss off,' he interrupted, and turned towards the door and moved off, muttering to himself.

The man in the bed rolled over, sat up, and then swung his feet to the floor, and, immediately regretting the manoeuvre, sat with his head in his hands, hungover. He waited for a moment, and then blearily opened his eyes, stood up, crossed naked to the window, and looked down into the valley. Already it was warm, and in a few hours the game in the bush would start seeking shade from the sun.

He turned, yawned, scratched himself, and pulled the sheet off the bed. He wrapped it around his body, made his way down the passage to the kitchen. He stopped in front of the fridge, opened it and pulled out a very cold beer, bashed off the cap on the door catch, and took a long swig.

Jackson looked on disapprovingly, and eventually the man

said, '*Babalas,*' – hangover – and took another swig. The old man retained the mother hen look for a moment, and then grinned widely, his missing teeth testament to his own drunken nights and fights. He did, in fact, consider hangovers extremely amusing – as long as he wasn't the victim.

'The madam will go?' Jackson said.

'Which madam?'

Jackson nodded towards the living room, and proceeded to say how when he had been young he never forgot to satisfy a maiden who was willing.

'Jackson, when you are young there were no maidens. You mounted she-baboons in the bush.'

Jackson cackled, delighted with his master's grasp of history, and acceptance of his venerable age, and watched him walk delicately through the lounge.

Max Seager was 29 that year, but felt a great deal older. He was tall, just over six foot, and heavily muscled. His skin was burnt a lovely brown by the sun but he was carrying a few kilos more than he should have, and the bags under his eyes were the product of too many late nights. His thick brown hair was brushed straight back, but the stubble at his chin was fair. It was a lean face and when one looked into his eyes, one got the impression that, like so many policemen, he had seen too much. In spite of this he was quick to laugh, and his humour was at times sardonic and cynical.

He stopped in the centre of the room and surveyed the scene before him. The figure lay sprawled beneath a brightly printed fabric on the couch, one long elegant leg extended to the floor. From the opposite end the tasselled mane of auburn hair moved as the girl stretched like a cat, and the fabric was drawn slowly over and down her face. She peered, blinked and finally muttered, 'You must be Maxim. Was it a toga party, or do you always dress like that?'

He bellowed to the servant, 'Jackson, more coffee,' before turning back to the couch. 'Don't call me Maxim. My name is Max and you looked like something Picasso fucked up in that.' He was now grinning. It was a wide, honest expression and made him look like a little boy. Women loved it.

'Yes it's charming isn't it. Curtain, was it?'

They sat and drank coffee, and talked with the camaraderie of those who have been drunk together, never quite knowing what was said to whom, and so assuming everything was said, and now lifelong friends as a result.

She went home eventually, and he settled down to packing the things he was taking and decided what to leave and for whom.

That evening he was leaving the country. To his way of thinking not so much emigrating, or deserting, or even escaping like a refugee. He was leaving because it was no longer what it was, and like a man leaving his arm after an amputation, he would survive. He would just never be the same again.

He was born in 1951, part of the baby boom that had even affected the Crown colony of Southern Rhodesia. His father had been a farmer and after the war had settled a piece of brush down in the Tuli Circle area. The farm had never done well as a cropping concern and in the spring of 1954 Errol Seager had decided to breed cattle instead and announced the fact that the lunch table. He never looked back, and the farm prospered, his son by then a strapping healthy boy, had watched with fascination as the first Afrikander stock arrived by truck, and been completely awed by the ball, and in particular the size of its testicles. A herd boy had explained in Ndebele, the local language, that enormous sacks in fact contained two grapefruit, and any time the young boss Max wanted one to just go and pick it out.

Some two years later he tried and received a thunderous kick to his chest that should by all reason have killed him. It didn't but it cured any ambition of being a rancher, a decision his father tried constantly to change.

Time went by, and as he grew up he did as much as any on any Rhodesian farm, albeit with a healthy respect for bulls, but his decision was made. He wanted to be a policeman.

He grew fast and at the age of eight was as tall as many twelve-year-olds. He treated the farm as his own play area, and would run long distances to his own secret locations. He was a lonely boy, and when his friendships with the Black children his own age finally came, his parents didn't discourage the notion. He was very soon completely fluent in Ndebele, and the natural leader of his own little band.

Perhaps his strangest friendship was that with the aging father of the farm's 'spanner boy'. The old man would sit in the shade for hours, instructing his wide-eyed child in the ways of the Matabele kings, of hunting, of women, which he didn't really understand, and lastly and more importantly of the superstitions and crafts of the Ngangas, the healers.

The tuition was basic, and really no more than an introduction, but it was to serve Max well in the years to come, where as a Patrol Officer in the remote areas of the Zambezi valley, and later in the beerhalls of Bulawayo, he would have an uncanny understanding of the way the minds of the rural Blacks operated. The old man also taught the boy to read tracks, known here as spoor, and how to find honey in the bush, and many other things of interest to old men and small boys.

At the end of his eighth year he was sent away to boarding school, and from that day on the visits to the farm would be the happiest days of his life.

By his thirteenth year Max was a very good looking young man, his grey eyes and quick smile were noticed by girls older than he, but noticed no more than by a friend of his mother. She had come to visit the family from South Africa, and on this occasion had begun behaving strangely from the start. It had been three years since her last visit, and in that time Max had grown several inches, and matured tremendously. He was still, however, only a boy and her seduction took place one hot Saturday afternoon, while his parents were at a cattle sale, and the friend had feigned a headache.

Her name was Marcie. She was tall with thick brown hair, and long, tanned legs. She painted her toenails almost daily and it began that way on the veranda. One long leg drawn up, resting her chin on her knee she had looked up to see young Max staring intently between her thighs. Her skirt had tucked up, and the white edge of her panties showed, stark in contrast to the copper brown of her heavy thighs. She slowly relaxed the raised leg, and as his knee dropped to the side the gap between her legs grew and so did Max's eyes.

She continued the languid strokes of the polish brush across her manicured toes, and eventually asked the boy if he liked painted toenails.

He stammered a reply, and she asked him if he wanted to do it. He nodded and timidly stepped forward, going down on bended knee before her like she was a goddess. To Max she was, and when she said, 'Kiss my foot,' he did. She instructed him to kiss higher, and higher, until his face was inches away from her crotch, and when she held his head with one hand, and with the other pulled her panties to one side with a long, red fingernail, he closed his eyes, unable to believe what was happening. Four times that afternoon, in the heat of her bedroom, she showed him how to give her exquisite pleasure. And four times she gave him the same.

And so Max entered the first stages of manhood, and acquired skills and appetites that would plague his father, and left the district's parents breathing sights of relief when he finally left for the Police Training School at Morris Depot in Salisbury. Not everyone was so keen to see him go. Three or four of the district's raunchier wives who compared notes on these things thought it was the passing of an era, and one took to drink.

Immediately on arrival at Morris Depot, he was seen as something more than the average recruit, and proved it many times. His aptitude and ability to assimilate facts and present them surprised even the hardest sceptics, and six months later Max passed out as top recruit. He was posted to a remote Police Camp located near Binga, and his fluence in Ndebele was quickly put to use. He spent the next two years there, and by the time he was transferred to Bulawayo Central, he was a Section Officer in CID.

He had already begun to use his knowledge of witchcraft to help smooth the path for whatever investigation he was working on. Just the suggestion of it was enough to elicit cooperation from the hardest criminal, and Max knew he was onto a winner. For the rest of his time with the British South Africa Police he fed the rumours and never denied them, even to white colleagues. He was the officer who used the power of the Ngangas to catch thieves.

He was never short of girlfriends, but somehow he never seemed to get close to any of them. He was, however, very popular on the social circuit in Bulawayo, although always remaining slightly aloof from it. At twenty-four he applied for and was accepted into the rapidly expanding Special Branch, and was posted to Kariba, to all intents and purposes a very promising young officer, and being carefully watched from above by those men who choose who shall be promoted and who shan't.

And then the emergency increased and escalated into a war, and Max's little Special Branch operation suddenly became the centre for intelligence gathering for a theatre of anti-insurgency operations that involved hundreds of troops covering thousands of square miles. In the beginning he flourished and gained a reputation for good solid 'int' coming from a network of loyal Blacks and Special Branch constables deep in the Tribal Trust Lands.

Backing this up with his reputation for using witchcraft to smell out the *Gandangas* – the terrorists – the capture ratio in the Kariba Police District was disproportionately high. He was quickly promoted to Inspector and when he was twenty-six two things happened that significantly changed his life. His parents were killed in a car crash, following the detonation of a landmine, and he met Svea de Villiers, and fell in love.

The two events were related, of this there was no doubt. While not close to his parents in the traditional sense, they had always been there on the farm, and the infrequent trips Max had made back down to the Tuli Circle to see them had always been times of relaxation and a very real break from the pressures of his job. His mother, a woman who seemed to be perpetually baking or wandering through the large gardens with a pair of shears, assumed that he never ate from one trip home to the next and fed him vast quantities of food, and made pointed comments that it was time to find a nice girl and settle down.

His father, a quiet and thoughtful man with an eye for good lines in a cattle beast and a taste for malt whisky, would occasionally tell her to leave the boy alone, and sit and watch his son listen patiently to his mother's gossip.

When his parents slept during the hot afternoons, he would take the Land Rover and drive down to the dam, or visit the by now ancient Matabele at whose feet he had sat as a child and listened to the stories. The huts where the *madoda* – old man – lived were away from the main compound, high on the western slope of a small hill, and he was openly practicing the arts and crafts of the witch doctor, a practice officially frowned upon but still prevalent in rural areas.

On one visit the old man told Max that there were *Gandangas* in the area, and that the spirits told of a time when they that came in the night would rule. Max, a realist, knew this would be the case eventually. Majority rule would come.

That night, while his mother was in the kitchen, he told his father he believed there was a terrorist presence in the area. The next week, his father, who had a healthy respect for his son's ability to judge these things, erected a security fence, and installed a fire-park around the house. Errol Seager and his wife were never actually attacked while on the farm. He had the reputation of being a fair man who had spent money on building a school on his farm for the local children, a clinic for his labour force, although small, and paid well over the accepted wage. More to the point, he also had a reputation for being an outstanding rifle shot, a man who never missed what he aimed at, and when he had installed the fire-park he had done so in full view of his work force, knowing that the word would get back to the terrorists that this house was bad news.

The arrangement consisted of grenades mounted on poles eighteen inches above ground level immediately inside the fence, and spaced evenly. There were also eight home-made claymore mines in the network. Ploughshares embedded in concrete, with iron filings, nuts, bolts and other nasty, sharp bits of metal that would, upon detonation from the house, blast a swath in a 100-degree arc and kill anything within range.

Errol Seager didn't know the precise range because he never tripped any of the devices, but neither did anyone else, and as a deterrent to anyone wanting to attack the house it seemed to work.

Then in February of that year, the couple had been driving on a dirt road to visit friends. They were late, and Seager was driving faster than was his usual practice in order to arrive before dusk fell, at which point vehicles on the road would become sitting ducks for ambush. They hit the TM-57 anti-vehicle mine at the narrow edge to a cattle grid only six miles from the home of their friends.

The Land Rover, adequately mine protected with steel plating beneath the wheel arches, was blown into the air and landed on its roof, but because it was moving fast it skidded forty yards and finally impacted with a large granite boulder, a piece of which, like an accusing finger, penetrated the windshield, killing both the occupants.

The effect of the deaths of his parents on Max, who had always been something of a loner, was to drive him deeper into his shell, and he threw himself into his work with a vengeance. His arrest rate soared, and he drove his men with a seemingly endless source of energy. Eventually he was sent on leave by his Member-in-Charge, who began to fear for the health of his bright young department head.

It was while on leave that year in Durban, South Africa, that he had met Svea de Villiers, who by coincidence had just moved back to stay with her parents on a Karoi farm only an hour's fast drive Kariba. She was holidaying in Durban, and the pair met when Svea, sitting sipping a cold drink on the veranda of the Edward Hotel, had been singled out by two cocky young salesmen from Johannesburg as being available. When politely rebuffed, one had become insulting, and finally Max on the next table had turned and asked them to leave her alone. They began on him, and when one said, 'You just want to try to fuck her yourself, man!' Max had risen to his feet. The fellow had completely misinterpreted the lazy smile, and by the time he registered that the glitter in the slate-grey eyes was not humour, it was too late. Months of frustration burned itself out in one punch that left the salesman in the Royal Durban Infirmary with a broken jaw and needing seventeen stitches in his mouth.

The manager had asked Max to leave and as he had done so the girl followed him down the steps. She caught up with him outside on the pavement and thanked him for his intervention, and when he turned and looked at her, she got a funny, goosy feeling that she had recognised long ago as pure attraction.

He finally said, 'A bit of overkill, I'm afraid... he'll be okay.' He turned and walked over, then stopped, turned back, and said, 'Would you like an ice cream?'

While her mind whirled and wondered what sort of man in 1977 offered a girl an ice cream, she heard her own voice say, 'Yes, please.'

Svea was tall and big-boned and a natural honey blonde, and where the sun had bleached her hair it was yellow like farm butter. Her eyes were very large and cornflower blue, and the faint freckles across her nose were accentuated by the deep tan. She was high-breasted with wide hips that dropped away to long legs. Her thighs were heavier than she would have wished, but the calves were perfect, and her feet were slender with the toenails painted apricot. Max noted this when she stopped to pull her sandals off, and approved. He had always liked painted nails but was never very sure why.

For the rest of the time they had been virtually inseparable, swimming, walking, eating together. Svea had begun to draw him out of himself, and she loved to hear him laugh. On the third day they were eating hot dogs and she spilled mustard down her shirt front. He pulled a hankie out and cleaned the offending liquid away, and when he looked up she was watching him and completely at a loss for words. He did the next thing he could think of. He kissed her, and that night they made love in the double bed in his room. She was initially terrified at the ferocity of his passion, but as things progressed, he calmed down and was more gentle. By the end of the week he was completely and hopelessly in love, and she knew it and was delighted. She had felt like that by the end of her first ice cream cone.

They travelled back to Rhodesia together, and spent their first night back in Max's house on the heights over the lake, and the next day he had driven her back to her parents' farm outside Karoi.

Svea's arrival back on the de Villiers farm always managed to throw the place into a happy turmoil, with her father escaping out to the lands until the place had quietened down. Mother chatting, servants greeting, dogs barking, and today's arrival was no different, even as it dawned on Svea's parents that this was the young man their daughter had told them of on the phone.

John de Villiers was in the local Police Reserve, and an active member of the Police Anti-Terrorist Unit in the area. He spent most of his time while on service working on intelligence leads generated by Kariba's Inspector Seager, and held the name in awe. If Seager said there were hostiles in a kraal line – a line of huts – then there were. Simple as that. He was delighted to offer his hospitality and the evening was long and drunken, Svea sitting at Max's feet on the living room floor, his hands running through the hair at the back of her neck, and the other nursing one of her father's enormous Scotches, produced for the occasion.

Max spent the night in the spare room, and although getting up twice to take phone calls, was rested and away by dawn, back to Kariba. Only the next day did the district gossip tell that Support Unit had contacted a large group some thirty miles from the farm, moving towards Chinamora Tribal Trust Lands, and some police chap from Kariba had a confirmed visual sighting of the tail end of the group off in the bush, and had called in the helicopters from the temporary base at Makuti.

A pattern soon developed, Max driving down a couple of evenings a week, until the spare room began to pall, and sneaking through to Svea in the night, while exciting, was not ideal, and he suggested she move into his place on the heights. She agreed, to the dismay of her mother, and so began the happiest years of Max's life.

2

The next two years sped by and Seager was to many observers a changed man. He slowed his walking pace enough for his Black staff to breathe a sigh of relief, for surely the Nangas had advised this, and for his more senior colleagues it was sly grins, and comments such as, 'Seager's smitten, thank Christ for that... the man wasn't mortal.' He surprised his Sergeant Major to the point of speechlessness one morning by stepping over a sweating terrorist suspect, doing press-ups in the sun, and as he did so, patting the man's filthy dreadlock-covered head and greeting him with a cheery, 'Good morning, munt.'

The house on the heights became a home. Its previous style of occupancy seemingly gone forever. It was a bachelor's house, with more beer in the fridge than food, and clothes strewn all over the floors. Max's servant picked them up and washed them, but that's where the cleaning stopped. Its masculine rooms were dusty, and the furniture and fittings were functional but with no thought given to appearance.

'It's comfortable,' Max had lamented as Svea threw out one old chair. She fired the servant and sent for an old man currently working on her father's farm. He had just retired from the army and was as crusty about cleanliness as she was, but of a rough and ready fashion that she knew Max would appreciate. He was Jackson Kariba, a Matabele and a man, and on his arrival they swept through the house like a storm. Within days it was ready. Curtains and drapes erected, new furniture installed with a little more regard to aesthetic appeal than the previous mismatched collection.

Food replaced the beer which was relegated to the fridge in

the garage, and suddenly it was no longer just a place where Max went to sleep. It was home, and few things gave him more pleasure than entering it.

Each evening he seemed to discover something new about this woman he loved. One night she was sitting on the veranda with a tiny bushbuck in her lap wrapped in a towel. It had been savaged by a dog, and when it died that night she cried. But that was not the end of the issue. The next day she surprised him by reeling off statistics of animals trapped in the poachers' snares, and announced that she was going to do something about it. She did, and began it by inviting to a braai the two local parks board chaps, people that Max had a nodding acquaintance with. The four became close friends, with Svea's harassment of them for not actually keel-hauling poachers as the butt of many jokes. She became active in the local conservation group, taught herself to paint in oils, and after throwing the first twenty canvases in the bin, bought them both a bottle of whisky with the proceeds from the first sale. They sat on the veranda that night and drank it, and finished the day making love in the big room overlooking the lake. Svea was, to Max, a constant source of stimulation, affection and love, and he reciprocated with a conviction that surprised even himself.

It was a situation that was not to last.

The war was intensifying, and by September of 1979, Max was rarely home. When he was, he seemed to brood for hours over his work, and Svea's ability to draw him out of it now seemed to be lost. He began taking her for granted and they began fighting.

The final straw came the following April when the Member-in-Charge, Max's boss and closest friend, was replaced by a Black officer of dubious ability. His appointment was political, and made a farce of good policing. He had called Max into his office for the third time in a week and attacked his professional ability. It had been too much for Max, who had walked out and gone and gotten drunk at the bar at Caribbea Bay. Three months later he resigned, but the damage was done. Svea had left, after announcing she was tired of Max's immaturity and he knew where to find her when he grew up.

He was too proud to admit she was right, and the days became weeks and the weeks months. Max began spending more time in the bush with Andre Van Wyk, who by now had left the Parks and Wildlife Department, and was running photo safaris. What time he spent in Kariba was painful, with the house a monument to his lost happiness. A hundred times he picked up the phone to call her, and when he eventually did, she told him she had met someone and they were going to get engaged. Max spent his time in the bush, silently and often deep in thought and it was testament to his friendship with Andre Van Wyk that Andre never mentioned the subject.

The country, by now governed by a party selected by the majority, was in a time of flux and change. Things were beginning to deteriorate, but what most concerned Max was that he was virtually unemployable. His career was over, and he now had too many enemies in the new regime to stay in the country indefinitely. After several months of consideration he decided to leave and start over somewhere else, like thousands of Rhodesians had done before him. The time had quickly passed, and with his hurt over Svea now a dull ache rather than actual pain, he set about making plans to go to Australia. It was simple enough. Pack a few things, exchange whatever currency he could, pull out the black market dollars he had been collecting, and go. And so he would. Tonight.

Svea arrived at noon, walking in as if she had never left. She had lost weight, and was very brown from the sun, but the unhappiness was in her eyes.

'I wasn't going to come...' she said.

'Yes you were. You phoned,' Max interrupted smugly.

'Only to tell your savage what to do for lunch, you pig!' she retaliated, and then she saw the laugh in his eyes and began to giggle.

'Hello, Max,' she offered.

'Hi, babe...'

She walked closer, and after a moment said, 'You're really going, aren't you, Max?'

He nodded, saying nothing. She came closer, and put her head against his chest and began to cry, the months of pain washing out of her.

'Hush, hush, baby. You're supposed to be happy. I hear you're getting married soon...'

She put her finger to his lips. 'Let's not talk about that Max. Please?'

And now here she was again.

They had carried a blanket out and eaten lunch under a big mopani tree, its thick foliage allowing occasional beams of sunlight through that dappled the ground like a leopard's spots and picked out highlights in Svea's hair. They had talked and laughed and eaten the food, Max tearing apart the cold chicken and handing pieces to her, and eating himself with an appetite that always surprised her. She liked watching him eat, because he did it seemingly without tasting, like a Jumbo Jet taking on fuel until the tanks were full, stopping only when he wanted to talk.

They drank cold white wine, a bottle of De Wetshof Sauvignon Blanc that he had hoarded from a shopping trip over the border in South Africa. For all his inability to taste food or appreciate it, Max certainly knew what wines he liked (and had once admitted to Svea that he had considered becoming a vintner). As the afternoon wore on, they got quietly mellow, and when the ants came across the blanket, towards the remains of the chicken, she to to her feet and, taking his hand, walked back to the house.

They made love on the bare mattress in his room, their sweat mingling like their lives had done, and afterwards Svea slept and he lay awake and watched her, etching her into his memory, because for Max Seager there would never be another one like this one.

Late in the afternoon she awoke and dressed, and without saying anything they walked out to the car. He gave her his collection of Nat King Cole albums, and a small present wrapped in brown paper. It contained a simple gold ring with a solitaire diamond, which he had bought as an engagement ring two years before but never got round to giving her. Svea dropped it into her pocket without looking, and, afraid to speak because of what she felt, drove away without looking back.

Which was just as well, because cowboys don't cry. It says so in the books, and Max had just run his hand across his eyes as if wiping away a tear.

He walked back into the kitchen, pulled a case of beer from the fridge, carried it onto the veranda, and as the sun began to fall over the lake, he cracked the cap from the first one and began to get drunk, listening to the elephants below the road.

Peit and Andre arrived as the sun fell, and the three of them sat and finished the case, and then began another. They spoke little, and eventually Peit finally said, 'Ro endegi... we better go.'

Jackson carried the bags to the car, and when Max, having had a last look around, walked out, he was by the gate, standing rather formally to attention.

'It is time, old one,' said Max.

'It is time, *Sekuru*,' said Jackson.

'You have money?'

'Yes, I have money.'

'When you finish here, go to the farm of boss Peit, he has three *mombes* for you.'

'Thank you, *Sekuru*,' said Jackson, grateful for the parting gift of three cattle, '*hamba gashle*.' Walk slowly and take care.

'*Hamba, gashle, Madoda.*' Go well, old one.

As Max turned, the old man drew up to full height and came to a snappy salute that proved his twenty years in the army hadn't been wasted, maintaining it till the Land Rover had passed through the gate and was moving down the road towards the lake, and the airport.

Peit and Andre said their goodbyes, gruffly and with a forced casualness, the way good friends do, exchanging addresses and making rendezvous for meetings they all knew they would never keep.

Within the hour Max was on the Harare flight, and within two was in the international departure lounge at the capital's airport, perched on a stool and drinking heavily, awaiting the boarding-call for his flight to Johannesburg.

Max was not a heavy drinker by habit, but on this particular evening he seemed to display all the signs. The orders were all for doubles, no ice, and with just the merest hint of a tonic over the massive gins. He was a man with a mission, and he succeeded admirably. By the time the flight was delayed and re-scheduled, and then finally boarded, he was as pissed as a rat, with his slow grin and boyish smile only occasionally masking the deep sadness he felt at leaving everything he loved.

It was the smile that got him onto the plane. The senior of the four cabin crew had experience with drunks, and while she may ordinarily have turned most passengers away from the door in that state, Max's smile broke the ice and she waved him to a seat at the rear where she could keep an eye on him.

He fell into the seat and went straight to sleep, and masking her own grin, she strapped him in herself. Her name was Jackie Sealdon and there was only one man in the world she loved and that was her big brother. He also had sad grey eyes.

As she turned to leave, she looked again and brushed a lock of hair from his face with her hand as a mother might do to her child, and then walked up the cabin to the three VIPs that Passenger Relations had advised her of.

As much as his smile got him onto the plane, Max's inebriated state certainly saved his life. In placing him at the rear, Jackie bypassed his seating placement of row 28, seat c, which was just as well because exactly four minutes later the aircraft impacted with the ground and row 28 was in the middle of a concertina effect that left all its occupants dead.

They weren't alone. Of the airliner's sixty passengers and seven crew, forty-nine of them died on impact or shortly afterwards.

In years to come, Max would, on the rare occasions that someone could convince him to talk about it, sheepishly admit that he had slept through the whole nightmare occurrence.

What he didn't know, when he came to an hour after the impact, was that the nightmare had only just begun.

The wreckage was, surprisingly, confined to a relatively small area. It was in five major pieces, with a myriad of smaller items of debris still on fire or smouldering. It was one of these pieces of smouldering wreckage that Max first saw when he came to.

He had considerable trouble focusing on the flickering object, and it was partly the effect of all the alcohol consumed in the previous hours, and partly concussion received as a result of a blow to the back of the cranial dome during the aircraft's careering passage over the ground prior to its breaking up.

The offending item was a Samsonite briefcase, which now lay roughly eight feet to Max's right, although he would never know what had hit him. He was sitting, leaning against a large rock, when his eyes eventually did focus on the scene around him, and he realised immediately what had happened.

'Sweet Jesus,' he muttered, and began to rise slowly to his feet. He promptly fell over as waves of nausea washed over him. He tried again, and a voice said, 'Steady there, sit down. I'll get the doctor.'

Max turned and looked up at the speaker. It was a woman, and in the flickering light all he could tell was that she had very short hair.

'No... wanna geddup.'

'Young man do as you are told!' It was a no-nonsense voice, and as Max did as he was told, he grinned to himself.

'I'll get the doctor. He wants to have a look at you.' She moved off and Max immediately, if groggily, stood up and began gingerly walking about, shaking his head as if to clear his mind.

He was recuperating rapidly, as those who are young and fit do. By the time the woman returned he was taking the in scene with the analytical mind of the man he was. She was joined by another figure, this time a man. He was tall, Max's own height, brisk and business-like.

'Up and walking. Good! Slowly slowly, if you please... Right, let's see that cut. Head down.' He flicked on a torch briefly, then lifted Max's face and shone it into his eyes, looking for a reaction.

'Can't do anything about the cut. Headache?' he asked.

'Yes. A beauty,' Max said.

The doctor chuckled, and said, 'Half the bump and half hangover I would say. Just sit down for a while.'

'No,' said Max. 'I want to do something. How long have we been down?'

'About an hour. And thirty-six lifetimes... so far.'

'What can I do?'

'Nothing. Just sit.'

'Bullshit to that, Doc.'

The doctor sighed. 'All right,' he said tiredly. 'There is something you can do. Over there is a young girl. She is dying and there is nothing I can do for her. Just go and sit with her, talk to her. It won't be long now. Will you do that for me?'

Max nodded, and moved off in the direction the doctor had indicated.

The night was very dark, and he picked his way carefully using the light from the odd piece of still-burning debris where he could. He hit his shin against something sharp, and heard the familiar tinkle of glass above his muttered curse. He bent and investigated and found he had a virtually intact beverage trolley right in front of him, end up but with much of its contents undamaged.

He moved on an eventually found the girl. She was sitting, her back supported by a section of a wing, her lower body covered by a cabin blanket. Max went straight back to the trolley and ripped back one of its buckled drawers, and began to rummage through the contents. Taking two handfuls of miniatures, he walked quickly back to the girl, stopping at a suitcase lying forlornly spilt on the ground. He took two large garments and made his way to where the girl lay, spread the first piece of cloth on the ground, pulled the top from the miniature and sprinkled the contents over it. He did the same again, this time smelling the liquid, and grinning to himself. He then rolled it into a tight ball and poured a third bottle over it, before setting it on the ground in front of them. The whole time the girl seemed to watch dispassionately.

Finally, he produced an aging Zippo lighter and set the little bundle alight. It immediately began to burn cheerfully, and he turned and looked at his charge for the first time in any kind of light.

'Hi,' he said. 'I'm Max. Can I sit with you?'

The girl looked puzzled. In the fire light the man looked familiar. She smiled weakly and nodded very gently, before closing her eyes for a moment. Across her forehead someone had written something. Max looked closer and made out the word MORPHINE 12, and a scrawl. He made a mental note that the doctor was organised, and looked down at the blanked. The mid-section was red with blood, and the stain was slowly spreading.

'Why did they do it again?' she asked in a little voice.

'Do what, my girl?'

'It's finished... why again?'

'Shush now.'

'Stella.'

'Hello Stella. I'm Max.'

'No, not Stella... John saw it. He said.'

The fire was dying down, and Max pulled another miniature from his pocket and added it to the flames. It flared blue and white, and in the dancing light Max saw she was wearing the uniform of a stewardess, and she seemed to stare vacantly into the darkness. He took her hand, she squeezed his, and said, 'You're like my big brother...'

Max sat and held her hand, and twenty-five minutes later she died. That made Jackie Sealdon the forty-ninth death that night, and the last person to die of injuries directly attributable to the crash.

But then the day was only forty-three minutes old, and a lot can happen in a day.

3

Max sat with her a moment longer, then got to his feet and went off into the night to find the doctor. He stopped once or twice, when the clouds allowed the moon a fleeting chance to gently illuminate the area. Each time he looked about himself at the vegetation and the ground surface, and tried for a horizon, each time trying to establish where they were. Depending on the route taken by the aircraft, they could be anywhere in the lowveld, and almost certainly still in Zimbabwe.

But from what he had seen, it was not lowveld-type bush. Too sparse, too abused, more the type of stuff found in a tribal trust land. He found the doctor, who was tending a group of people lined up in shallow depression, all prone, and some very still indeed.

He was bent over a man, changing the rough dressing on a sucking chest wound. There were the low cries of lightly wounded but deeply shocked victims and several of the figures in the line-up were already dead, their faces covered with whatever came to hand, an attempt to give the death a dignity it had lost in its own mechanics, of haemorrhage, crushed bones, severed tissue and the smell of the excrement released when the bodies' muscles finally and irrevocably relaxed.

The doctor stepped over one such victim and bent to look at the next live one.

'Stella's dead,' said Max.

The doctor looked up at him, and Max squatted. 'Stella the stewardess. She died a few minutes ago.'

'Oh. Thank you for doing that for me. Her name was Jackie. She was only a child...' He bent and began to move his fingers lightly along the lower abdomen of his patient, felling for swelling.

'Anything I can do?' Said Max.

'Yes,' replied the doctor. 'See if you can find anything for these people to drink. There is a group of unhurt over there at the base of that rock. Make them all drink something if you can. All right?'

Max nodded, and moved off, heading back to the beverages trolley he had so recently plundered.

As he moved, he was thinking, juggling pieces that didn't fit. He remembered the last time he had walked through the wreckage of a crashed airliner. Smaller but just as violent. It was Vickers Viscount, one of several owned and operated by Air Rhodesia, and when he had walked through its remains it had been scattered across the sparse, rocky bush in the tribal trust lands below Kariba, three years previously. He remembered a young soldier crying, and a civil aviation expert called Hoskins, who shuffled over and told him it wasn't a crash. It wasn't an accident. It was deliberate.

He remembered asking if it was a bomb, and he remembered Hoskins saying no, it wasn't a bomb, it was a missile. Surface-to-Air Missile Type Seven, probably. The Sovbloc military alpha duo-syllabic designation was Strella, and it was very effective within its operating limitations.

The Rhodesians had never really believed that anyone would shoot down a civilian airliner. Even towards the end they were still surprised at the barbarity of the acts committed in its name.

Max approached the trolley, and began plundering its contents a second time, his thoughts on what the stewardess had said.

'John saw it... he said so.'

He thought about her, a young girl lying dead under a man-made fabric blanket in the middle of nowhere. He never even

knew her surname. Stella who? No, not Stella. Jackie. Jackie who? Where did he get Stella from? Ah, yes. She had said Stella. Duo-syllabic like the other. He kept thinking over her words.
'Why again... John saw it... he said why again...'
No, not Stella. She said Strella. STRELLA. STRELLA.
Oh, sweet Jesus, not again, not a fucking missile.
'John saw it, he said why again?'
A missile again?
Stella. Strella. STRELLA. STRELLA. STRELLA.
And then he was up on his feet again and moving.

He ran back into the depression fast and lightly, belying his size and moved straight to the doctor.

'That was quick. Did you get the water or something?'

'No,' Max said. 'Not yet. Listen, Doc, are any of the cockpit crew still alive?'

'No. They are all dead.'

'Are you sure?'

'Of course I'm sure,' the doctor nearly snarled.

'Did you know their names?' The doctor frowned and Max gripped the man's arm. 'DID YOU KNOW THEIR NAMES?'

'What is this about?'

'DID YOU?'

'No... but Jackie asked after them. The one was Captain Farlow or Thurlow or something, one was Carl, and one was John.'

'Are you sure?'

The doctor looked at Max, and in the flickering light the man's eyes seemed to glitter. 'Yes,' he said. 'I am sure those are the names she asked after.'

There was a pause, and eventually Max said to himself, 'They did it again.'

He stood up, and brushed his hand through his hair, wincing

when he touched the cut. 'I'll get those drinks,' he said, wandering away.

Now at the trolley for the third time, Max worked quickly and silently. He separated all the bottles into two piles, one alcoholic and the other soft. He then took one third of the soft drinks, dropped them into his shirt front and walked back to the small party in the depression.

He squatted before the doctor, who was by now with an elderly man bleeding from his head, and with clear plasma suppurating from a burn down the side of his face and neck.

Max dropped half the drinks on the ground, the tins and bottles making an inappropriately festive little tinkle as they hit.

'Doctor, I have reason to believe this aircraft was revved.'

The man looked up, tiredness overriding all else in his face. 'What did you say?'

'We were revved. Shot down. Attacked. This aircraft was hit by a missile or missiles.'

'Young man, you are concussed...'

'No, I'm not. I'm fine. And I have reason to believe –'

The doctor interrupted him. 'Who would do such a thing? Don't be ridiculous.'

By this stage, the woman with the no-nonsense voice had joined them from the group further up the line.

She introduce herself. 'I'm Sister Mary Theresa, Chilundi Mission.'

'That's nice,' said Max, rather patronisingly. 'Look, Doctor, Jackie said several things.'

'She was dying and people say strange things. Now, please, don't be ridiculous.'

'They fucking well did it before – twice!' Max said, raising his voice higher than he'd intended to. 'Now I'm going to talk to those people up there.'

He moved off quickly, as did Sister Mary Theresa, visibly upset by what she had heard. Almost as soon as she had gone Max reappeared and squatted down beside the doctor.

'Doc, I'm sorry I shouted, but this is the sitrep. These hills about are full of caches left from the war. All it needs is some trigger happy terrorist with a SAM Seven, and it's done. They are pathetically simple to use and devastatingly effective. Look around you. Now then, it's unlikely that any tribesmen got hold of one or two of these things. So it's probably army people. Their discipline is atrocious, and some of them would do this just to see if it works. Either way, come dawn we are going to have visitors and either way there can't be witnesses to this. Whether it was a breach of discipline, or on orders for some reason, we are all in grave danger staying here. The first people at this scene may not be rescuers. They well be the perpetrators. Do you copy me, Doctor?'

The man said nothing, just stared off into the night.

Max stood and move off towards the big rock to find the unhurt. They deserved to know the situation, and he would tell them.

He found them sitting quietly in the dark, on first appearances as if waiting patiently for a bus. Once closer, he did a quick head count, and quickly looked them over. On the left there was a middle-aged couple. He was thin and slightly built, his thinning grey hair neatly parted. He wore rimless spectacles and watched Max's approach earnestly, as if expecting good news. The woman sat immediately in front of him and was swaying back and forth in a bovine fashion. Her eyes had the strange, vacant quality one sees in victims of shell-shock, when the brain simply shuts down operations. The senses retreat in complete disarray while the brain tries to assimilate the latest horror, quantify it, and act on the information. Sometimes the brain just can't handle the data, and once it reaches that stage of horrific, like a computer with an insoluble equation it churns itself to exhaustion. Whether in milliseconds or months, the effect is the same. It can right itself very quickly or be that way until external help aids it in sorting the images into forms the organism can handle. This woman, Max could see, was certainly a casualty, if only in the mental sense.

Max immediately classified her as a problem and swept his view to the right. A much younger woman sat cross-legged. Her wide thighs were well tanned, and where her lap should have been lay a child, cradled between her legs. A little blonde head with a mass of curly hair snuggled in towards the woman's stomach stirred briefly, and the woman's hand dropped and stroked the little body, which was wrapped in what looked to be an overcoat of some kind.

The woman looked up at Max and smiled. She was blonde like the child and well groomed. Her hair was tied at the nape of her neck and although heavier than she could have been, she was certainly attractive.

Max smiled. That's better, he thought, and as he turned to the far right, a match flared in the dark, and for the first time he got a good look at another one of the party. She was young, very attractive, and perched on a rock, one elegant leg over the other like it was the most natural thing in the world to survive air accidents in the African bush. Her hair was dark and cut so it fell either side of her face like Garbo in her heyday. Her eyes were alive, and as the match died she blew a stream of smoke nervously into the night.

Christ, though Max, the stiff upper lip and all that.

Now his grin broadened, and he crouched down, balancing on the balls of his feet. The group, with the exception of the older woman, were all looking at him. Fuck it, he thought, I'll tell it how it is.

'My name is Max, and I want you all to listen very carefully to what I have to say.'

He paused, checked that he had all their attention, and then continued, telling them that he believed the crash was no accident, and that he felt for the safety it might be a good idea to move off into the bush a bit, and see who came at first light before exposing themselves.

'But who would do such a thing?' demanded the old man from behind his companion.

'It's been done before,' said Max.

'I believe I know of the incidents of which you speak. Firstly, they took place during a war, and secondly, I'm not so sure they actually took place at all. My wife and I have many friends amongst the natives and I can't imagine any man doing this to his fellow man. I am of the cloth,' he added somewhat unnecessarily, and then introduced himself. 'I am the Reverend Collingwood, and this is my wife Frances.'

Max nodded as if he expected nothing else, and said, 'Well, in ten minutes I'm going. If any of you wish to join me you are welcome. I would seriously recommend it.'

He turned and was walking away when the mother spoke.

'I'm not sure that you are entirely correct,' she said. 'But I've lived in Africa all my life and nothing is impossible. If you don't mind, my daughter and I will join you.' And again the smile.

'Not at all, Mrs?'

'Johnson. Helen Johnson. And this is Sarah.'

'Fine. I'll get a few things and be back in a minute. Then we'll go.'

Then the svelte creature on the rock spoke. 'Can I come? I feel like a walk.'

Christ, thought Max, she thinks this is the bottom end of daddy's estate. 'Sure you can,' he said.

'I'm Vicki Waters. You are?'

'Seager. Call me Max. I'll be back shortly. Can you walk in those shoes?'

'They will be all right. We're not going far, are we?'

Max gave a half-smile and moved off into the dark, towards where the body of the stewardess lay and where he had found the beverage trolley.

He knew exactly what he was searching for, and in only a few minutes was looking for the doctor, a light climber's pack hung over one shoulder. Its original contents were strewn across the wreck site, and Max had repacked it with the items he wanted.

He found the doctor leaning tiredly against a tree within sight of the row of wounded. A cigarette lay perched between his lips, and as Max approached he took it out and said, 'I think you are right.'

Max, expecting another battle to convince him, was stunned. 'What?'

'I said I think you are right.'

'Why?' Max asked quickly, the ex-Special Branch Inspector never far below the surface.

The doctor took another puff on the cigarette and said, 'One of the dead, before he died was very concerned about his briefcase. Wouldn't let the good sister take it from him. After he died I had a look.'

'Well?'

'Seen the papers recently?'

'No. I've been in the bush. Why?'

'The Maiden Commission. A Brit and American fact finding team looking at their aid and its uses. Depending on the Commission's findings all British and American aid to this country could stop immediately. This is the report – here in this case.'

He held it up in the moonlight.

'And?' Urged Max.

'The last thirty pages are conclusion. I went for that. It is very damning and I would say that it would spell the end of aid to this little banana republic.'

'That's reason enough,' said Max. 'Those bastards could salt away millions in the next year. They would kill to get another year's handouts.'

'I would have put it more articulately, but I concur.' He paused, and then said, 'You had better be on your way. Dawn in the next three hours or so.'

'I'm taking three of them. The reverend's wife?'

'Leave her. A liability in that state. I'll get them down here after you've gone. I hope you're wrong. I surely do.'

'Why don't you come? There's nothing more you can do here,' said Max.

'Hippocratic oath and all that,' the doctor smiled ruefully. 'Couldn't leave them, not after what they've been through.' He put out his hand. 'Good luck.'

'Thanks,' Max said quietly, and turned to walk away. As he did so, the man spoke again.

'Do something for me will you. Phone my wife. Cochran's the name. We're in the book. Just tell her... tell her...'

He trailed off, but his expression said plenty. *You'll know what to tell her, what to say.* Max nodded just the once, and moved off into the night.

4

Max went quickly back to the group, stopping twice on the way at large suitcases and rifling through the contents and selecting items. It was clothing he was after, dark coloured or greens and browns. It was difficult to tell in the dark, so using the acid test for any camouflage he threw it onto the ground and whatever was difficult to see, he thrust in the pack.

A minute or two later he wandered very casually into the rocks and said in a cheerful tone, 'Right, let's go walkies.'

Mrs Johnson rose to her feet, her sleeping child squirming briefly in the coat. 'Can we head for water?' She said. 'Sarah will be thirsty when she wakes.'

Max liked that. Thinking ahead. 'Organised already,' he said.

'Miss Waters, are you ready?' Said Mrs Johnson.

'Yes... hold on. Any herds of lions around here?'

'They come in prides, and I shouldn't think so,' said Mrs Johnson patiently, adding, 'Would you agree Mr Seager?'

Max looked at her, and even in the bad light could see the twinkle in her eyes, the humour lying just below the surface.

'Absolutely,' he said. 'Haven't seen a herd of lions in these parts for days.'

'You two,' said the girl, hand on hip, 'are taking the piss.'

Helen Johnson gave a low chuckle, turned to Max and said, 'Lead on Macduff,' and as they moved past the Reverend and his still swaying wife, she said, 'We're off for a walk. We'll see you in the morning.'

Max kept them moving, picking their way slowly through the rocks until at one point the whole southern part of the sky cleared of the moving cloud and he got a bearing.

'Right, this way,' he said, stepping up the pace a little.

'Which way?' Asked Helen. Max pointing in the direction they were moving.

'How can you tell?' She said.

'Got a look at the stars a minute ago and picked out the Southern Cross. We go this way, which means we're moving east.'

'Oh goody,' chimed in Miss Waters. 'If we go far enough we can have a G&T at Raffles.'

Max turned and gave her a withering glance. She lowered her head and gave a little, 'Sorry,' and watched him from under raised eyebrows. He eventually grinned and she burst into laughter. It was a rich, pealing sound and was very infectious. Soon he joined in.

They lapsed into silence again, and when Max thought they were just over a mile from the wreck he swung them left and up the sides of a kopje. It was a long, gentle rise that levelled off with a small plateau one third of the way up. Here he had them stop, and he turned and said, 'Okay. Let's rest here and see what the dawn brings. I'm going up the hill to watch. It will be light soon and if I'm right, then I'm going to go back and try for some more stuff so I don't want you people to move. Say here till I get back. Helen, in the pack you'll find some tins of drinks and bottles from the wreck. You will also find some practically coloured clothing. Change what you can. You especially, Miss Waters. Get rid of that white sweater.'

'I will not,' she retorted. 'It's cashmere!'

'It may well be, but it's also visible from half a mile. So please change it.'

She went silent for a moment, and then said softly, 'You really think they're going to do something awful, don't you?'

Max nodded.

'A gut feeling or something more?' She asked.

'A little circumstantial evidence. But, as you said, mostly gut feeling. I used to make my living that way, by believing my instincts. And this, Miss Waters, stinks of something very nasty.'

'Please call me Vicki,' she said, with forced normality, then added, 'In an hour it will be too warm for the bloody jersey anyway.'

Max smiled his thanks and moved up the hill with long and easy loping strides. He looked very competent and very strong, and suddenly she was glad he was there.

Max eventually settled in a small depression on the western slope of the hill. Below him he could see the slope fall away. At first light the whole area would be visible. For the first time since the crash he was alone and had time to think, and he used it as best he could. He began by going through his pockets. Swiss Army knife, lighter, matches to replace the lighter that was very fickle, some coins and notes, his passport, traveller's cheques, and a worn receipt from somewhere or other.

He looked around. The ground they had covered was sparse, abused. That would make it Tribal Trust lands, but how far south? Daylight would offer assistance because the vegetation would give a clue, and then what? Find a road? No, he thought, that could be hostile. Let's wait and see. He wished he had taken his binoculars from the Land Rover at the airport, and he wished it wasn't two women and a child with him, but most of all he wished it hadn't happened.

Because Max's mind was stuck on a question: had they done it before? The answer came from his own memories.

The chopper had landed them very close. There was Max Seager, his Member in Charge, a fellow called Sandy Gaul, and

Sergeant Major Chibanda. The disaster was in their administrative area and it was their scene for the policing effort.

Overhead, the Police Air Wing single-engine was still circling as it had been since finding the wreck half an hour earlier, impotent and angry. The crew on board had called in the reaction force and then waited, unable to help further.

The helicopter had put troops onto the ground to secure the area and assist as the first civilian specialists were called from their homes and their gin and tonics.

The young soldier was resting on his haunches, the backs of his thighs tight to his calves. He balanced himself on his rifle, its camouflage paint job a copy of the fatigues he wore. They themselves were cut down, the shirt sleeveless, and the shorts more at home on a rugby field. He wore training shoes without socks and a face veil was wrapped round his head keeping the sweat from his eyes. He was young, probably a year ago in school, but his eyes were old. He leant on the rifle but own in the dirt, so it was like a crutch, the wiry muscles in his forearms contoured in the flickering light of the flares like a Michelangelo sculpture.

An aircraft returning home from a resort full of happy, laughing people crashing and killing many is a tragedy fit to undermine the faith of the most resolute. To have lived through it would have been reason enough for life, by any standard.

But to have lived through it and then be put to death for no more than surviving the experience would be unthinkable.

That's why the young soldier was crying.

He had seen attacks on soft targets before. He had seen the weak and the helpless become victims, he had seen his own friends and comrades die or be maimed, but he had never seen a young girl raped and then bayoneted after surviving an air crash.

He had never seen a group of what were survivors, thirsty

and begging for water and help, systematically killed in such a barbaric fashion.

He had seen things, this young soldier. But this went beyond the pale so he did all he could, which was to cry. To cry for them, to cry for the world that allowed it to happen, for the country he loved that was dying, and for a childhood he never had.

At dawn, the moment the sun gave sufficient light for a sparrow to follow tracks, they would follow up on the spoor and kill the men who did this thing. A good sparrow – the name given to trackers because of their bobbing motion as they run – can track at six or seven miles an hour on clear, fresh tracks and as soon as the light was sufficient they would go. There were others scattered around the site. Young, hard, very fit men, the finest bush troops in the world. Men of the Rhodesian Light Infantry, specifically 2 Commando.

Max Seager walked up to the soldier. 'I'm Seager. Kariba Special Branch. Please show me what you have found.'

He stood up, wiped the moisture from his face with a grimy hand and looked at Seager. 'You just wait for the dawn, jong. Then we go. Long culling ek se! Come see what they did to the young girl. We will cull them.'

He walked away into the dark towards a set of flares burning behind a screen of groundsheet suspended on branches.

The night was long and filled with comings and goings. First was a troop of Support Unit, paramilitary police, who would hold the area at daylight while the army moved onto the chase. They were followed by Civil Aviation people, and within an hour of first light, Seager had all he needed. He called for uniformed branch to take over, and went to find the officer commanding the army men, who still relaxed about the site, resting while they could.

The officer, however, was not.

He was sitting hunched over a radio with a sergeant and the unfortunate man whose back it was on.

'You the boss?' asked Seager.

'Standby,' he said, and then mumbled into the handset for a while, finally ripping the headset off his ears.

'Sergeant Nicholas?' He called.

'Sah!' barked another man off in the dark. He appeared a moment later.

'Get Timson and Warren out on the spoor. Start them with torches. These bloody bigfooted coppers will stuff up my tracks,' the officer said.

He turned and faced Seager. In the flickering light the bags beneath his eyes, although testament to his tiredness, were the only indicator. The rest of him was pure professional soldier, his beret covered in the powdery dust and creased shirt only enhanced the image. The pips at his shoulders identified him as a Captain, and he was young enough for that to be impressive.

'I'm the boss,' he said. 'Pascoe. RLI. Who might you be?'

'Seager. Kariba SB,' said Seager.

'That's nice, but you can't fucking come. You won't be able to keep up.'

'That's nice. I don't want to come. I have intelligent things to do,' quipped Seager.

The soldier grinned, and the crows' feet around his eyes deepened. 'I've heard about you,' he said. 'They say your int is good.'

'Just lucky,' said Seager. 'Can we talk?'

'Sure. Want a cup of coffee? Over here.'

Captain Pascoe didn't bother with the services of an orderly. He made and poured the coffee himself.

'I want a live one,' Seager said. 'Just one, alive enough to talk.'

'Ooh. I don't know about that. Give it a try, but these things are hard to plan. I'm not going to tell my boys to button off. I don't need a mutiny,' said Pascoe.

They would know more disobey this man than they would the Commander of the Army, thought Seager. He had that air about him.

They were then interrupted by one of the Civil Aviation people wanting access to the section of the plane which was cordoned off. The man's name was Hoskins, and his lank hair fell onto the pebble lenses he needed to see through.

Seager called the section officer in charge of the Support Unit and asked him to detail a guard for the gentleman and then allow him to go wherever he pleased. He moved off, and the two men fell in either side of him. One, a tall, blonde youngster, carried an MAG on a sling and the weight didn't seem to bother him at all.

Suddenly, the dawn began, and Pascoe excused himself to get his unit on the move. They were all over the site, and as the Sergeant moved amongst them they moved towards a central point, and began shrugging off excess equipment, which would be moved up later by helicopter if necessary.

Off to the left, someone gave a whistle, and the Sergeant began bellowing orders.

The trackers had found the spoor.

In no time the stick had formed up in a distinctive diamond head formation, the trackers sixty yards out in front with two or three riflemen as escort, and behind the main body of twenty-two or twenty-three men. Only the radio operator sat dejectedly under a tree, his big green burden propped up against a rack.

'They always leave me behind... fuckssakes!' he muttered to no one, but was overheard by Seager, who grinned.

Pascoe arrived, and was ignored by the irritated radioman.

'Right, I have a couple of K-Car helicopters standing by at Karoi. I'll bring them in when needed. You can get a ride on one of them if you like, but no guarantees on live ones, okay?' Pascoe said.

Seager nodded, and as Pascoe walked away Seager called to him, 'Pascoe, how do you keep up with such short legs?'

The reply was muffled and four-lettered, but not without a grin.

They moved out immediately, and within seconds were gone from sight. Seager got back into his work. His member in charge had arrived back and would want a report.

The next hour seemed to pass very quickly for Seager who sat beneath a tree and, sipping tea from a stolen mug, began making plans for his investigation. Reliable information out of the area had been scarce for some time following the recruitment of Seager's best source into the army. He had tried to talk the man out of it through several intermediaries but had failed. Someone in the area had to be found who would place the same importance on the job, and not just for beer money or fear of security force retribution.

He was still there when Hoskins the Civil Aviation expert appeared looking flustered. 'Inspector,' he said hesitantly, 'something here doesn't gel.'

'What?' Seager was irritated at the intrusion.

'It's the starboard engine pylon. It's been damaged,' Hoskins said.

'It would be. It crashed into the ground.' The man looked hurt by Seager's patronising tone.

'Sorry,' said Seager. 'That was uncalled for. What about the pylon?'

The man cheered up immediately. 'It's more the type of damage. I'd say it was explosives.'

Seager stood up. 'Explosives? Do you mean a bomb?'

'Oh good Lord no, wrong type for a bomb. No... I'll have to try the lab first, of course.'

'Fuck the lab,' interrupted Seager. 'Speak your mind man!'

Hoskins took a breath before speaking. 'The damage was externally applied. The force came from the outside of the aircraft. So I am pretty sure this aircraft was hit by a missile. I'll be able to tell you the type later. All right?'

'A missile?' blurted Seager. 'Are you sure?'

'Yes,' said Hoskins. 'I am sure. I'll tell you what type in a moment. My chaps have got fragments.'

With that, he walked away, back towards his people, who were bent over a trestle table in the hard morning light.

So they finally did it, thought Seager. There had been rumours of surface-to-air missiles in their arsenals, but everyone assumed they were for the protection of the training camps which, although they were deep inside Zambia and Mozambique, were no longer safe from the tiny but audacious Rhodesian Air Force. There were a few, Seager included, who believed it would only be a matter of time before they carried the missiles into the country and attempted to use them on civil air traffic.

First they shot the plane down and then they killed the survivors. Civilians who were returning from a weekend frolicking in the sun at Kariba, small, healthy children tanned by the sun, women clutching large bags filled with sun tan lotion and spare towels gossiping about who they had seen with whom at Caribbea Bay. Lovers taking a weekend away from the laid back colonial bustle of Salisbury to watch the red sunsets and the game, and to lose a few dollars over the baize. There would have been a honeymoon couple or two, and they had already found the passports of a family from Australia, and two Canadians.

Now they were leaving in body bags, the victims of the ultimate atrocity on a continent where violence was a way of life, and where the savagery was only paralleled by the beauty.

Seager had a quick look around for Sandy Gaul, and not being able to find him, walked straight back to the RLI radio operator.

'Can you contact Pascoe on that thing?' Seager asked, pointing at the radio.

'Course I fucking can,' he blurted, his Cockney accent as strong as the day he left London. 'Well, I can when it fucking works.'

'Try it, will you?' Seager showed the man his warrant card.

'Cor, Old Bill! All right. I'll give it a go for you.'

He made contact immediately, and handed Seager the headset and mike.

'Pascoe? Seager here.'

'Copy you fives. Go.'

'Target revved in flight, repeat revved in flight. Possibly by Sierra Alpha Mike Figures Seven. Did you copy that?'

'Confirm Sierra Mike Alpha Mike Seven over.'

'Roger that,' confirmed Seager.

'Don't like your chances of a live one now!'

'Need one more than ever, Pascoe. Good hunting! Over.'

There was just a sibilant clicking hiss as Pascoe signed off, and Seager handed the headset and mike back to the operator. The man was pulling off an auxiliary set himself.

'That gen, sir? A fucking missile?' He was incredulous.

'Affirmative,' said Seager, walking away.

'Arseholes. Always leave me behind. This is one fucking punch-up I do want to be in...' he trailed off, complaining to himself.

Seager found Sandy Gaul twenty minutes later as a Land Rover skidded to a half in the dust. Constable Chikunde always fancied himself as Aari Vatanen and loved driving to prove it. Gaul climbed from the cab and shook his head. Chikunde's driving was a lost cause.

'Sandy,' Seager began, 'the sitrep here is shit.'

The man listened as he lit his pipe, and as Seager finished he looked up, his eyes full of anger.

'Find these men for me, Max. I want to hang them from the gallows in Salisbury. What do you need?'

'This area is stuffed, sir. I suggest that when you go down to Combined and the Commissioner to tell them this, we freeze and let the scouts in. My source left here some time ago and I haven't got another.'

'All right, Max. I'll do that. Get on the phone to Reid-Daly's Command and let them know the situation. They will be dead keen on this one. Tell them I'm going down to Salisbury now and they will get orders within the next few hours.'

'I'll get a chopper organised,' Seager said, and walked back to the still muttering radioman.

They never did contact the group that did it. In a mad dash for the river the terrorists covered seventy-odd miles in a day and a half and disappeared either over the border or into the deep bush. Seager's sources and the massive energy spent by the Selous Scouts frustratingly turned up nothing except the usual after-the-fact leads. They found out who fed them, where they slept the night before, who the mujibas were – the young boys who ran their messages – but never the actual group.

A Selous Scout sniper shot a commissar at range with a soft nose hunting bullet two months later, and his record was particularly bad. Many hoped he was the man who had set up the attack. The following February there was a second successful attack. Yes, they had done it before.

The dawn came quickly, as it does in Africa. One minute it was black, and then suddenly the sun was up. The light was soft and on the western slope Max was still in darkness, but below on the scrub-covered red earth where the wreck lay it began as a deep blue and rapidly turned colourful as the sun's first rays reflected the hues and tints.

Max rolled forward and lay across a flat rock looking at the distance. Already he could identify parts of the wreck and see figures moving about. Two figures. He began to calculate the distance. Must be near to a thousand yards down the slope. As he watched, one figure moved away from the wreck and walked some distance into the bush before stopping at a fallen tree. The figure moved back a moment later. Someone taking a leak, thought Max. He looked up and into the distance again.

A man standing at ground level has a visible horizon of eighteen miles over flat water. Up here he would judge it nearer sixty miles before the haze began to obscure colour and definition.

He got to his feet and walked round to the other side of the kopje. Off to the east was the blue wall of some high ground. Very high, the sun just peeping over the top. Now he knew where he was. Max had been near here during the war on several occasions. The blue ranges were the Eastern Highlands, and if he was correct over his guess, between them and those mountains was Cashel Valley, the Sabi River and the main highway south to Birchenough Bridge.

He moved back to his place on the rock and waited. He would not have to wait long.

Max heard it first. The familiar whine of an engine working at high revs. It took him a minute to see it as its camouflage was effective, but there, coming from the north, slowly picking its way through the rocks and bush was a Mercedes Unimog in the colours of the Zimbabwe Army. It was a friendly-looking vehicle that had earned the nickname 'twofive' from the troops in the war because of its complicated gearing and subsequent military definition. As he looked, he could now pick out troops moving in an extended line across the ground ahead of the truck, and he judged the distance as a kilometre away from the wreck.

Not long now, he thought to himself.

Then he heard his name called softly, and the girl came into view. He whispered to her and she moved towards him.

'Lie here,' Max said. 'If any of them has a pair of field glasses they will pick you out.'

He was pleased to see she had changed into a khaki shirt. It was many sizes too large, and made her look rather small.

'Have they come?' She asked, peering over the edge. 'Sarah is awake and a bit niggly... I'm not much good with kids.'

'Sshh,' he murmured, and pointed.

'Oh, yes. I see,' she said. 'That line isn't very straight.'

Max looked down the hill, and she was right. The far end of the line was struggling. He looked back at her quizzically.

'Daddy's in the army,' she explained. 'Well, he was. Retired now. He liked straight lines.'

Jesus, Max thought. A real little Sloane Ranger, this one.

'Pay Corps, was he?' Max ventured.

'Not likely,' she said. 'He said they were all wankers. He called himself a runt or something like that.'

'Grunt,' he corrected. 'Means infantry.'

'That's right. He only retired last year. Now he runs a security company.'

This is getting interesting, thought Max.

'What regiment?' He asked, innocently.

'The Paras, but he was seconded to NATO for the last three years, and lots of trips up to Manchester.'

Not likely, thought Max. More like Hereford, Bradbury Lines, he grinned to himself. Daddy is a hard man, but he wouldn't tell his daughter that.

'Right. Quiet now, girl. They're closing fast.'

Below them troops ran into the wreck site, and then through it into the bush.

'That's not right,' said Max. 'Fuck.'

'Why?' She asked.

'Quiet,' he snapped.

The vehicle pulled up in amongst the wreckage, and Max could see men jump down and a figure separate from the wreck and walk to them. The troops were sweeping through the area either side of the site.

'Fuck,' he said again.

'What?' She demanded, caught up in his tension.

'They're doing a sweep. It means they're looking for others. They're not offering assistance. They are securing the area for action. They're fucking well going to do it, the bastards.'

And as he finished speaking, it began. The gunfire was quite clear from where they were. It went on for a full minute, and the single shots began as they finished off those that lived through the crash, the murder and the final onslaught.

Beside him, the girl began to slowly breathe again. 'Oh my God, no. They can't...' and she began to cry. 'But they were wounded, and hurt, and they're not soldiers. They're just people.'

Max turned. 'Go back to Helen and Sarah and stay there. Tell Helen it's happened and to hide until I get back.'

'Where are you going?'

'We're going to need more stuff. I'm going back down there.'

'You can't. They'll kill you.'

'They tried that for five years. Don't worry. Wait for me at the place and don't move into the open. Go now, or I'll tell your dad you disobeyed orders.'

She smiled weakly and crawled round to the back of the rock, and out of sight.

Max looked back down the hill. The troops were pouring drums over the ground, and over the bodies, and as he began carefully down the slope they set fire to the area. Convenient, he thought. No survivors, all bodies burned beyond recognition. How long till they did a body count and found four missing? How long till someone picked up the tracks leaving the site? That was still possible even with all the movement in the last ten minutes which would have obscured the tracks.

Where now? Out to the road. That was a start, and depending on what chase was given they could decide from there.

Helen Johnson sat watching Sarah play with three stones on the ground in front of her. She smoked her seventh to last cigarette, and wondered how long the tinned juice would last. When that was gone Sarah would have to drink the Perrier water, and that little experiment had been tried before without success. She smiled as Sarah dropped a stone onto her foot and muttered, 'Ow', and admitted to herself that this little child was the most precious thing in the world.

They had tried for seven years to have a child, she and her husband. It had been the saviour of their marriage at the time, and with all the irony that fate throws up, within six months of Sarah's birth, Donald Johnson had died, a victim of an ambush on a remote farming community road. He had been about to visit a client at the time, a further irony in that over all the time Donald had spent in the bush in uniform he had never been scratched yet on one of his infrequent trips out of Salisbury on business he died a death of unbelievable violence. The police had spared her the details, but several of Don's friends had seen the reports and admitted to Helen one drunken night that Don was alive when they got to him, and that they 'did things to him before he died'.

He was a careful man, and he had made arrangements for his wife and child should the unthinkable happen. A senior partner in the law firm he worked for pushed things through very quickly and Helen Johnson was fiscally comfortable for the rest of her life. It was poor consolation for the loss of the vibrant, intelligent, humorous man who she loved to distraction, but it did mean she was secure and Sarah was assured things later in her life. There were no other relatives at all, and two years later she still missed him terribly.

She came back to earth with a thump when Sarah stood before her and held out both hands, fists closed and palms facing downward. It was a new game and involved telling which hand the stone was in. It was really very obvious because her little hand could barely contain the stone she had chosen but her mother made great play of pondering it before choosing the wrong hand. Little Sarah broke into fits of giggles at her cleverness, and was still giggling when the distant sound of gunfire echoed over the hill.

Helen swept her child up, and held her close, then said, almost to herself and with infinite sadness, 'Oh dear,' before the first tear coursed silently down her cheek. Sarah, instantly aware of the change of mood, sat quietly in her mother's lap, looking up every now and then disturbed by it all.

For little Sarah Johnson, the nightmare had begun.

5

Now on the flat, Max began to move very carefully indeed towards the wreck. He reckoned on it taking him up to an hour to cover the distance going very slowly, looking for pickets, searchers or someone just taking a piss. Anyone seeing him would be the end, because as long as no one knew they had survived they had a chance of just walking clear. It could be days before they tallied bodies against the manifest, and then they may just put it down to some administrative error anyway.

He was confident in his ability to move through the bush undetected and he needed stuff from the wreck, so he kept going, intending to swing wide an approach from a flank.

Vicki Waters, holding back her tears and her shock, tried to walk elegantly into the clearing where the other two were waiting, but her quivering lip and red eyes revealed what she had just witnessed.

She walked firmly up to the pair, and said, 'Max said to say they had done it and we are to hide here somewhere, so I think we...' and she began to cry again before settling down to the ground like a deflating balloon. 'They just shot them all,' she said through tears. 'All those wounded people. They just...' The dignity vanished and suddenly she was just a nineteen-year-old girl a long way from home and very, very frightened.

'Vicki,' Helen said, 'listen to me now. We are clear of the area and they don't know we're here. We are quite safe. Max will be back soon and he will know what to do.'

'They'll kill us too,' Vicky sobbed. 'I know they will.'

Strengthening her voice to the point where she knew she

sounded like her mother, Helen said bluntly, 'Listen to me young lady. They have just killed a lot of people. We must get clear. Someone must tell the world what happened here. So don't sit there and sob! Pull yourself together. You, Sarah, Max and I are walking out of here. Believe it!'

Vicki sniffed and nodded twice.

'Right. Good,' said Helen, her voice softer now. 'Come with me. We're going to find some place to wait for Mr Seager.'

Dear God, she thought, help us now. Don't let them find us. Give my little one a chance, please, God?

Max was now only two hundred yards from the wreckage, sitting absolutely still at the base of a mopani tree. As he sat, he silently thanked fate for his choice of clothing when leaving Kariba, the brown and beige checked shirt and fawn pants blended perfectly with the trees and long strands of dry grass at this feet.

He sat absolutely still because it is movement that the eye sees. When colours blend, it doesn't distinguish form, only movement. He sat absolutely still because two Black soldiers were walking across his line of sight only fifteen yards away. They were chattering and they stopped briefly to light cigarettes. They were speaking Shona, not one of Max's strong points but the sense was that a search had begun, just to be sure, and these two resented having to get involved, for hadn't they finished everyone at the main place?

But the complaints weren't too loud because these people feared their officer more than anything else on earth, and besides, they were part of the elite Sixth Brigade, who provided the president's own bodyguard, and followed orders without question, and they were proud of it. Even killing women lying helpless.

Max waited until they were some forty yards away and moved again till he could see the main site. The fire had died down now, and a smell of cooked meat lay over the area. It was also immediately obvious that he would get no closer as there were still troops everywhere, and he silently began to retrace his steps, going to ground on two occasions when he heard voices.

On the second, he made a discovery.

He had rolled into cover behind a fallen tree, and as he raised his eyes to watch the movement in front, he had found himself looking at a piece of worn caramel-coloured leather, only inches from his face. He looked again, and pulled it clear. It was a briefcase, and he instantly pieced together two memories: the case at the wreck that the doctor had, and the figure walking clear at dawn. That figure had been getting rid of the case.

Max stuffed it back, and as he did so the handle came away in his hand. He looked at it, and a few seconds later shoved it back. He moved away again to the kopje and back to his companions. As he left he looked around, marking the place. If it was important enough for someone to die for, he may want to come back some time and retrieve it. Right now, though, all he wanted was to get clear without attracting attention – which removing the case might have done – and be back in time to move the others before the search extended that far.

Five hundred yards from the clearing, Max slowed down and began to move carefully over the shallow rise in front. He stopped, squatted and watched for a moment, looking for movement, and silently thanking his bush education and the men who'd given it to him. One phrase stuck in his mind: 'Always move downwind. Stop often, and when you do, freeze. Animals see movement, and you must too. Look for the flicker of an ear, or a tail swish. And never hurry.'

Now he applied those lessons to men with guns.

The sun was high in the sky, and he had to cover as much ground as possible before nightfall, and try for food for the child. He increased his pace.

Sarah had been quiet for what seemed like a lifetime, and to most little girls an hour often does. She had sat at her mother's feet and watched an ant for a while, and then moved the fingers on each hand in turn, trying to get them to do it together. She gave it another try, and was really concentrating, which was why she never noticed the dung beetle making his way steadily towards her foot, rolling his piece of dung before him, and minding his own business.

At this precise moment, two soldiers ambled into the clearing, only a few leaves covering their hiding place. Helen Johnson saw them, and very slowly put her finger to her lips, looking at Vicki with a warning to be silent.

The dung beetle, a prize specimen about an inch long, with enormous horns above the hard shell of his head, chose that moment to roll his ball of dung into Sarah's right foot. The nudge was very gentle really, and accustomed to find things he couldn't roll his ball over, the beetle climbed over the dung, intending to roll it back and try for a different route towards his nest. His delicate front legs touched Sarah's foot, and that she felt. She looked away from her fingers, and down at the ground. And shrieked, loudly.

Her mother swept her up in an instant, saw the cause of the problem and immediately looked back at the two men on the edge of the clearing, who were easily visible through the leaves of the bush which was concealing her. She looked back at the child, whispered at her to be very quiet, and then looked at Vicki, who by now had lost all the colour in her face, and was sickly pale.

'I think they heard,' Helen whispered to the terrified girl. 'If they head this way, take Sarah out the back of the trees. I'll talk to them.'

'No,' interrupted Vicki. 'They'll hurt you.'

'They're all corruptible,' Helen said. 'I'll try money, and if that doesn't work, I'll... I'll try something else.'

Feeling in his pockets for his cigarettes, the soldier paused at the edge of the clearing, thinking this would do nicely as a spot to sit for a while, and then go back down the hill and say it had been searched. He had plenty of cigarettes as the wreck had provided well for looting. He had also found a pair of silky women's panties, which would come in useful when he got back to Harare. He knew a girl there who would be very grateful for them, and would show her appreciation in just the way he liked.

He turned to see where his companion was, and as he did so, heard a high-pitched squeal from the bush to his right.

'What was that?' he called, his hand frozen in his pocket clutching his cigarettes.

'Eh?' his companion replied.

Stupid pig, thought the soldier. Your mother mated with a baboon to have you.

'The noise,' he said impatiently.

'What noise?'

'Idiot,' said the soldier, and began to move towards the place where it came from, pulling the smokes clear and lighting one. He had only covered twenty feet when out of the bushes stepped a woman from his dreams.

He blinked, and looked again, and she was still there. Yellow hair, white skin, and heavy. Perfect.

He lifted his rifle threateningly, and at the same time wondered what do to next.

The woman smiled at him, and said in bad Shona, 'Take me from here safely and I will give you money. Much money.'

The soldier decided this was too good an opportunity to miss. He turned to the other stunned soldier, and said, 'Go tell the lieutenant that we have a live one here. But take your time. I'm going to have some fun first. You can have her when you get back.'

Yeah, he thought, you and all the rest.

He watched the other soldier run away, then turned back to the woman. She was no longer smiling. He walked to her quickly, enjoying her fear, then slapped her twice on the side of the face, and punched her in the stomach. She dropped to her knees, retching.

Max was at the base of the slope and began moving easily upward. He had bypassed several groups of soldiers, but the searching was random and without pattern. Max thought their search was a routine covering of an area rather than looking for anything specific.

That was when he heard the running footsteps coming down the hillside towards him.

He froze, listening intently. Close and getting closer, heavy steps, thudding. A man. That meant they had been found! He hadn't heard gunfire, and all the groups of soldiers he'd seen were pairs, which meant there was one up top and one going back with the news.

Stop him, Max thought. I have to stop him.

The basis of all the eastern martial arts is the tuition of students by a master. The tuition is pure parrot-fashion imitation of set moves, moves refined down the centuries and very effective. The student learns these by hours of practice and imitation, until they become instinctive. The moves are tied into set defensive patterns and usually followed by an offensive blow to a specific point on the opponent's body.

In theory a skilled exponent of most styles can block and retaliate in milliseconds in response to any type of blow or attack by one or more attackers. Most styles can be immediately put into offensive mode by simply omitting the defensive moves, and going straight into a full-strength attacking blow.

Max didn't know any of this, so he went back to basics. Neanderthal basics.

As the soldier ran round the corner of the track, Max hit him full in the face with a rock the size of a grapefruit. The impact made a sound like a dropped watermelon, and the man fell to the ground like a ragdoll, his face concaved by the force of the strike from top lip to mid-forehead, and obviously as dead as a doornail.

Max didn't stop to make sure. He set off straight up the hill as fast as he could, his legs pumping like a sprinter.

In the clearing, Max was greeted by a scene from a nightmare. On the ground in front of him was a rifle with a blood-stained bayonet still attached, and a few yards away a soldier on top of Helen, who was obviously badly wounded.

He crossed the clearing like a leopard, scooping up the rifle and bayonet, and lunged with it at the grunting man.

Twice in his career Max had killed in the line of duty. The first occasion was in a raid on an illegal beerhall. It was a shebeen selling illegal beer and cheap spirits to anyone who entered. Run in the back of a store, it operate illegally, an was the subject of this particular action because the owner, an African woman, had been cutting the cheap gin with wood alcohol, and two deaths had resulted.

Shebeens were frequented by a variety of customers. Some ordinary people, some of life's losers, and, like anywhere, some of the local underworld types. Patrol Officer Max Seager had entered the premises with two African constables, and placed the owner under arrest. There was the usual shrieking, wailing and cry of innocence, and amid the noise no one noticed the very large man at the back of the room rise to his feet holding an iron cooking pot. He swung wildly and hit the first constable on the back of the head. The man staggered and the two fell to the floor together.

The attacker rose, but the constable remained prone. He

reached for the pot again and looked up at Max, his wild eyes betraying the poison in his veins. Max looked on coolly, staying absolutely still. It was only when the man dropped the pot in favour of the injured constable's Greener shotgun that Max pulled out his own 9mm Browning and called out to him, 'Friend, do not die for a moment's anger. Put the gun down. It is time now. Do not do this. Place the gun down and come peacefully.'

The fellow misjudged the young policeman, and lifted the shotgun, ready to fire, his crazy eyes rolling in his head. Max shot him twice in the chest, the 9mm rounds throwing the man back over the tin seats.

Max had never liked guns, always seeing them as a tool to use as a last resort. He liked them even less after that day.

The second occasion was a drugged-up Black teenage boy. He had taken too much of some substance which forensics had never identified, and was holding a three-year-old African child hostage. It was his sister, his mother having slept with a German tourist at Fort Victoria for five dollars. At the time, those of mixed blood were accepted by neither side, and years of resentment building up exploded here. The boy had already killed his mother with a kitchen knife, stabbing her repeatedly in the neck and chest. His little brother he had simply beaten to death with a budza, the mattock generic to the continent of peasant farmers.

Now he sat with his strangely silent baby sister between his knees holding her by the neck with one hand and threatening to kill her. Max, the senior officer at the scene in the township, had done the necessary and eventually shot the boy with a high-powered rifle from the back of a parked bus. The hundreds of spectators looked with new respect as Max simply drove away after the incident with all the cool in the world. What they didn't know was that he drove straight to a bar and got drunk, and was later collected by his boss, who had scoured the area's licensed premises looking for his young colleague. He himself had done it once and knew how Max felt.

But this was different. This was the first time Max had killed in hot rage and it was different. It was the most basic emotions at work. Anger, hatred, fear and revenge.

Max drove the point of the bayonet through the soldier's neck and up into the skull cavity with such force it lifted the rapist clear of the ground like a puppet jerked back on a string.

Max gently rolled Helen over, his hand covering the terrible wounds in her back. She was losing strength fast, and shock was taking over.

'Promise me, Max,' she said weakly, 'promise you'll take care of her. There's no one else... she's all alone now.'

He nodded quickly. With his adrenalin pumping and sweat running down his face, he didn't know what to say.

'Say you promise, Max. Please.'

'I promise. Don't worry, Helen. I'll see to it. I'll get her clear.'

Helen began to cough and gouts of dark blood filled her mouth. She began to quiver and twitch, and only a few seconds later lay completely still.

Eventually, Max stood, and then uncharacteristically kicked the dead man twice in the head, muttering, 'May you rot in hell,' surprising himself with his callousness.

But just as quickly, the anger subsided, and he stripped the body of its webbing and magazines for the soldier's Kalashnikov, as well as cigarettes, matches, and water canteen.

Leaving the bayonet still embedded in the soldier's head, he unclipped the weapon and slung it over his shoulder. He looked once down at Helen's body and then walked to the edge of the clearing carrying the looted kit.

It was catch twenty-two: leave the kit and hope the eventual searchers for the two missing men surmise that Helen killed them, and be without a weapon, or take the weapon and hope to stay out in front long enough to make it to the road and safety.

Max began softly calling Vicki's name, hoping she hadn't run too far.

He found her wedged into some rocks a hundred yards from the clearing, only appearing when she heard her name called. She had Sarah held close, and as Max neared she quizzed him with her eyes. He shook his head twice, hoping she wouldn't say anything in front of the child. He wasn't sure exactly what Sarah would understand from his gesture, but she could certainly feel the tension, her little body was tense and her eyes wide.

'Give me the pack,' Max said, smiling and speaking gently for the child's sake. 'We have to move fast now. They won't be far behind once they start looking.'

He quickly rearranged the contents at the bottom, spreading a rust-coloured towel over the tings and bottles to make a padded layer. He then put the pack on backwards, that is on his chest rather than his back, and looked at Sarah, still in Vicki's arms.

'Sarah,' Max said, 'we're going for a long walk so I'm going to put you in this cubby hole, and you can see out of the top. Is that all right?'

She just stared, her big blue eyes taking him in, and then one grubby knuckle came up and she shyly rubbed the corner of one eye, and frowned before saying, 'Mummy?' in a little questioning voice.

He thought for a second, leant forward and took her from Vicki, lowering her into the pack facing him.

'We will see Mummy later,' he lied. What the fuck do you say at a moment like this? He thought. He patted her gingerly through the side of the pack. It didn't see very comforting, but Max didn't have much experience of these things. He could only liken it to comforting a dog.

This was a long, long way from anything he had experienced before, and rather scary. He turned to Vicki and said, 'Right, let's go. That way. No talking until I say so, and if you see me stop, then do exactly as I do. Okay?'

Vicki nodded and they moved off down the eastern slope of the kopje.

Max set a fast pace and for the first few minutes kept checking to see if she was managing to keep up, and was surprised to see she was without problems, her long legs matching him stride for stride.

Good girl, he thought, keep that up and we're halfway there.

He moved very carefully at first, but as they cleared the area he moved faster, the girl behind and to his left, the rifle at the ready and his eyes constantly scanning the bush ahead of them, and while he walked he began thinking, and putting the pieces together, and planning the next move. He began by once again counting the assets, and then adding them to the weapon and water, as well as magazines. He looked down at it as he walked and remember what he had learned about this particular rifle. It was an AK-47, manufactured in the Soviet Union, but the original design was stolen from the Germans. Its curved magazine contained thirty rounds and he had five magazines. It was capable of firing on full automatic or single shot, and was accurate up to four hundred yards.

Its best features were its simplicity and its ruggedness. Max had dug up an arms cache in the Zambezi Valley during the war, and had pulled one such weapon from the dirt, its mechanism seemingly clogged with mud and sand. He cocked it and pulled the trigger and it fired perfectly. It was only then that he believed the stories, that his assault rifle was the best bush gun about. Never needed cleaning, simple to operate and very tough. Just the thing for badly trained, illiterate men.

Its disadvantages were that it fired an intermediate round

rather than a lone one, which meant its range was limited, and so was its hitting power. But for what Max needed it was perfect.

He had a quart of water, which meant they could skirt things till dark. Sarah would need plenty of water.

Max thought the road couldn't have been more than fifty miles away, so if they could move at three or four miles an hour they would be there by tomorrow night at the latest. Call it three days allowing for holdups. He would need food soon.

Max looked down at his little passenger. Her head was out of the top of the pack like a baby kangaroo, and she was watching him warily. There were now, he estimated, about five miles from the wreck and moving well.

He kept it up for another hour, and then Vicki began to slow down, and he called a halt, moving them into a thicket to rest for a while. He pulled Sarah from the pack so she could stretch her legs and she just stood and looked at him.

'Mummy?' she said.

'We will see Mummy later. Would you like a drink?' She shook her head but he dug into the pack and produced some orange juice in a tin. As he opened it, she watched and he handed it to her. Sarah sipped it, and then began to drink it in deep draughts until it was finished.

'More?' She half-nodded then began to shake her head as if unsure. She looked uncomfortable and was fidgeting.

Max turned to Vicki and held out a bottle of mineral water. 'Oh yes,' she said. 'I'm parched.' She took the bottle and drank. 'What now, Max?'

'Slowly,' he said. 'Make it last. It will be three days before we make the road.'

'Are they following, do you think?' Then, fearfully, 'What? Three days?'

He nodded. 'It's about fifty miles, I think. Once there we get help the best way we can. They will be looking for us, after that scene up there on the kopje. They may extend the search past the road. They will have to stop us now. They know there are survivors. They know there are witnesses. So we move east and we keep moving until we are safe.'

Sarah was still fidgeting. Oh fuck, Max thought. She needs a wee. What now? For help, he looked at Vicki. She hadn't noticed anything.

He thought of another life rule: if in doubt, ask.

'Do you want a wee-wee?'

Sarah nodded unhappily.

'Ah,' said Vicki, 'okay. Pants down, I suppose?'

'Right,' said Max, and as he rose to his feet, little Sarah who couldn't understand the delay and couldn't hold on any longer, just let go.

Her face was such a picture of embarrassed relief that Max started to chuckle, and while she settled down to finish it like a lady, he looked at Vicki and, accompanied by a very Gallic shrug, whispered, 'What now?'

In return, Vicki copied the gesture.

Oh shit, she was no help. Okay, Max thought. Simple enough. She's just another person, same as the rest of us, only smaller. Talk to her. As her? No? What the hell...

'Finished?' he said cheerfully, as Sarah rose unsteadily, beginning to pick at her wet panties with her fingers. She nodded, a bit uncertain of who was to do what next.

'Brookies off, then.' Max lent forward, and she put up a hand to steady herself and held up her dress with the other hand. He stooped and she took hold of his arm, and he pulled the damp panties down so she could step out of them. He slung them over the pack, pleased with the efficiency and success of his efforts.

Then he remembered where they were and why they were there, and said, 'Okay, let's move on. We'll go slowly, and Sarah can walk for a while.'

He tied the panties on the base of the pack to dry, put it over his back this time, and picked up the rifle. Finally, he held out his hand.

Sarah looked but wouldn't take it.

'Come on,' he said. 'Hold my hand.'

She stared back at him. 'Mummy?'

'Mummy's not here, angel. Just me and Vicki. You want to come with us?'

Sarah looked around, and then turned to Max and nodded. He put out his hand again, and she took his index finger and held it tightly. Poor little mite, he thought. Don't worry, we'll get you out of this and then we'll find your relatives, or something. There must be someone...

The little group moved off, the child on one side of Max and Vicki on the other, carefully picking a track that would be visible from the front so that when he needed to he could look back and see if there was anyone on the spoor as they moved into the valley floor.

That was the crux of the issue. If the soldiers had a tracker then the chase would be brief. But if not, and the search was patterned, then they had a good chance. Please God, he thought, no sparrow, not until it rains at least.

There were clouds to the east, and as the day warmed up it may mean rain by the afternoon. Max wanted a cigarette but would save that for later when they were well clear, because you can smell tobacco smoke a long way away in the bush. It's an alien smell, and they needed to be as one with the grass and stunted vegetation about them.

Presently little Sarah began to falter and slow down, so without stopping he picked her up and held her in one arm and pushed on. She was soon asleep, her head resting on his shoulder. Max was surprised at how heavy she was, and suddenly admired mothers who carried children like this for hours while shopping or walking.

'What do we know about this little one?' He said softly to Vicki.

Running a hand through her hair, she moved up from her place a pace behind and to the left, until she was alongside Max. She was sweating freely, and now wishing she had worn better shoes. Vicki often travelled in tennis shoes for comfort's sake, but on this occasion had opted for a more fashionable pair as the flight was short.

'Not much,' she said. 'Only what Helen told me while we were waiting for you. No other relatives, that I do know. Her husband died in the war and neither of them had any other family left. Sarah is about to turn three in, I think, March, Helen said. Very bright for her age.'

'What do you know about kids?'

'Ah... I was afraid you were going to ask that. Nothing. Don't really understand them. Only daughter and all that. Sometimes wished I had troops of brothers. Daddy would have liked that. As it was, I was it, so I got dragged off and taught how to shoot pheasants and things.'

'How old are you? And don't tell me ladies never say.'

She laughed. 'I'm nineteen,' she admitted, and then looked almost wistful. 'I had my coming out ball last year, but looking around her I think someone missed the point.'

They walked on in silence, Max considering what he had learned, and considering the irony of it all. Of all the people he could have been thrown in with under these circumstances, it was three-year-old orphan girl and a nineteen-year-old Sloane Ranger.

All things considered, the girl was showing considerable physical strength and mental fortitude. There were others who would have been very different.

Max picked out a point ahead, and swung towards it, intending to stop there for a while and produce the dry biscuits and potato chips he had removed from the wreck's beverage trolley.

Tonight they would need something more substantial. Getting hold of that would be interesting, he thought. This was Tribal Trust Lands, and devoid of anything in the way of small game. The best he could hope for would be some poor bastard's goat or maybe a chicken or two if he got close enough to a kraal. Worry about that later, he decided.

'Let's take a break,' he said. 'Talk, relax, sleep for a while if you like. But all very quietly, please.'

'And you?' Vicki asked through a mouthful of biscuit. 'The mysterious Mr Seager. What about you? How did you know what they'd done? Are you an aviation expert, or a soldier? You could be a soldier. I know lots of them. You're like some of the chaps who used to come back to the house with Daddy years ago. Mess manners not so hot, but very competent when it counts. That's you. Competent, swear too much, but competent.'

Max smiled. The three of them were sitting quietly in the space, concealed, he hoped, as well as was possible.

'I was a policeman until recently,' he said.

'You, a policeman? Never. They are an ordinary sort of people who lack imagination,' Vicki countered with a smile.

'I had a patch up in the north, at Kariba. We don't all lack imagination. I was Special Branch. There was lots of that.'

She looked up, interested. No longer chitchat. 'Special Branch? We have them in England. Political and subversives, isn't it?'

'Yes, in brief. Lots of intelligence work, lots of puzzles, with answers that usually kill people. Solve the puzzle and stop someone dying.'

'How did you know about the soldiers coming to the plane?'

She wasn't going to let up on that, he could see.

'Something the stewardess said, and then playing the puzzle.'

There was a length pause, which Max eventually broke. 'What happened back at the clearing? Did they see you, or what?'

It was warm under the shade of the sparse leaves above them. The air was hot and still and it seemed incredibly quiet.

'It was silly, really. Sarah was being very good, just sitting quietly, until she got a fright. An enormous beetle touched her foot and she gave a little shriek. They were close enough to hear. Helen thought she could bribe them...'

He was silent after that. The killing of two men in two minutes was something he had not thought about until now, and justifiable as it was, it was still an action he would spend some time regretting. Regretting putting everyone in that position, as well. He shouldn't have tried to go back to the wreck, he knew that now. But then, who knows what would have happened if he didn't?

'We'll stay here for another hour,' he said, 'and then move on. Sleep if you can because we will be moving tonight as long as there is a moon.'

Sarah woke eventually and ate a couple of the biscuits, and drank a tin of juice, following it with some water from the canteen. Max had to hold it for her because it was too heavy, but she seemed to enjoy the water running down her front, and wanted to make mud pies in the puddle it left.

She asked for her mother again, but didn't seem unduly worried when Max again said, 'Later.'

Once night fell it might be different, and he was glad he had brought the coat she had spent last night in. It was something that smelled of her mother, something familiar, and he thought that might be helpful.

They moved again in mid-afternoon, Sarah walking at first and then riding in the pack, this time on Max's back. Vicki followed and chatted softly to the child, pointing out birds and things as they went.

By nightfall they were well into the broad valley, and by eight Max halted them quietly. He had smelled woodsmoke.

6

'You two stay here. I'm going in there to try for some food,' Max said. 'I'll be an hour, no longer. While I'm away, collect some wood for a small fire.' He indicated the sleeping child. 'If she wakes up, just cuddle her till I get back.

He rummaged through the outer pockets of the pack and produced the only item he had kept from the original contents. A small torch.

He moved off, rifle, torch, and webbing only, at a steady jog towards the smell. Upwind.

It wasn't far. Maybe a mile later he heard the sounds of livestock moving and a few yards past that the outline of a kraal came into view against the night sky. The line of huts with a thatched fence joining them was in bad repair, and from the cooking smoke only two of the huts were occupied. Max let his eyes adjust to complete night sight, which can only be done while still, and then went in closer.

Off to the right was a smaller hut with a ramp arrangement, its conical roof a miniature version of the main hut. Chicken house or grain store, he thought. Goats moving behind him now added to that ultimate African smell, the smell of a camp or compound. It's a mixture of woodsmoke, animals' dust and the musty smell that humans give their dwellings after prolonged occupation, but mostly the smell of stale woodsmoke.

Max loved it. It was the smell of his childhood, and then he decided how he was going to get food without stealing or hurting anyone in the process. He didn't have to wait long and the candidate was ideal.

An old man appeared from the main hut, stooped with age

but still agile enough, it seemed, to live out here. Usually when one reaches such an age one's children take care of you. Not this one. Not yet anyway.

He squatted by the fire and added a few twigs, and then blew his nose noisily into his hand, flicking the offending mucus into the night.

Max grinned to himself. Perfect.

'Old man,' he called in perfect Shona.

The old fellow spun about and looked around.

'Old man,' again.

'Who calls from the darkness? Don't try to rob me. I have my spears and am not so old as to be like a woman.'

Max grinned even wider.

'Old man, listen, for I shall speak only the once. I am a *svikiro* and I am travelling to the mountains to talk to the spirits. I travel with them now so I shall not enter your camp or they will burn out your eyes, and your crop shall not grow for a thousand years. Do not look this way!'

'Aiieee!' the old man wailed, sure that this encounter with a spirit medium meant his certain death.

'Bring food for our journey. Bring *sudza*, salt and some *hookoos*. Bring water and I shall lead them from this place and you shall be safe. Furthermore, do this thing well, and speak of it to no one and I shall ask the spirits to leave you much *mali*. You shall find it here where I speak from at dawn. But,' Max boomed in a perfect Highveld accent, 'speak of this night and you will see my companions again!'

The old man hurried to his feet and scuttled about his tasks.

He was back in a short time, an old sack held in front of him. He lowered his head so as not to see the spirits and be blinded, and shuffled forwards until Max said, 'Halt there, old one. Leave the bag and return to your fire and sleep softly, for tonight the aura of my visit will protect you and yours. Return here in the light of day, and find *mali,* but remember my words.'

The old fellow nodded, dropped the bag, and scurried back to the fire, not looking back once.

Max pulled out some money from his pocket. The bills were all twenties and he left two. Ten times the worth of the goods, and probably more money than the old man had ever seen.

He scooped up the bag and disappeared into the night, jogging again, now downwind. Every now and then something in the bag moved and squawked. *Hookoo.* Roast chicken tonight, he thought to himself, and picked up the pace, moving well in the moonlight. Still no sign of rain, though. Max wanted rain to cover their tracks.

He was back at the camp within the time he had allowed, and called softly as he approached. Vicki was sitting huddled with Sarah, awake but still in the pack, at the base of a tree.

'Right, let's find a place for the fire, and eat,' he said smugly.

'I'm famished,' Vicki said. 'What did you get?'

'It's not takeaway stroganoff, but it is going to have to do.'

They found a place in the rock where the glow from a small fire wouldn't be seen other than from directly above, and for once the old Zippo worked first time and soon a fire was burning cheerfully.

Max inspected the contents of the bag. Two live chickens, one dead and pretty well cleaned, a small bag of salt, some mealie meal, an old plastic detergent bottle of what turned out to be water, and finally a tin of bully beef.

He made sudza – cornmeal porridge – and cooked the whole chicken, and they cleaned it to the skeleton. He had sarah on his lap and was feeding her the small pieces of white meat from the breast, and small handfuls of sudza. Eventually she wiped a greasy hand across her mouth, settled on his lap and fell asleep. He wrapped her in the coat, and lay her down beside him. He reached into his pocked and extracted his second cigarette of the day, and lit it with a great display, mimicking a popular cigarette commercial full of macho men and campfires. Vicki laughed and they began to talk quietly.

'Are we safe here?' She said.

'Relatively. They don't like moving at night, especially searching. You miss things at night, so we're safe enough for now.'

'Good,' she said, and proceeded to take off her shoes to massage her feet. 'We must have walked a hundred miles today.'

Max gave a short laugh. 'Shit, I wish we had. More like twenty, my girl.'

'Is that all? Shit...' she surprised herself. 'See? Now I'm swearing too. It's all your fault.'

'It's tough in the bush.'

'Mummy would positively freak if she heard me say that word.'

'You're fucking joking!' He needled.

She threw a shoe at him. 'You're disgusting... but nice. Like a battered tomcat.'

They were silent, and thoughtful for a minute, that contentment that comes with being bone tired and having eaten well.

'If my friends could see me now. V. J. Waters on the run through the African bush, lions everywhere...'

'V. J.?'

'Victoria Jessica.'

You don't look like a Vicki, he thought. You look like a Jessica, but out here Jessica would be contrived. Jessie would work better.

'Has no one ever called you Jessie?'

'Jessie,' she said, 'sounds like the heroine from some penny dreadful novel.'

'Don't pontificate,' he said. 'It's not becoming in a girl of your age.'

She laughed again. It was a nice sound, clear and strong.

'I want a bath,' she said.

'Go to sleep.'

'Yes, daddy.'

'Now who takes the piss?' he challenged.

Later, as the camp slept, he climbed up the large rock with the rifle and sat watching, perfectly still. Eventually, satisfied that they were alone, he climbed back down and lay beside the child, and was soon asleep, one hand cradling the weapon. It had become like an extension of his arm already.

He was awake well before dawn, and quickly circled the camp twice stopping and listening, smelling the air, making sure they were alone. The wind had changed and now came from the east, so no smoke from the old man's kraal, which lay to the south.

Max had slept lightly but well, the child having woken twice in the night. They went through the wee-wee ritual, this time with more success, Max able to get her panties off in time, as they were only just dry from the first mistake after being left on a stone by the fire. She cried both times before drifting back into fitful sleep, an the second time it was in his lap as he sat against the rock talking softly to her.

Now he scraped what sudza was left from the old pot the man had given him with the sack, and these he rolled into little balls and softened with water so they would be edible later in the morning.

He woke Vicki, who sat up quickly and looked about her.

'It's okay,' he said. 'Let's put some miles between us and this place before light. We move in five minutes.'

She nodded and rubbed her eyes, and at that time she looked so young and helpless Max had to remind himself she was nineteen.

She pulled her shoes and socks closer to her, and shook one sock clear of dust.

'Do the same with the shoes,' Max said.

'Why?' she asked, in a croaky first-thing-in-the-morning voice.

'You never know what might have crawled in there in the night,' he replied.

She made an awful face and shook the shoes out, ready to leap away if anything fell from them which crawled, stung, bit or breathed.

'Max, can't we just go home? I never did like camping or that sort of thing.'

Max grinned. 'Two minutes, milady.'

'Piss off. I'm not human until I've had several cups of coffee!' She thought for a moment, and then added, 'I would die for a cup of coffee. Bugger it!' She stepped onto a sharp stone.

Max had put Sarah, still asleep and wrapped in the coat, straight into the pack and was already walking, so he stopped and turned.

'Christ, spare me,' he muttered, watching Vicki hop with one shoe on and the other in her hand.

'He already did,' she said. 'Now stand still while I lean on you. That's the trouble with you colonials – no manners.' And with that he began to laugh, and she did too.

'Right, I'm ready,' and she pranced off, leading the way.

'Oi, David Livingstone,' Max called. 'This way,' shaking his head in amazement. She was certainly a lively companion.

They moved slowly at first, but then as the light spread its warmth across the cobalt sky they began to move faster. The country was much the same as the previous day. Stunted bush, sparse grass, and erosion testament to the bad land management often to be found in the tribal-owned areas of the country. No fertilisation, no rotation of crops, no farming at all. Clear it, plant it and bugger it, as the saying went.

Twice in the morning they saw small herds of cattle at a distance and they skirted widely because where there are cattle there are herders.

They talked at times, and Sarah walked for a while, and they found themselves at the base of a small kopje. There they halted, and built a small fire just enough to cook more sudza, and while the water was heating Max jogged up the hill to see what lay ahead.

He moved round so he climbed the eastern slope, and making sure he provided no silhouette, he sat and scanned the horizon. The blue slabs of the mountains were certainly closer, but what immediately caught his eye was the much thicker, greener vegetation running in a winding strip in the midview. Distanced maybe six or seven miles away, what he had seen was the Sabi River. It had to be the Sabi, he thought, it was the only river that size running north-south. That meant the road was only a couple of miles the other side. Be there by dark, if they moved it. Max was elated, and began to move downward when he thought he had better have a quick look to the west, and make sure they weren't being followed.

He did so, and they were.

There off in the bus, only a mile away, was a line of men extended and moving steadily. Bastards, he thought. Just leave us alone. We have had enough. He looked again and watched for a moment. The line moved slowly, which told Max it was likely they had no tracker. They were just doing their best, and constantly losing the spoor.

Then he felt the wind shift, turned and ran down the hill. The fire – they would smell the smoke. He had to kill the fire and then shoot through real quick. Oh fuck, Max said to himself. I thought we had lost them! Bastards, he though as he ran. Those bastards.

*

Almost two hundred miles away, to the northwest, in the capital, an angry dark sky began to deliver rain in sheets of water onto the hot streets and red tin roofs. In the suburbs, brilliantly coloured bougainvillaea and hibiscus cowered under the onslaught above ground, while below, their roots waited for the life-giving liquid to seep down.

Small children scurried for shelter under bits of cardboard and plastic, and people on bicycles put their heads down and pedalled harder. Servants ran to washing lines to take in the morning's work, and on the Royal Salisbury Golf Course two men shrugged, and continued playing.

Not a mile from their green, another two men were less fatalistic. They were in the lavishly decorated townhouse of the minister. His wife didn't live there – she had the family home in Borrowdale's sprawling respectability. This was the place the minister kept for his less formal assignations, his current one being a Moroccan-born French girl of very dubious background. She spoke virtually no English, and certainly no Shona, the minister's native language. But she wasn't there for her languages or conversational skills.

She was there because she had a beautiful, curved figure, and red hair, which the minister found particularly exotic and exciting, and was available to the minister whenever and however he wanted her.

Right now she was on her knees in front of him, as he sat with a whisky in one hand while the other gripped her red hair as her head moved up and down in his lap. He was in the moment, relishing the sensation of her mouth and the power the act gave him.

So much so that when the front doorbell of the house rang for the first time, he ignored it.

The second ring was accompanied by a fist banging on the wooden panels. Now he was angry, and couldn't concentrate.

The minister cursed, pushed the girl away, and without doing up his fly or making any effort to cover himself, he crossed to the window and peered out towards the door.

He turned back to the girl and, pushing his cock back into his trousers, said, 'Upstairs. I'll call you down when I want you.'

The girl shrugged, smiling, he thought, like a simpleton.

He jerked his thumb upwards impatiently, and muttered, 'Stupid slut,' in Shona.

She nodded, showing she understood the gesture, and said in perfect Arabic, 'You'll get yours you fat pig,' while still smiling like an adoring idiot, and then set off for the stairs. In fact, she understood far more than she let on, even the Shona words. She had had the houseboy teach her bits over the weeks, and the work was beginning to pay off.

The minister reached the front door, and swung it open, smiling the winning smile of every successful politician. 'My dear Heine,' he said. 'How nice to see you. Come in.' He stepped back to allow the visitor to enter the room.

The man was tall with blonde hair, and a conservative suit of black wool covered his athletic frame. In spite of the humid air, he wasn't sweating. Not at all. However, he was wet thanks to the rain pounding down outside. The short run from his car had been long enough for that.

He was Heine Guttman, officially catalogued as a commercial attaché at the Embassy of the Democratic Republic of Germany, but in reality was the senior operating field officer the whole of southern Africa for the Stasi, his country's secret police who worked hand-in-glove with the KGB. He held the rank of Colonel, and was usually very cool and collected.

But not today.

'Comrade Minister,' he said. 'Our little problem...'

'Ah, yes, Heine. Terrible! An air crash, how unfortunate that there were no survivors!' He began to laugh, his dark face wobbling like a blackcurrant jelly. 'Don't worry, Heine, he is dead. Orpheus is dead. There were no survivors.' He laughed again.

Now the visitor spoke, his voice close to a hiss. 'But there were survivors, comrade. Someone got away. A little birdy told me, my fat friend, that someone got away!'

'It couldn't be him... the chances of that one man surviving it were infinitesimal.' He made the word sound like *infaantesamaaal*.

'Whoever it is,' said Heine, 'killed two of your people. Your supposed elite. Up close, comrade, one with a bayonet and one with a rock. That's no ordinary citizen. It could be Orpheus. You must find him! There is too much at stake here. We have done years of work!'

'We are searching now,' the minister said, no longer laughing. 'I have a whole platoon searching. We will find him.'

The German reminded him of a puff-adder, and he was in too deep. There was no backing out now. He had taken too much from them. He had to deliver.

'You will increase the search area, put in more men,' the German ordered. 'Find him and kill him or you are finished... we are all finished!' With that, he turned and walked to the door.

Upstairs, the girl who had heard the voices and felt the tension, but understood little through the closed doors, was disappointed. When he was angry or upset, the minister was often hard on her. She heard him stomping up the stairs, and as the door opened, she forced a smile onto her face.

'Hello, my fat little pig,' she said in Arabic.

*

Max burst into the camp. 'They're coming, about half an hour away.' He squatted, breathless, and began pouring handfuls of dirt onto the small fire. 'Get Sarah into the pack, put the pot and stuff in the sack. Now.'

He stood and walked three feet to a large boulder, before stooping, catching his hands under it, and beginning to lift.

Vicki watched astonished as the muscles in his arms rippled and then set as he breathed out sharply, then lifted. The cords along his back and shoulders stood proud and then suddenly he was standing up, the rock in his arms. He staggered three steps back and lowered it over the spot where the fire had been.

'Let them find that,' he said, 'the fuckers.'

He went back to the place he had lifted the rock from and swept his hand over the depression, clearing the imprint. 'Let's go,' he said.

Max slung Sarah over his shoulder, and grabbing the rifle and sack, began to jog away, leaping on stones wherever possible.

'Do it like I am,' he said. 'Makes us difficult to follow.'

Vicki began running after him over the stones as if she was crossing a stream, and in the backpack Sarah started to cry.

They moved like that for two hundred yards. Max stopped, and said, 'Now we go north for a couple of miles. They will continue to look for tracks to the east. Then we cut back to the river. Ready?'

The sweating, breathless girl nodded twice, unable to speak, and he set off at a steady mile-eating pace just short of a trot.

'Come on, Vicki, you're doing well,' he said. 'Breathe deeply.'

They'll search that hill well, he thought. Could be there for a couple of hours. By then we'll have swung east and be halfway to the river.

Sarah's crying had subsided into an unhappy sobbing, and while Max walked he moved the pack to his front and began talking to her.

7

Dusk was settling its soft mantle over the bush, but the sky wasn't its habitual breath-taking red. Behind them in the west, angry storm clouds had moved in, at their centre a massive cumulonimbus, with its towering anvil-shaped column piercing the heavens sixty thousand feet above. The wind was gusting at their backs, as Max led the group down the steep bank onto the river flat; he was becoming increasingly concerned that the storm might arrive at the river before they did, and make crossing it impossible.

If his plan had worked, then two or three miles south of them the searchers would still be looking for spoor as they pushed on towards the river. The hunters would know that once across, and near the road, the chances of their quarry escaping increased dramatically.

Max stopped and looked back at the sky. It had gone from blue through white to dirty yellow, and was now dark grey with ominous black areas below the column. The wind had freshened and he could smell the sweet humidity that always accompanies rain in Africa. As a boy he had loved to stand in the rain and just smell that sweetness, but today it carried menace and foreboding. As he turned, a bolt of lightning lit the sky, zigzagging upwards, and he unconsciously began to count. One, two, three, four – and then the thunder pealed and rumbled invisibly across the sky. Four miles away and probably moving at at least that speed towards them, he thought. Which gave them less than an hour.

'Let's move it,' he said, echoing perfectly Vicki's thoughts.

Sarah began to cry again in the pack, and he smiled at her,

saying, 'It's just the man with the drum in the sky. Don't worry little one.'

Vicki was also scared. Born and brought up in the tame, picture-book prettiness of Hertfordshire, she had seen rain. Every day in boring relentless greyness it rained in England. She had seen storms before, too, but never anything like this and never in the open. The top of the cloud was now out of sight above them, but the column was still in the last light of the day at thirty thousand feet, and she could see the swirling blackness of the storm centre. Vicki wondered if this was the kind of storm that ripped off aeroplane wings.

'We stick to the trees now,' Max said. 'The lightning,' was the only explanation he offered, and the only one necessary. Another clap of thunder rolled across the sky like a distant artillery barrage and Vicki hurried after him.

'It's good,' he said, 'as there'll be no tracks to follow, lots of noise and poor visibility.'

He did not say that the river could be impassable in half an hour, and could remain that way for at least a day. He wanted her to see the storm as an ally, helping them to hide.

Forsaking security for speed, they moved along a worn path towards the river's edge. On both sides of the path heavy green bush guarded the fertile alluvial soils from men and erosion alike, while at its edges sat formidable acacia thorn bushes, that even a cape buffalo would avoid.

As they walked, Max took the plastic water bottle the old man had given him and emptied it onto the ground. He looked at the canteen at his waist and decided to keep that. He released the two chickens.

By now it was dark, and the wind swirled leaves onto the path. Thunder came again, like bass drums and big guns, and then fell the rain.

'Come on, we must run now,' he shouted, and with Vicki trailing behind him he jogged the last hundred yards to the water's edge, down the eroded bank and onto the shingle shore. Before them, black and a hundred yards wide, was the river. The watershed behind them had fed the main flow with rain water, and already the mass moved with a dull roar. Usually it was a rather gentle, relaxed affair, wide and shallow, but the season's good rains meant it was high, and getting higher by the minute.

'Can you swim?' He shouted through the teeming rain and watched her nod in reply.

He pushed the empty water bottle back into the pack, where it would act as a makeshift buoyancy aid, and pulled Sarah closer to his boy, with the bottle behind her. She had stopped crying, but was shivering with right and cold, and was making a steady, agitated noise each time she breathed out. He swung the rifle over his shoulder.

'Hold onto the pack strap,' Max said to Vicki. 'We walk till it's too deep, then swim. Don't fight the current, go with it.'

With that, he stepped into the first foamy inches and moved straight out. It was very, very dark, and the noise from the flowing water and the rain made talking impossible, so putting complete in him, Vicki she took hold of the shoulder strap and stepped into the water, bumping into him reassuringly each time he paused to feel the bottom ahead.

The current tugged at her legs and once she slipped, only for a large hand to reach back and pull her to her feet. She looked up, and Max had a broad smile on his face. Christ, he was actually smiling! Was he enjoying this?

They moved on and it got deeper by the step, and then they were floating. He pulled Vicki round to the front with Sarah between them, and they were bobbing up and down, the bottle in the pack helping keep them afloat, and Max shouting the whole time.

'Just hold on... doing fine... nearly there...' And then they bumped into a log, and it floated away. Max was kicking his feet, and lifting his head up using the current, and Vicki prayed to a God she had spoken a lot to in the last thirty hours, and then her feet touched something solid and they were in waist-deep water and only forty yards from the other bank, and the child clung on like a limpet through the pack.

With almost obscene strength, Max used one arm to pick Vicki out of the water and like St Christopher in the stories he waded to the bank, and through the roaring of the water and the driving rain she could hear his laughter.

'We're clear,' he bellowed over the noise. 'They'll be stuck in there all night!'

His grin was so infectious that Vicki, too, began to laugh, and Sarah raised her head from inside the pack and stopped her shivering long enough to look. She didn't understand, but the tension was gone and when Max laughed his body shook, and that felt nice against her, curled up against his chest inside the pack.

Max unslung the rifle, and taking Vicki's hand, began to climb the bank. He would keep them moving until they hit the road.

*

Johannes Van Heerden looked from the sliding windows of his Land Rover and saw the storm ahead. If it kept moving east it would miss his farm, but with some luck he would get the rain into the dam as it flowed across his farm in the stream from the highlands. He was pleased. So far the season had been good, with plenty of rain, and his mealies needed the *come-come*, as the locals called it. The others in the valley had long ago switched to vegetables and fruit trees, but he had stayed with maize, and it had paid off. He would get a good price this year, and with almost a thousand acres of mealies in, he could order a new truck, put a new roof on the sheds, and mike a sizeable payment to the bank for the mortgage on the second farm.

Yes, it was a good season.

It would also be the third season since his grandson had been on the farm to help, and that was also good, because Johannes was no longer a young man. He would be seventy-three on Christmas Eve, and although he still rose at dawn and did a day's work, he now wanted to spend time just sitting on the stoop and watching the birds drink, and maybe visit old Koos Van Wyk on Rooiplaas. His wife Marta was also no longer young, and having Jannick home was also a great comfort to her. He was the only son of their daughter Suzanne who, God rest her soul, had died with her husband when Jannie was a small boy. Jannie was brought up by his grandparents, who were old-fashioned, God-fearing people, who believed in stern discipline and lots of love. The shambok still lay over the mantlepiece, and over the last fifty years it had been used to discipline children, dogs, and the occasional local farm worker alike. Jannie Meyer is a good boy, thought Johannes.

The rain began to splatter against the windscreen, and he turned on the wipers, reminding himself to get new blades. The bulbs on the seat beside him had come from Chipinge, and he would be home in an hour and would get the generator running, and fix those lights in the sheds.

He would have been home sooner but for the roadblock a few miles back. This one was different to the usual, he'd noticed. It wasn't just a cursory look in boot. They were looking for something specific, and the vehicles coming the other way were being completely emptied.

Silently, Johannes wished the best possible luck to whoever they were after.

*

Max let go of Vicki's hand and shifting Sarah to his knee, he dropped onto his haunches. She was still shivering. Poor little thing, he thought, you're tired, hungry, wet and terrified. He held her closer, and finally opened his shirt, stripped her of her dress, and put her inside the shirt, hard against his chest, and did the buttons up around her as high as they would go.

He was warm from the exertion, and almost immediately the child's shivering subsided, and she sat, very quietly, with her head against his chest. He stuffed her dress into his pocket, and turned to Vicki

'Right,' he said. 'That's the road. We're going to wait for someone who looks okay and then you are going to step out into the road and wave them down. I'll be right behind you.'

She looked at him in the darkness, her hair lying in rats' tails around her head.

'It has to be you,' he said. 'They will never stop for a man at night. Don't worry. If they're hostiles...' He trailed off, not needing to say the obvious.

'How do we know if they're friendly?' She asked sensibly.

'Type of vehicle, condition of the engine, speed they're going...' he paused. 'Don't worry. I'll tell you when to step out.'

They waited for three or four minutes, and then heard the familiar whine of a truck. Max watched it approach from the mound he was on. High headlights traveling very quickly, engine straining... African driver, new truck, short wheelbase... army.

The next was an old pick-up, overloaded and chugging northwards, then a bus, unmistakeable even at night, and then from the south, a vehicle moving steadily, which dipped its lights as the bus approached, Land Rover, new by the engine sound, got to be a friendly, thought Max. Courteous driver, slow and steady into the bend, dipping its lights.

'This one, Vicki. Hurry, now!'

He pushed her down the mound and followed three or four feet behind, and crouched at the road below the shoulder while she stood up, head high, and as it neared, she waved her hand then stepped out into the road. Please God, let it be a friendly, he thought.

The vehicle immediately began to slow, and then the brakes went on hard and it skidded to a halt, pointing straight ahead. Vicki stepped round to the side, and hoping Max was there behind her, she leant in through the window which had been slid open from the inside.

'Excuse me,' she began timidly, thinking, Max, where the hell are you?

The face that looked back was that of a European. An old man, his face wrinkled with the years, and in the light from the dashboard she could see the deep tan, his face the colour of copper against his white shirt.

'We need a lift.' She stopped as the barrel of Max's gun brushed past her cheek. There was a pause that seemed long, but in reality could only have been three or four seconds, and then the old man spoke.

'I am an old man and am not afraid to die. But I think you are. So pull your trigger Englander, or get in the truck. They're looking for someone, and that is I think you, yes?' He paused. 'Come, we'll go the back way. There are roadblocks. Come...'

He pulled the latch and the door swung open.

'Hurry, girl, you in the front. Man, you in the back.' And with that, he slipped the gear into first, and as the doors slammed he pulled away.

No one spoke until they were moving at some speed along the still wet asphalt, the hum of the tyres as distinctive to the Land Rover as its uncomfortable seating.

'My name is Johannes Van Heerden, and before I decide what do to, answer me one question. Did you commit any crime?'

Max looked up, and the man's eyes were on him in the rear view mirror. 'Yes,' he said. 'But they started it.'

Van Heerden nodded, and drove on in silence for a while, before saying, 'I have a farm, up in the valley there –' he pointed into the night '– you shall be safe there while I hear your tale. Then we shall see what must be done.'

Right then, Sarah stirred, and he saw the movement in the mirror.

'Is that a child? You should have said so. There in the basket –' he pointed towards Vicki's feet '– coffee and some sandwiches, and behind you in the back, there's a blanket. It's dry, and smells of nothing more than my dogs.' He smiled to himself. '*Kinder on der plaas*. It's been a long time.'

Sarah ate three of the sandwiches and then sipped at a cup of the hot, sweet coffee that Max held for her, and then as the vehicle turned off the road into the hills, he wrapped her in the old rug and she snuggled herself into his lap and was soon deep asleep, the way small children always do in cars at night.

The route took them high into the valley on an old road, and all were silent as they began to move through mealie lands, the high tassels the height of the vehicle's roof.

'Welcome to Canaan,' Johannes said, as the lights of the house came into view and they turned into a gravel driveway.

The vehicle moved up the shallow gradient of the drive and through the gates of the security fence, a twelve-foot high hurricane wire arrangement topped with barbed wire. It was in two separate concentric perimeters six feet apart, and Max, though possibly with mines in that space once upon a time, but removed by now after the formal cessation of hostilities.

The house itself was a long, low arrangement with a veranda running the length of the front. Commonly called a stoep, it was the traditional red polished concrete, and gleamed dully under the exposed lights in the overhanging ceiling. Bougainvillea grew up along one pillar and long the roof, its red blossoms vivid on the edge of the darkness.

As the Land Rover pulled to a halt, two bull terriers muscled up to the doors, snuffling and wagging tails with such vigour that their whole back-ends swung like badly towed caravans.

The man turned and spoke. 'Come inside. We will eat soon, and then I will hear your tale.'

Max, with Sarah asleep in his arms, stepped down from his side, Vicki simultaneously alighting from her front passenger door. One of the bull terriers immediately stopped the happy wagging, and lowered his head, staring up through his little piggy eyes. Vicki slowly lowered herself to her knees and extended one hand, palm down. The dog advanced, slowly and suspiciously, until he could smell the hand, which he did, before allowing her to gently rub behind one battered and scarred ear.

'You know dogs,' the man said. 'Come inside. The servants should have gone home to the compound, so you will not be seen.'

Max walked towards the steps, and one of the dogs followed him warily. The living room was exactly as he expected, a traditional Rhodesian farm home. Game skins on the floor between two very good Persian rugs, and a large, overstuffed suite in an attractive floral pattern dominated the room. A large fireplace with horse brasses around the mantle was the centre of attention rather than the old black and white television in one corner. There were hand-crocheted doilies on the tables, and the room smelled of dogs, brandy and the freshly cut flowers in the large vase on the coffee table. A bookshelf ran the length of one wall and was full of what must have been thousands of paperbacks, hardback volumes, reference books and sources of information on every subject from anthrax to practical midwifery. It was a room that had been lived in.

Max looked at his host. 'Thank you,' he said.

The old man crinkled up his weathered face, and he smiled. 'Think nothing, boy,' he said, turning towards the passage and bellowing, 'Marta, come, woman, we have guests. They are hungry and tired.'

He paced out of the door and Max put Sarah in one of the chairs, and lowered the pack to the floor by the door before clearing the weapon. He put that by the door, too. Vicki subsided into a chair, and suddenly leapt to her feet. 'I'm filthy!' She exclaimed, turning to look and see if she had marked the chair and cushions.

Just then Van Heerden entered the room, and was followed by a small, slim woman of roughly the same age as him. Her grey hair was pulled back into a bun and she wore a floor length dress with an apron. Her face was one of those that one associates with women who brook no nonsense but contradicted that apparent hardness with soft eyes and laugh lines in amongst the genuine wrinkles of age.

'My wife Marta,' said Van Heerden, the pride in his voice obvious.

Vicki and Max introduced themselves, Max brushing his hand self-consciously against his thigh before taking her firm grip.

Marta immediately turned to the sleeping bundle on the chair, and peeling back the blanket from Sarah's face, she sniffed.

'Johannes, this smells of your dogs. I'll wash it tomorrow.' She turned to Vicki. 'Your daughter?'

'No,' interrupted Max. 'Her mother is dead. The soldiers...'

She nodded, and swept the child up in her arms.

'Right. We will eat in an hour. I'll put this one in a bath. You two may use the other bathroom. Share the water or you'll run out. Johannes will put out some clean clothing.'

She broke into rapid Afrikaans, with a stream of instructions to her husband.

'I will ask my grandson to join us for the meal. He will listen as well, and he will know what must be done. Come and bathe. Max, you need one if you don't mind me saying so.' Her eyes flecked with mischief, and she strode ahead down the passage with Sarah, chuckling to herself.

Out of gallantry, Max allowed Vicki the water first. While waiting in the lounge, he looked at the old photos on the mantlepiece, and made friends with both dogs. He stood as Johannes entered the room with a tray, and placed it on the coffee table.

Without asking he took the cap off a bottle of beer and held it out to Max, who took it, grunted his thanks, tilted it, and drank deeply. 'Drink, my friend,' said Johannes. 'There's a hobo more where that came from.'

He poured his own into a glass before settling into a chair. 'Now tell me what my wife need not hear. Speak while the women have other things to do.'

Max settled himself into the other large armchair, his long legs stretched out in front, and thought to himself, how much do I say, and how much will he believe?

'Any reports of an air crash in the past few days?' He began cautiously.

'Marta mentioned something. Unconfirmed, but fears are held for the safety or some such,' Johannes replied.

Max nodded. He had expected something vague like that.

'Two nights ago...' Jesus, he thought, was it only two nights ago? 'Two nights ago, one went down in the T.T.L. on the other side of the river from where you picked us up. I suspected it had been revved, and four of us went for a walk to wait and see. I was right. They came at first light, the army, and shot those left at the wreck. They had to leave no witnesses because the plane was shot down and no one must know. I thought we had got away, but they picked up our spoor somehow. Now they have to get us and kill us. We have stories they can squash. The little girl's mother was the fourth of us. They got her, and then there were three.'

Johannes sat quietly and looked at Max, his expression not so much one of shock, but of sadness. Eventually Max spoke again.

'That's the truth of it. I appreciate your stopping for us. We will be on our way at first light because the longer we are here the nearer they get, and the more danger you and Mrs Van Heerden are in.'

'I believe you, boy,' Johannes said. 'I have lived in Africa all my life. I was born here and raised here, and there is nothing that would surprise me. But what now? You will not be safe anywhere until you are out of the country. They have roadblocks everywhere. The roads are thick with troops.'

He paused and patted his pockets, and eventually produced a pipe and a pouch of tobacco and began to fill it. He continued, 'They will hunt you. You will have to lead them to a place where they will be disadvantaged by their numbers. Wait for Jannie. He will know what to do. That's my grandson.'

I don't need advice, thought Max unfairly. I need help. I need the dogs at my heels, and three or four days to get clear. I need someone to take Vicki and Sarah to safety, and then I'll run those fuckers ragged. I need to get nasty. I need to have nothing to lose.

'Can you help me with some supplies?' He asked.

'Make a list and then I'll add to it. I spent forty years hunting in this bush, I have what you'll need. Another drink? No? Well, after forty years I'll have what you need.'

He spoke the way old men do, often repeating himself and thinking aloud.

Then the two dogs rose as one and scrambled towards the door, and Max leapt for the weapon, jamming a magazine into the base. He was cocking the rifle as the door swung open.

'Woah there, I'm with the good guys,' said the arrival. He was tall, taller than Max's six foot, but lean and very fit-looking. He had long blonde hair that had just been washed and was wet against his scalp. His face was tanned the colour of copper, and he had the old man's sky blue eyes. He was younger than Max expected, but was obviously the grandson they had spoken of.

'You must be Jannie,' Max said, lowering the gun and putting out his hand.

'I am. Jannie Meyer.' He took the proffered hand.

'Max Seager. Sorry about that.'

Johannes spoke. 'Well?'

'Relax Oupa, I had a look around. It's clear, the gates are locked, and the workers are down in the compound.' He looked at Max, dropped the affectionate tone he'd used with his grandfather, and said, 'What's the sitrep?'

As Max began the story, Jannie crossed to the coffee table and took one of the beers. He drank from the bottle, listening and occasionally questioning.

'What shoulder flashes?'

'Sixth Brigade,' replied Max. Jannie nodded as if he expected nothing else.

'Tracker?'

'No, just a couple who picked the odd bit of spoor, and then lost it.'

'If it was Sixth Brigade they won't give up. Their officers are too scared of the boss. But why? Why the drama?' He trailed off.

And then in walked Mrs Van Heerden with Sarah in her arms. She was all bathed and clean, hair brushed and in an old shirt with the sleeves rolled up, but still looking very miserable and confused. The woman put her down and she looked around the room of strangers and immediately crossed to Max, who bent and picked her up.

'Hello princess. Nice bath?' She nodded, and he ran a finger down her nose, and for the first time she smiled, not knowing what else to do.

Jannie looked a little confused, and as Vicki entered the room his confusion turned to bewilderment. Max turned to look, and saw why. She looked stunning, her hair washed and dried, wearing a simple high necked lacy blouse that had belonged to Mrs Van Heerden. A floor length black skirt completed the outfit. For the first time Max actually saw just how attractive she was. Until now she had been a lively liability, but here indoors with people she was in her element.

She smiled and said, 'Hello. You must be Jannie. Your grandmother has been telling us all about you.' She crossed the floor and held out her hand. 'I'm Vicki Waters.'

Jannie, who had never seen anything so beautiful, simply stood with his mouth open, and Vicki said, 'Max, I believe we're dressing for dinner. Go and have a bath,' not taking her eyes off Jannie for a second.

Max stifled a laugh. 'Yes, Vicki,' he said, and putting Sarah down he walked towards the passage. Behind him, everything seemed to happen at once. Jannie recovered his composure enough to speak, Johannes leapt to his feet, yelling for the servants to bring drinks before remembering they had been sent home, and Marta Van Heerden, who at sixty-seven years of age had seen young men with that look in their eye a thousand times but had never seen it returned with the panache of this one, smiled to herself and wondered what the world had come to.

Max, once in the bathroom, looked in the mirror and tried unsuccessfully to see how the cut on his head was doing. He touched it gingerly, and swore softly when he hurt himself, shrugged and began to strip out of the damp clothing which he threw into a heap on the floor. He looked and there on the chair were fresh khakis laid out along with a big fluffy towel. He lowered himself into the rapidly cooling water left by Vicki, and gave a long, contented sigh. He then became aware he was being watched. He turned, and there at the door was Sarah, with the same agitated look that had preceded their first attempt at a ladies' toilet.

'Wee-wees?'

She nodded quickly, and remembering the first time and its time frame, he climbed from the bath, wrapped a towel round himself, picked her up and put her on the toilet. Shit, he thought, what if she falls in? The hole in the centre of the seat was, he thought, proportionally similar to him on a forty-four gallon drum.

Sarah, however, had done all this before, and simply leant back and balanced herself with her hands on the seat. Right, thought Max. For modesty's sake he began rummaging through the shampoo bottles for something to use on his hair, when she said the first words other than 'Mummy' since the crash.

'I'm ready,' she said.

Ready? Ready for what? He thought, delighted that she had begun to talk, but confused all the same.

He was rescued by Mrs Van Heerden, who did the necessary, and as she left with Sarah, said to Max, 'Always be gentle. The skin is very soft.'

Right, he thought, add toilet paper to the list, and got back into the now even less hot bath.

A head popped round the door. 'Aren't you finished yet? Hurry up. I'm famished. That man is gorgeous, by the way.'

'Bugger off and let me finish in peace,' he interrupted, and Vicki left, her laughter pealing down the hall.

Tomorrow it starts again, he thought. Laugh now, my girl, because tomorrow it starts again, because we can't stay in here and they're looking for us out there, so tomorrow it starts again.

Eventually bathed and dressed, Max joined the rest in the dining room. It was a long room with a huge walnut table in the middle, and a sideboard unit that looked as though the family had come up on the first wagons from the Cape.

Mrs Van Heerden served the food. It was hot and nourishing, and it just seemed to keep coming. Sarah refused to go to her bed, and eventually fell asleep on the sofa in the adjoining lounge. Mrs Van Heerden seemed to enjoy the house full of people, and the conversation skirted the reason for their presence for as long as it could it had to arise, and when it did there was moment's silence, awkward and unwanted as a gatecrasher at a party.

Max broke it. 'You say you saw troops deployed on the roads. That means they have covered the obvious routes. They will keep hunting, that I agree with. Every hour we're here or anywhere, we put the lives of others at equal risk, so we must go alone and go where they least expect us to. Which is into the bush, and south. We must head for the border.'

Jannie nodded his head, in full agreement. 'It's the only way. Go for the deep bush, run them a wild chase, the longer it goes on the more sloppy they will get. Stay clear of the roads, and clear of any people.'

There was a pause then as Jannie refilled his glass from the water jug and sipped it thoughtfully.

'How far is the border?' Asked Vicki.

'Ah,' he said. 'I thought you might ask that. About two hundred and fifty miles.'

'Two hundred and fifty miles?' She replied, as if she hadn't heard right the first time.

'That's as the crow flies,' said Max. 'Our route and going carefully... call it double. Five hundred or more.'

8

Vicki rose to her feet with all the dignity of a dowager duchess, and said, 'Can I have a word with you please, Max?' And swept from the room.

He stood, said, 'Excuse me,' to his hosts, and followed her into the lounge.

'Max, this isn't funny anymore. We got away from the wreck. We've been chased, had one of our group killed, nearly drowned, and I have had enough. I don't want to walk five hundred miles bloody anywhere!'

Her eyes sparked with anger, and her cheeks were flushed, and when she tossed her head her hair swung back, exposing her lovely neck. Max was painfully reminded of Svea.

'Listen, my girl,' he began.

'Don't *my girl* me!' she snorted.

'Just listen for a minute. You're not in Kent, or in some second rate film script. This is real. They want to kill us. They have to kill us, and they will keep searching this area until they do. They have killed one of us already, and will kill anyone to cover this thing up, including the people in the room next door. Now, I made Helen a promise, to get Sarah clear. I'm going to do that without involving anyone if I can help it, but you are involved so if you want to be a selfish little bitch then you stay here in the morning when they offer to hide you, because they are good people and they will. And you will be their deaths as surely as if you'd shot them yourself. Do you understand me? We have to go. We have to.'

Vicki seemed to deflate under his onslaught, and sat down and began to cry, her hand occasionally stroking Sarah's sleeping form. Eventually she wiped her eyes and stood up, smiling bravely.

'Okay, Max. We go in the morning. Shall we return to the party?'

With that, she took his arm and they went back to the dining room, but the mood was gone. Jannie and Johannes were poring over a map, making a list and arguing in Afrikaans over some point or other, and Marta had gone to make coffee. There was much to do before bed, much to be sorted and packed into one heavy and one light pack.

'Max, look here,' said Jannie. 'We get you to the bridge in the morning, and then you swing west.'

Max joined Jannie at the map, and Vicki sat and watched the man in whose hands her life would be for the next days and weeks while they crossed five hundred miles of bush and tried to evade an army that wanted them dead.

The next hour was spent in planning, consultation, revision and rejection of much... keep to the bush, never cross a clearing where you can help it, don't wash as they will smell soap after a while and if you must, use ration soap, if you think they are near, eat then move on before sleeping, backtrack, cross tracks, always seek to confuse... all this from Jannie who seemed very knowledgeable about being chased through bush. Eventually Max asked him who he'd been with in the war.

'Started with the game department, he said, using the old colonial term for the Department of Parks and Wildlife, 'then R.L.I., did the squadron selection course, and then joined Reid-Daly's mob.'

With those words he had summed up what Max knew must have been the career path of most of the small band of elite soldiers that were Ron Reid-Daly's Selous Scouts. To have been in the parks as a warden was qualification enough, but to add to that time with the Rhodesian Light Infantry, and then into the Special Air Service Regiment meant that Jannie had all the rare qualities that those who select look for in men they will place for weeks at a time deep in hostile territory, alone and living off the land, gathering information and often moving close to enemy camps. This man was certainly worth listening to. Max had visited their training camp outside Kariba on several occasions and watched them train, eating carrion, handling every hardship, brushing up their linguistic capabilities so their local accents were near-perfect, and the constant weeding out of those who weren't capable of handling the loneliness and the fear for weeks at a time.

'If you must contact, do it at range. They don't like long shots. It's all the encouragement they need to give it up. It's the delay between the hit and the report of the rifle that unnerves them. Long shots are dealer's choice.'

Then Marta came in with coffee and took Vicki to one side, speaking quietly. Max turned and watched Vicki shake her head and smile her thanks for the offer, and he turned back to Jannie.

'I'll give you a silenced .22 for small game, look at water holes at dusk, and just hit the small stuff. When you have finished, spread the remains for the jackals. If they are close, bury it deep or sling it up a tree so it looks like it was left by a leopard...' He paused and lit a cigarette. 'Never smoke if they are close. You can smell it a click away. See it from even further at night...' His advice went on and on.

Marta joined them and began giving Max instructions on the best way to handle Sarah on the trip while Jannie moved off and sat with Vicki to chat to her.

We seem to overcome his initial shyness, Max smiled to himself.

'Are you listening to me?' Marta broke in.

Max nodded guiltily, like a small boy caught out, and she continued.

'There is, in the box, malaria tablets, one a week, make her take them or she will die out there. There's antihistamine, where you have children and bugs they will meet, and there will be tears. Always keep her clean, use the soap and wash her hair regularly or she will get lice. I have put clean underwear in the pack. Change her daily or you will have infections. There are water tablets for her. You are a great bit oaf and can drink the water anywhere, but hers must be clean. There are salt tablets and battle dressings, and tampons for the girl. She was too shy to ask for them but I keep plenty in the story for the servants who care to use them.'

And on it went.

Johannes came in and placed some items on the table. He said nothing, and when Mrs Van Heerden had finished, Max went through them. All were good and well used. Compass, tent fly, groundsheet, a heavy-bladed skinning knife, camouflage face cream which was obviously Jannie's, face veils floppy bush hats, camo shirt, three pairs of khaki shorts, and then the things he had listed. Odd items, but all useful.

Max filled the pack, then emptied and repacked it a second time, only then satisfied that he had what he wanted where he wanted it. He walked into the lounge where the conversation had dried up in the awkward way it does when a young man is with a young woman and chaperoned by a formidable presence like Marta Van Heerden. As Max entered, he bent and picked up Sarah, and the older woman spoke.

'Time for sleep, Max, you have a long way to go tomorrow,' was all she said, all but winking at him. He agreed, and said to Vicki, 'See you in the morning.' He winked at her and she gave him a ferocious look while Jannie, in all innocence, stood to formally shake Max's hand. This man, thought Max, was a lamb to the slaughter. Jannie was besotted, and all the confidence over the maps at the end of the table had given way and suddenly here in the presence of this very elegant young lady out of the London debs' party list he was a true innocent.

Max left them to it and, carrying Sarah, was shown by Mrs Van Heerden to a guest room. Its large double bed was welcoming beyond belief. He put Sarah in one side, and as he did so Mrs Van Heerden said, 'You will need luck, and God's help. If you have never prayed before, then do it now, for the sake if the child if not for you. I shall pray until I hear that you are safe.'

'Thank you,' he said softly, walked to her and kissed her cheek. 'Sleep well.'

Max spent the next twenty minutes writing three letters, one to Svea, one to Andre, and one addressed to Johannesburg in South Africa. He sealed them in envelopes that were in the side table's drawer, and fell into a deep sleep. In the night little Sarah, sleeping restlessly, rolled into him, and his large arm crossed over her and held her close, and the strange bond between man and child strengthened.

Max awoke just before dawn and leaving Sarah to sleep on, he silently padded the length of the long passage to wake Vicki. She reluctantly opened he eyes as he shook her, and muttered something at him as he turned the lights on, and as he stepped back into the hall he was met by a mug of tea offered from the bony old hand of Johannes.

'Mangwanani,' he said, the Shona morning greeting.

'Cheers,' Max replied, taking the mug.

'Jannie has gone for the truck. He's going to Fort Vic today and can take a load of wood for a friend of mine there. You and the women will be in the centre of the load and he will let you off at the bridge. They are lazy and will not search a whole load. Now come. Marta has cooked.'

The sky began its chameleon change and as they sat at the kitchen table Vicki joined them and it was her remark of 'sailor's warning' that made him look again at the sky. It was red where the sun was rising, a deep almost tomato colour. He nodded, saying, 'Mightn't be so bad, could wash tracks away,' and continued eating from the mound of Boerwors sausage and eggs placed before him. Then he turned to listen to the heavy engine noise of a truck in the driveway, and he looked at Johannes.

'It's mine,' the old man said, before indicating to his left, where a canvas duffle bag sat. 'In there, some utensils, canteen, salt, vitamins, onion flavour herbs, tins for the child, some of my kudu biltong, sandwiches for today, coffee, tea, a thermos flask, solid fuel burner, and other things.' With that, he winked at Vicki, who looked thoroughly nonplussed, and then happy as Jannie entered the room.

'Morning all,' he bellowed, grinning at everyone and dropping into a seat beside Vickie who smiled coyly.

'Just coffee, please Ouma,' he said. 'I ate at my place.'

'Nonsense boy,' she replied. 'All you eat is peanut butter on toast. Now eat this!' She thrust another portion of the same vast dimensions as Max's in front of Jannie, who shook his head and got stuck in.

'Every morning for two years, ever since I moved out,' he mumbled between mouthfuls, 'I say no thanks, and every morning for two years I get fed like there is no more later.'

He smiled at his grandmother, who retaliated with an affectionate, 'Silly boy.'

'Another good night on Canaan last night,' Jannie continued. 'Joshua found Lemon on the job with his wife and took to him with a budza handle. He seems okay but you'd better keep an eye on him today.'

'Lemon?' queried the old man. 'Didn't know he had it in him,' and he began to chuckle.

'Save that talk for the barns, you two,' admonished Marta. 'We have a lady present.'

'Don't worry about me, Mrs Van Heerden,' Vicki said. 'My father is an army man. And besides, I thought lemon was a fruit,' she finished with a butter-wouldn't-melt-in-my-mouth expression.

Max stifled a laugh, Jannie looked astonished, and Johannes almost choked on his coffee as Marta Van Heerden turned and looked at the girl over her rimless glasses, hands on her hips, as Vicki looked back all innocence and sweetness like a convent girl.

'Mr Seager, your trek won't be boring with this one,' she said, beginning to laugh loudly, and was soon joined by Vicki.

That woke up Sarah, who appeared in the doorway a moment later, and soon she was on Max's lap eating scrambled eggs from a bowl with little rabbits running round the edge. There was a picture on the bottom and Max was equally interested in its appearance so he helped her eat the eggs and made funny noises whenever he saw another part of the picture emerge.

'I think you two have the same mental age,' quipped Vicki, smiling over her cup.

There was a pause, and the spell was broken when Jannie looked at his watch and said, 'Time to go.'

They finished the distribution of the foodstuffs and last minute bits between the two packs that Jannie had provided and were in the driveway not ten minutes later. Sarah was in a cream dress, with a floppy hat several sizes too large for her on her head, and a jersey to guard against the morning chill.

Max slung the packs into the hollow centre of the wood load and onto the mattress that covered the truck bed. They said their goodbyes with the same intensity of emotion one would expect to see between friends of long standing. As Johannes handed Max the silenced .22, he said, 'Shoot straight kerel,' the catchphrase of the Boers who demolished Lord Buller's British forces in 1899. Max smiled and took the old man's hand.

'Thank you, Johannes. There are three letters on the bedside table. Will you post them for me? I'll be in touch from Messina.'

'You do that. Merry Christmas and *totsiens*.' Until we meet again.

Only then did Max realise it was just three weeks till Christmas. Where would it find them?

Vicki's eyes were moist as she hugged Marta, and saying nothing she clambered aboard the truck, Max following with Sarah. Jannie, his dogs in the cab already, began to carefully pack the long cords of mopani and masasa wood into the gap, and soon there was only the odd chink of light reaching the three contained within.

Max picked up the Kalashnikov he took from the dead soldier who brutalised Helen, loaded a magazine from the webbing, and cocked the action.

'I want a gun,' said Vicki, gesturing at the Kalashnikov.

Max breathed deeply. The most dangerous thing in the world is someone with a gun who is frightened. The second most dangerous thing in the world is someone with a gun who doesn't know just how dangerous they are. Combine both and the thought is unpleasant, which is why Max hesitated before answering, someone stupidly, 'Why?'

Vicki's answer was delivered with conviction. 'Because two are better than one, because I will never have done to me what they did to our friend, because it's my life, because I want to be able to hit back, and because I am my father's daughter.'

'Have you ever seen someone shot?' He asked. 'It's not very nice. Why don't you leave that to me?'

'I'm not a bloody child, Max. I'm in this as deep as you are. I don't want to be helpless. I don't want to be shot like an animal. I have used shotguns, and fired Daddy's pistol on the range.' She paused for a moment, double checking she was certain about what she was saying. 'I want a gun, and I want you to show me how to use it.'

Max looked at her for a moment, then shrugged his shoulders, conceding her point.

'Right. I'll just pop down the store and get another...' His attempt at humour fell flat. Vicki frowned at him.

'Okay, Vicki. Firstly, this is not a gun. It's a rifle.' He held the Kalashnikov up. 'It is designed to do one thing and one thing only, and that's to kill. The Americans have a saying: "A gun is a funny animal. You very rarely need one, but when you do there's nothing quite like it." Well, that's true. You will carry it, love it, sleep with it, and you will never put it out of reach. You will love it like your man, because when you need it, it will save your life.'

She nodded.

'This,' Max continued, 'is a German-designed weapon, copied and refined by the Russians. It's made by Kalashnikov and is their model 47. It fires an intermediate round, which means it's got more power than a pistol but less than a true rifle. That also means its range is limited, and so is its hitting power, but for you it's ideal. It's the finest assault rifle ever built. Now watch me carefully. This is the foresight.' His hand moved along the barrel in the half-light from the chinks of sunshine as he ran through the weapon's nomenclature.

They managed twenty more minutes, and then Sarah began to get bored and niggly, and they stopped the lesson while Vicki took Sarah onto her lap and started playing a game. Max ferreted around the pack and produced a boiled sweet, which distracted, and he and Vicki took up where they had left off with her lesson. He left stripping the Kalashnikov until they were in good light and somewhere they might not need it instantly, and went onto grips and bringing the weapon to bear again and again and again, then clearing and changing mags, again and again and again.

'Now,' Max said, 'operating it.' It's got two modes. Single shot, which means it's like a sports shotgun. One shot for each trigger pull. Then automatic. Don't ever squeeze off more than two or three on auto or you'll use the rounds too quickly, burn out the barrel and send the last few at the sky. Okay?'

She nodded. 'Where's the button?'

'What button?'

'For the switch to automatic. Lots of bullets.'

'It's here, this lever,' and on it went.

The truck pulled onto the main road and Max stopped the instruction and said, 'We're now on the road. If we stop for any reason, please be very, very quiet. Take Sarah and give me the rifle.'

He stopped and chambered a round into the .22, which lay by his side, and cracked the Kalashnikov in his left arm.

They lapsed into silence, and as Sarah fidgeted in Vicki's lap, Max wished she would go to sleep, unfairly since she had only woken up an hour ago. The truck rumbled on, its diesel engine throbbing reassuringly, pushing them nearer and nearer the border by the minute. Sarah stopped fidgeting and turned to look through the gloom at Max.

'Where's Mummy?'

'She's gone away, Sarah.'

'Why?'

'She had to.' Max was in turmoil. Sarah was at last beginning to talk and he didn't want to drive her back into silence with anything she couldn't understand. He couldn't believe her resilience up to this point. Last night she had been scared, wet, cold and confused. Now here she was, not twelve hours later, talking to him as if all that was forgotten.

'Will you stay with me and Vicki?' Max said. 'Keep us company and look after us?'

She nodded quickly, looked across at Max then back at Vicki.

'Vicki is pretty. Will I be pretty when I'm big?'

They both laughed, and Vicki said, 'You're pretty now, angel, the prettiest girl in the world.'

She smiled again, her first since her bath last night, and for the first time Max thought maybe, just maybe, she'll get through this without being totally fucked up.

*

As the truck rolled on, Max's mind travelled back to the last time an airliner had been shot down in Rhodesia, up on his patch in the Chinamore Tribal Trust Lands south of Kariba. There had been people who waked clear from that one too, had waked the distance to the main Salisbury/Kariba road, and had been there by dawn. The difference was the distance was shorter, and the whole area was swarming with security forces on their side.

This time, it was a younger child, an English girl with no conception of what she was in for, and the distance was immeasurably longer, the country far more hostile, and this time the army looking for them wanted to finish the job.

On the positive side, they had a gun, they knew they were being hunted, and for the moment they had a start. Max himself added as a plus. He was young, fit, aggressive and not unexperienced in the bush, and while he wasn't in Jannie's league, he could give anyone a run for their money. But he wished there was enough light in their hideaway to read the map in the pack's side pocket.

The second time he had joined the 2 Commando sticks who had reacted to the scene, the pursuit had once again been lead by the young R.L.I. Lieutenant named Pascoe. This time he had again refused to let Max join the hunt, but he had just tacked himself onto the end of one of the patrols, and Max had been in the field with them for almost eighteen hours before Pascoe realised he was with them.

'I thought I told you that you couldn't come.'

'You did. But I've always been a difficult bastard. Besides, it's my area. I go where I like.'

Pascoe stared and then grinned. 'Well, let's see if you can keep up. They have swung east again,' he said, before they moved off again.

Helicopters dropped food to them and they ate on the move, sometimes jogging on the spoor while the trackers could move that fast, and on the second day the group they were hunting split, and Max went with the sergeant and nine troopers westwards, on the trail of the smaller of the two groups.

Pascoe's section of ten men contacted the main group at two the following afternoon, and in a brief but vicious contact killed five of the insurgents and took one prisoner. The man died on his way to hospital. It wasn't altruism that made them try everything to save his life – if he died they would learn nothing from him. Unfortunately the contact had taken place at a range of nine feet, and the shotgun blast had removed his left leg above the knee. The massive trauma and blood loss had been too much for his system, and he had gone into deep shock despite desperate attempts by the medic to keep him alive and available for questioning. Max's group had chased as far as the river and then stopped short of creating an international incident by following the group into Zambia's farcical version of neutrality.

*

From hunter to the hunted.

It was only a few minutes later that the truck began to grind to a halt.

'Too soon. Must be a roadblock,' said Max. 'Sarah, you must be very quiet now. Bad men, bad, bad men, all right?' She nodded, feeling the tension in the air. 'Sit with Vicki, and be very quiet.'

Max passed her over, and scooping up the Kalashnikov, cocked the action and swung to his knees facing the rear, where the cords had been stacked after their entrance.

The truck stopped and with the engine running, Max found it hard to hear what was going on. He remained on high alert in case they began unloading.

But a minute or two later they began to move again, and he settled back and relaxed. He slipped the weapon onto safe, and lying it down beside him, he looked at the child and said, 'Did I ever tell you the story about how the elephant got his long trunk?'

The truck rolled on and finally began to come to a halt again, then turned up a side road, coming to a stop two minutes later.

As soon as the engine had died, Max said, 'Walkies time, I think.'

'It's clear. We'll have to move.' Jannie's voice came through the stacked wood like a spirit speaking from the past.

The cords began disappearing, and light flooded into the chamber. Eventually Vicki scrambled out and took Sarah from Max, who followed. He squinted in the sunlight.

'Let's shove this stuff back,' he said, and throwing the pack to the ground along with the two weapons, helped Jannie restack the timber. He walked round to the front of the truck and swung open the side door, took the two dogs from the high cab, and dropped them to the ground. They began snuffling around, and one cocked his leg against the tyre while the other, the bigger of the pair, muscled over to Sarah who gave a little squeal and squatted down so she was face to face with the animal. His great pink tongue came out and wiped itself across her face, and she giggled.

'Aggro you bugger, behave yourself,' said Jannie good-naturedly.

'Aggro?' said Max.

'Yes,' said Jannie sheepishly. 'When the monitoring force were here they were pups and always fighting with each other. One said they were always full of aggro and looking for bovver. So that's their names. He's Aggro and the other one there pissing against the truck is Bovver. They're good dogs.'

He grinned, went back to the cab and pulled a canvas-wrapped item from behind the back of the seats.

'Let's walk into the trees there,' he said.

As they walked, Vicki asked, 'Was that a roadblock back there?'

'Yes. They wouldn't unload all the timber. Too much work, and they didn't search the cab because of the dogs...' he trailed off, and lead them into the trees and pointed down the hill.

'Down there is the Birchenough Bridge,' Jannie said. Max nodded and looked down the valley. To the west were low hills and more Tribal Trust Lands and on the other side of the river the bush was thick and inviting, forming a narrow ribbon between the river and the road.

'I reckon you should head straight down and re-cross the river tomorrow morning, back into the T.T.L. It's not too stuffed by the river, not too much bush, then swing back towards the Chirinda Forest, and maybe stay inside the road from there on. Keep near the river so you'll always have water. Remember, if the hunted thinks like the hunter, he will win. Good luck.'

He began unwrapping the canvas from the item he had brought from the cab. 'I have something you may want to take along...'

He pulled the wrapping clear and stood back. Max looked, grinned and then said, 'Christ, Jannie, now you're talking!'

There in the canvas spread over the ground was an FN FAL, one of the first assault rifles ever manufactured, and still one of the best. Here was a gun Max knew. Its heavy barrel allowed it to fire on full automatic without immediate damage. It fired 7.62

long rounds at a rate of 650 a minute with a muzzle velocity of 840 metres per second. The bullets would go right through small tree trunks and through whoever was on the other side. With a weight of just over 14lbs with the bipod, flash eliminator and magazine it wasn't light, but it was worth its weight in gold for the firepower it could deliver. The bonus was that this weapon was fitted with a sling and a big variable telescopic sight that would allow Max to contact at distance. This was obviously what Jannie had meant when he talked of the long shot being dealer's choice.

Max looked at Vicki. 'You knew, didn't you.'

'Do you think I would have asked you for a gun if I didn't think there was a second one coming from somewhere?'

'Smartarse!' He replied, delighted with the new addition.

'There are fifteen magazines in that webbing,' Jannie said, 'and some fawn spray paint. I suggest you alter the camo as the last place I took it was into trees, which is why it's that colour.'

He was referring to mottled dark green/light green colour of the butt and external parts.

'Last but not least,' Jannie continued. 'A couple of Zulus, and this I brought along for Vicki.' He held out a smaller, oil fabric-wrapped parcel and Vicki took it. She unwrapped it and pulled clear an old button-down holster on a canvas belt. She opened the flap and pulled the gun. It was a Browning Hi-Power 9mm, and she hefted it gingerly.

'There's only the one mag for that gat, so hold off on any target practice, and save the rounds for the real thing. Let's hope they never get that close.'

'Thanks, Jannie,' Max said. 'This gear really helps even the odds. I hope like hell that none of it gets used, but they will be comforting to have on hand.' He held out his hand. 'We'll be in touch.'

They shook, and Max took Sarah by the hand, beginning to

move slowly down the hill, slinging the pack with his other hand, and cradling two guns most uncomfortably. He went a short way and paused, adjusting everything to wait for Vicki, who was bidding a lingering farewell.

A few minutes later she appeared, hefting the unaccustomed weight of the Kalashnikov, the pistol already on her hip, and her smaller pack riding high on her back. She had also procured some training shoes from somewhere and had ditched the other pair.

They moved easily for the first hour, and immediately picked up the pace once Sarah was in the original small climber's pack on Max's chest. He looked rather like a parachutist, with loads back and front, but considerably more menacing with the long barrel of the FN extending beyond the front pack. He had the sling over his right shoulder, and his right arm resting on the working parts, but within inches of the trigger, and the weapon was cocked and off safe. He knew if he fell he would have the possibility of accidental discharge, but took that risk in order to have firepower available instantly.

From the back, Vicki watched him, his long legs moving effortlessly over the rocks and uneven ground as they descended into the river valley proper, the hair at his collar curling into thick waves.

She had always wanted curly hair and this irritated her. This very masculine man who probably washed his hair with soap, never used conditioner and probably had it cut by whoever was nearest at the time had beautiful wavy hair.

'Bastard,' she said, *sotto voce*.

'What?' He asked.

'Bastard.' This time louder.

'Why?' He said, intrigued.

'Just because.'

'Because what?'

'Because you have wavy hair and I don't. It's not fair,' she said in a mock sulk.

Max began to laugh. 'Silly girl.'

'Watch it or I'll chatter all the way to the border.'

'Sshh!'

'Still a bastard.'

The final word gained, she lapsed into silence. They reached the valley floor a few minutes later and moved along it parallel to the river for the next hour. Then finally Max called the first halt of they day. They rested a while, drank some water and while Sarah played timidly with the pack straps Max began to outline his plan to Vicki.

'We go under the bridge, spend a couple of days on the other side and swing back near Rupisi. We keep near the river all the way until it crosses into Mozambique. Then maybe follow it anyway. We'll try for twenty miles a day for the first few days, then take it from there. Ever been hiking or camping?'

'No, not really. I went to France once to a campsite near Cannes with a couple of girl friends from school. The showers were full of vomiting Australians and it just seemed to rain all the time.'

Max was sceptical at her seemingly casual attitude to everything. He himself was scared, and was not looking forward to a five hundred mile covert march with a girl and a child, but Vicki seemed to either not care or understand what they were in for. But she sure was brave, he knew that for certain.

'It can be fun, or it can be shit,' he said, 'and on a trek like this it will be both. If you see anything you don't like the look of, tell me. If it looks alive, or it's people, just freeze. If you are absolutely still they will find it hard to see you...'

'What if you're in front, and I see it? You won't see me freeze.'

'You won't see it first. I will. Just do as I do, or as I tell you. But should that ever happen click your finger softly. As we move on I'll show you how to make audible signals but for the moment let's take things as they come, and not overdo the paranoia. They may well have stopped searching or swung west again, or have gone into Mozambique.'

Have they hell, he thought realistically. They're here, all around us, and they're not going to give up.

'Let's go,' he said, and scooping up and now silent Sarah he popped her back into the pack and set off.

10

They moved well throughout the day, stopping twice more and at dusk Max turned them back towards the river, and crossed into the Tribal Trust Lands, wading through the water which was still muddy from the previous night's rain. The red-sky-in-the-morning warning hadn't materialised, the rain clouds scudding their way eastward late in the morning, and as night fell the air was hot and dry.

When they halted, a kilometre from the river, and settled into a rocky enclave for the night, they were all tired and dirty. Max dropped his kit, asked Vicki to amuse Sarah for a few minutes, and stalked away from the enclave, the long barrel of the FN leading the way. He was back in a short time, and laying down the weapon he began to set up their first camp. It was basic. A tentfly and lightweight sleeping bag for little Sarah, and the luxury of a small fire deep in the rocks. With the wind coming from the north, Max considered the risk justifiable for the morale it would provide on their first night out.

He kept her going by giving Sarah baked beans, which he was right in assuming all children like, and he and Vicki ate biltong, fruit and large mugs of instant coffee.

'This,' she said, cupping a mug, 'is sheer bliss.'

He looked up from his stare into the small flames, and in the soft yellow light she saw him smile.

'Legs sore?' He asked.

'A little. Got a good blister.'

'Don't let it cost you your life.'

'What?'

'Your rifle is out of reach,' he snarled. 'What did I say? Never do that! Never!'

'Oh Max, for Christ's sake.'

'He won't save you. That fucking rifle will.'

They lapsed into silence and eventually as he poured the last of the hot coffee into their mugs, he settled back and pulled a very sleepy child into his lap. He looked at Vicki. 'You're going to have to accept disciplines that take troops two months to learn in two days. We are too slack. We have a fire going, and anyone could smell it downwind. Neither of us has any night sight. In reality, there should be no fire, no talking, no smoking, and above all absolute quiet. Always. But for the sake of settling into our little walk easily, we'll start off gently.'

She got up and walked to where her rifle leant against the rock by the tentfly and came back to the fire, settling into her spot like she was at a cricket match, relaxing on the grass.

'You swear too much,' she murmured.

His smile slowly returned, and she continued. 'Jannie told me about you.'

'Oh,' Max said. 'Must have been informative as I only met the guy yesterday.'

'He said you were an evil bastard and used svikas or something.'

Max stifled a laugh. '*Svikiros*,' he corrected.

'What's that?'

'African spirit mediums. For years while I was in the police I used a very limited knowledge of basic witchcraft to help in my work.'

'Well, Jannie said you even scared the shit out of him.'

Max's mind was racing as he tried to place Jannie's face in an investigation team that may have witnessed his style.

'Jannie is being very flattering. The unit he was with had a training camp and extensive operations in my area. The Special Branch of the British South Africa Police, by the nature of their intelligence gathering role, had very close ties with that unit. We got the int and gave what we could to them. They followed it up and did the nasty bits. If Jannie said I was an evil bastard, that's the pot calling a very clean kettle black. Those blokes? Jesus.'

She gave him a lordly stare, and said, 'Well I think he's very nice.'

'Yeah,' said Max. 'I'd noticed.'

'Anyway,' she finished, ignoring his sarcasm, 'he said that if I stuck with you and did what I was told I'd be okay. He's really cute. Mum would freak, of course, he'd be all right.'

'Vicki, you're jumping the gun, aren't you? You met him once, and we have to clear here first before your mother can disapprove. And Jannie would fit into high society London and the debs' season like Genghis Khan at a tea party.'

'They can't be that bad,' she said. 'He really is very sweet.'

'Bollocks. Let me tell you about the men who made up the Selous Scouts.'

'The who?'

'The Selous Scouts. They were originally recruited from various places, such as Squadron R.A.R., R.L.I., and the Game Department, with the express intent of having them infiltrate terrorist camps, formations and then cull whoever they could. They were selected for knowledge they already possessed, African language skills, military skills, tracking skills, and the ability to move in the bush, live off the land for extended periods in hostile areas, sleeping like an animal, eating whatever they could find or kill, all the time a long way from safety and often in danger from both sides. They were then further trained, often by each other, and operated in groups as small as two or three, or as large as sixty or seventy depending on what the job was. They accounted for well over half the kills in the whole war and formed less than five per cent of the troops in the field. In time their role was extended to actual assaults deep inside Mozambique and Zambia, in the most cheeky and cocky manner imaginable. They took great pleasure in abusing anyone in authority and answered to their boss only. Show me a white guy who will wear terrorist kit, black up his face and walk around amongst them, speaking their language better than them, then piss off back into the bush and eat snakes and things, and I'll show you a guy who is anything but sweet.'

'Well, he was sweet to me. Sounds like you would have been more home with them than the police.'

The fire was dying low by then and the night seemed to close around them. Sarah stirred in Max's lap as he rose, trying to disturb her as little as possible, and put her into the sleeping bag in the tentfly, and crossed back to the fire. He scooped up his rifle and holding it in the crook of his arm left the camp silently again for a look around.

They slept the three of them together, with Vicki eventually rolling backward until Max's bulk was comfortably close to her back, and an hour before dawn he was lighting a solid fuel lump in the burner to heat water for tea, before moving on.

*

Back in the capital the Comrade Minister was becoming increasingly concerned. He was in no doubt that the man they sought to kill was dead. Whoever had walked clear of the crash was still clear, and that person had probably killed the two soldiers. The body of the woman was also a problem because it indicated that there might be more than one group in the clear. All this was, however, minor in its irritations compared to the German.

Yes, Heine Guttman was a problem.

Heine Guttman didn't like taking chances, and would do whatever was necessary to make sure the situation was resolved to his satisfaction. Furthermore, the first person who would feel the full reptilian wrath of Mr Guttman would be he, the Honourable Comrade Minister.

He rolled his bulk from the nuptial bed and placed his large, flat feet firmly on the parquet floor, rose and walked to the elegant *en suite* bathroom, where he winced. There in the bath was the family's washing. His first wife, the only one resident in the Salisbury house, was not his greatest asset. She still insisted on doing all her own housework, and wandered round the house with a *duk* on her head and bare feet. In the laundry there was a brand new fully automatic washing machine but no, she had to bend over the bath and do it that way. He sometimes believed that she still thought she was a domestic servant in the home of a white family, and it wouldn't surprise him if he came home to find she'd taken in someone else's washing. She really couldn't come to terms with the changes in their lives, and their new, comparatively wealthy position.

He finished washing and dressed, then walked through to the kitchen and was given his tea in a large, chipped mug. He decided against again showing her the rows of bone china cups and saucers in the sideboard, and the Wedgewood teapot, and stood sipping the tea.

Looking out of the window, he watched from the corner of his eye as she settled on the kitchen step and began crocheting. He would make arrangements today to have her taken back to the modest two-room house he had in the Tribal Trust Lands. There she would be more at home, and he could send for his second wife.

Now that was an idea! She was only twenty-eight, sleek and fat like a shiny otter, and, while basically lazy, she would certainly fit better here. She had been expensive at two thousand dollars lobola, and as yet had not borne him any children.

But back to the present. He tipped the contents of the mug into the sink and paced from the house to where his driver lounged in the front seat of the Mercedes Benz in the driveway. The minister hurried to the rear door (it always pleased him to get to the door before the driver could jump from his seat to open it for him), swung it open and climbed in.

'The office, and hurry up you miserable piece of sheep shit,' he snapped.

He would phone the Brigade Commander at the base and have him put more men on the search, and then call the German. He began to sweat at the thought, and thought of something which would distract him. The redhead. Yes, before lunch he would see her at the townhouse.

*

As they pushed further south by the hour, Max was becoming concerned with Sarah's relapse into silence. While it was superficially useful in that any talking while on the move was unnecessary noise, he would rather have had to ask her to be quiet. He spent most of the morning as they moved talking to her, asking questions to which she nodded or shook her head, but said nothing.

Vicki behind him was a constant source of surprise. She was far fitter than he expected, and other than the odd good-natured grumble about the weight of the pack or the rifle she trudged along without comment, in spite of the heat and the flies. Her hair was now tied back in a ponytail and she was wearing shorts for the first time. Her long legs were white but her arms and face were already tanning, with the exception of her nose, which had burned and was about to peel.

It was mid-morning when Max waved them to a halt, and dropping Sarah and the packs, pulled the .22 from its normal spot wedged in the pack's frame.

'I'm going to try for some fresh food,' he said to Vicki. 'Try Sarah with some biltong. She's a Rhodie so should love it, and then get the solid fuel burner going and let's have tea. Okay?'

'Now you're talking,' Vicki said, mimicking his delight at the presentation of the FN.

Max walked off nearer the river and soon disappeared from sight. Vicki was surprised at how quickly he was virtually invisible in his fawn shorts and short, lost among the dry-looking bush.

As he neared the thicker bush, Max slung the FN over his back and took a handful of the small rounds for the snake gun. He noted with some satisfaction that in amongst the copper-jacketed, hard-nose bullets there was the odd hollow-point round. He loaded those into the magazine, chambered one round and began to walk very slowly into the bush. He didn't like hollow-points as a rule, but then he didn't like sports hunting either. He was here for food, and with the limited hitting power of the .22 he wanted all the advantages he could get.

It was surprisingly easy. Within fifteen minutes of entering the bush he saw a small movement off to his right. He froze, and when the movement repeated in the same spot he move forwards with the rifle at the ready.

The weapon was totally unnecessary, because there in the dry grass along the edge of a particularly thick piece of thorn bush was a small buck in a snare. As he approached it, it struggled fitfully, and emitted a low, mewling noise, obviously in agony, its long, graceful neck deeply and savagely cut by the rusting wire of the snare and choking every time it moved.

As Max knelt beside the creature, its terrified eyes rolled and it struggled even more.

Of all Africa's scourges, of all its savagery, its violence and its death, to Max the snare went beyond the pale.

Set by tribesmen and poachers who were often too lazy to check them daily, they put the trapped animal through many hours of unbelievable agony, before they died from blood loss, exhaustion, asphyxiation, thirst or hunger. That was if a roaming hyena or jackal didn't rip their exposed underbellies out while they struggled and cried. Yes, cried. Some small species of antelope cry like little babies when hurt.

Other larger species may break free from the snare eventually but carry the wire deeply embedded in their necks or legs until gangrene or maggots, or just infection eventually pull them to the ground, the dignity of their existence shattered by a long, slow, painful death. After that suffering, death would be a welcome end.

Max had, like any farm-bred child, seen the evidence of poachers' snares, and had grown up with the loathing deep in his soul. As a boy he had watched his father cut a young kudu from a snare, and then after attempting to treat the rotten wound, had done the only thing possible and shot the beast. Max had never forgotten the look in its eyes.

Some four days later, Errol Seager had found snares in the hut of one of his employees. They were expressly forbidden and the employees were often reminded of this. The labour force had ample rations of fresh meat available, in part to discourage the practice of poaching with snares.

Max's normally mild-mannered father a shocked his son by beating the offender with a shambok until his back bled, and telling the local member-in-charge to get off his farm when enquiries were made as to how the labourer arrived at his wounds. It should be said in Errol Seager's favour that the man was not dismissed. He had three children at the farm school and was normally a diligent fellow.

In recent years, Svea's passionate rhetoric on the subject and active work with game conservation had had its effect on Max, who was normally concerned only with his own sphere of operations. He had increased his head count and put three men on an anti-poaching patrol with the parks' board chaps and raised the government bounty on snares handed in. The expenses were hidden in the informers' payroll budget, and Max's little team had helped the battle daily with threats of everything from hanging to Svea's favoured keel-hauling, which the constables concerned loved in concept and used in threats at every opportunity, though never actually carried out.

'I'm so sorry,' Max said softly to the trapped buck, 'but I need you and where you're going there's no more pain and no more snares.'

With a lump in his throat and anger boiling up in his heart, Max cut the animal's suffering away with a swift stroke of his knife.

Unravelling the wire from its anchor he carried it and the dead buck to the river's edge, where he threw the snare as far as he could into the water, and set to skinning and gutting the carcass. Better, he thought, to do it here than with Vicki and Sarah watching.

After throwing the offal as far as he could into the flow of water, he began to make his way back to the camp, two rifles and the butchered meat re-wrapped in the skin over his shoulder.

If he had come across the poacher at that moment, Max would quite probably have given him a hollow-point round high in the thigh and sat and watched him die slowly, like the animals he had sent the same way. But fate is never that kind and the walk back was uneventful.

'I didn't hear a shot,' Vicki said brightly. 'Oh good, venison!'

'I didn't shoot it,' Max said. 'It was slowly strangling itself to death in some bloody snare. But we have fresh meat and we will need to eat it all tonight or it will go off.'

'The poor little thing. I just lost my appetite.'

'Don't worry. You'll get it back by tonight. Did Sarah eat anything? Or say anything?'

Vicki shook her head, and looked at where Sarah sat unhappily, the tea untouched beside her.

'I think,' Max said softly, 'it's dawning on her that things are a bit different now.'

He squatted and, with his rifle still in reach, poured the brown liquid from the pot into a mug and sipped it, watching the child. Eventually he stood and walked to where she sat and lowered himself down beside her.

'Don't you want your tea?'

She looked up, her big blue eyes like saucers, and shook her head twice.

'Can I taste it?'

She nodded, and he took the cup, sipped it, and smacked his lips.

'Oh, that's yummy. Much nicer than mine!'

It was an outright lie. Sarah's tea was milky and sweet, the result of a generous squeeze of the condensed milk tube. What was more she knew it, she had been patronised before. But it seemed to work because when Max went and sat down by the fire again she shyly followed him and stood very close, watching him. He put own his cup and swept her up in this arms, and planted big, noisy kisses on her cheek then leant back grinning. She wiped her cheek with the back of one hand and grinned too.

'Bath time for you tonight, my angel,' he warned, still smiling.

'I would kill for a bath,' said Vicki, joining in.

'Vicki,' said Max, 'for my girls, anything.'

They cleared the camp and moved out, running with the river, and by dusk they were on high ground overlooking the minor tributary, the main river three miles to the east.

Once again Max chose a place protected by rocks all round except for the entrance and a narrow, steep climb to the rear, and once again he did an immediate reconnaissance of the area before returning to make camp. After erecting the fly and making a small fire, he put a pot on the stones at the edge and added water, most of the hindquarter of the buck, and a small amount of Johannes Van Heerden's herbs, and a smattering of curry powder. That done, he ferreted around in the pack and finally found a piece of the rationed 'sunlight' soap, some no-more-tears shampoo and a clean T-shirt for each of them.

'Come on then,' he said to Sarah, picking her up, and headed down the hill towards the stream.

'Are there any crocodiles?' Vicki asked, peering into the narrow stream.

Max gave her a withering look and shook his head. He had picked a spot where the stream seemed to flow the strongest. If they were all to get bilharzia, they would get it sooner or later but on the grounds that later was better than sooner he had chosen a place where the fluke would have the hardest time staying still while waiting for a donor animal. There was an extremely remote chance that the water was clear, but having traversed areas of what Max now thought might be an African Purchase area it as unlikely. It only needed one person to crap into the water and the life cycle of the parasite would be completed.

'No, Vicki,' he said. 'No flat dogs.'

With that he began to strip his kit off, and left only in shorts began undressing Sarah, who by now was poking the water's edge with a stick. She allowed it without complaint when Max told her they were going for a swim.

Moments later he was sitting chest-deep on the sandy bottom, with Sarah's little white body squirming in his arms, trying to watch everything at once.

Duck or no dinner, he thought, and taking a mouthful of water, squirted her in the chest. She squealed and suddenly her normally morose expression changed and she was beaming at him, giggling and ready for a game.

He began the soap routine as part of the game and as Vicki settled into the water beside them, demurely covering her breasts, Max was feeling rather pleased with himself.

He was even more pleased a few minutes later when Sarah spoke her first words since two nights before at the farm. He had taken a small amount of shampoo and was gingerly rubbing it into her wet, blonde ringlets when she said, 'That's not how you do it!'

Max stopped, stunned. 'Show me,' he said, and she did, and like a parody of a children's shampoo commercial she began massaging the soapy bubbles on her head, little eyes screwed shut and he wanted to burst out laughing.

Vicki saw it coming and glared at him, and he looked suitably chastised as Sarah stopped the action, peeped through one eye and said, 'See?'

'Right,' Max said, and took over.

They were back in camp by full darkness, the pot bubbling happily on the dying flames, and as Sarah sat in Vicki's lap with her hair being brushed, Max built up the fire, adding another pot for coffee. Then he had a brain wave. He took a mug of water and mixed a liberal amount of the condensed milk into it. It was white, sweet and cool, and Sarah drank it without stopping. He made another, which she took more slowly, and after that wiped her mouth, and burped.

That set the mood for the evening. They all ate from the pot of venison stew. The buck – which Max thought was probably a Grant's Gazelle – had a strong flavour, and with the herbs and curry powder was very tasty. Max ate a second helping, and then a third, without talking, all the while feeding Sarah bits long after she had finished hers. She seemed to enjoy eating from his plate more than hers, an Max remembered his own childhood and the pleasure derived from eating things at the wrong time of day. Breakfast at night, during the calving when his father tried to be on hand for all the births, particularly the stud stock, meant that all the farm's routines went haywire and Errol Seager used the opportunity to inject some variety into his diet. Max's mother drew the line, however, at roast beef for breakfast, and would sit while her husband fed the young Max with whatever he was supposed to have been eating.

After coffee, Max wrapped the small buck fillets in tin foil and buried them in the ashes at the edge of the fire.

'As yet the Van Heerdens forgot nothing,' he said, marvelling at the items he kept finding in the various containers.

'They were nice...' mused Vicki, contented, clean and full.

'This country is full of people like that. Good, solid folk,' said Max. 'But many of them have gone now, drifted somewhere else.'

'Another place in the sun?'

'Yes, but there will never be another place like this.'

'Where were you stationed?' She said, settling back with another cup of coffee.

'Kariba. You should have gone to see that while you were here. The town overlooks the lake and the bush. It's high up on the hills over the gorge, and I could sit on my stoep and listen to the elephants in the bush below. There's a place down the lake a bit called Bumi. They built a hotel for the tourists there. Small, but a hotel. Cold beers and watch the game with a drink from the veranda outside the bar. Where else in the world can you see a pride of lions sashay across the road like it was put down for their convenience, wild lions, and no National Parks protection. Just wild Africa. It's the last place, Vicki. The world's last wilderness up there in the Zambezi Valley. Sunsets so red that you don't believe what you're seeing, and the quiet of the heat at midday when the only sound would be the cry of the fish eagle or the emerald doves away in the trees...'

'You're quite and orator, Max,' Vicki encouraged. 'What about people? Don't you think they need space?'

'Not here. Not here. Never. There are four billion people on this planet. We breed like no species the world has ever known. Of those four billion you could cull three billion tomorrow and the world would be better for it. But here, this is the last wilderness. We can't make lions or buffalo or leopard. Have you ever seen a leopard in the bush? No? Join the club. Most people never will. They are very shy, and very hard to see. But when you see one! When you see him, pacing into the trees like a teddy boy, all muscle and latent energy, and arrogance, and you realise there are very few left, you become extremist in your views. If someone said take your choice: no more leopards or no more Communists... I'll tell you what, don't bet on the toiling masses of reds out there.'

'You're not an extremist,' Vicki said. 'You're just a big softy. You want to personally protect all the animals, and the sunsets, and the cries of the fish eagles, and the silence...' She laughed softly. 'Max Seager the romantic.'

'And you. What of you, my little Sloane Ranger?'

Vicki grinned. 'How on earth did you hear about Sloane Rangers?'

Max's eyes narrowed for a moment as the memories bubbled up behind them. Somehow there in the firelight he softened, and for the first time since Svea's departure he spoke of her to another person.

'My lady... ex-lady... she spent a year in London, and somehow got into that scene. She was full of the stories when I met here, which was when she'd just got back.'

'Was she... nice?'

The story began to come, slowly at first, and then in long monologues Max described their life in the house at Kariba, the joys, the laughter and the happiness, and then the end, blaming himself.

'And by the time I would admit to myself that I was wrong and actually phoned her, it was too late. She's marrying someone else in February,' he trailed off.

'Sore,' said Vicki.

'Sure is,' said Max. 'But there's nothing I can do about it.'

He stood up, carried Sarah to her sleeping bag and zipped her in.

'Make some more coffee, will you?' He said.

'No. We're on rations. It won't last forever. You can have tea.' Her tone was challenging, but kind.

'Tart,' he said.

Vicki walked over and wrapped her arms around him, burying her head in his chest. 'Thanks for taking care of us,' she murmured.

Breakfast before first light was coffee and the slowly roasted meat from the previous evening, and they were on the move before the sun was up over Mount Selinda to the east. Max now wearing a camouflage T-shirt of Jannie's and a mottled green face veil around his head like a sweat band. It would be hot soon, and he was wishing his hair was shorter.

'Very macho,' said Vicki when she saw him.

She was never at her best in the mornings, Max had come to understand. She went through two stages. The first was bright cheeriness, and full of banter. That lasted about twenty minutes, as a rule, then she actually woke up and was grumpy for at least an hour, during which she would demonstrate the unenviable trait of accusing Max of whatever she was feeling. In this case, when he didn't reply immediately, she sallied forth again.

'God, I hate you. You're always so crabby in the mornings,' she muttered.

He stopped, looked at her, and smiled. Then walked on.

'The least you can do,' she said, 'is retaliate. That would be good manners. At least accuse me of nagging you.'

He stopped again and spoke. 'If you don't shut up, Vicki, you're going to get a slap on the arse.'

'That's better,' she said. 'Back to your usual charming self. Where to today Greystoke?'

'Who?'

'Greystoke.'

'Who's he?'

'Lord Greystoke. Alias Tarzan of the Apes.'

Max stopped, waited for her to catch up and slapped her bottom gently as she came level.

'Don't push your luck, madam,' he warned, grinning.

She gave a mock salute and pranced on ahead, the Kalashnikov ungainly in her hand and contrasting starkly with the fluid rotating motion of her bottom in the shorts, which Max, being a man, couldn't help noticing.

She was changing from grumpy to her normal good-spirited self, and the morning passed quickly, the group moving steadily back to the river at a tangent. For a few minutes they almost forgot why they were there, a mile and a half west of the Sabi River, level with the spot called Rupisi, and where the road ceases to be tarred and becomes graded dirt with a stamped gravel surface to cope with the rains.

The reminder of what they were really doing, when it came, was brutal. It shattered the happiness of what had been up until now really no more than an extended and intense camping trip, and once again became a chase. It also changed forever the life of Vicki Waters, for at precisely 1342hrs she took the life of another human being, for the first and last time.

11

He was Thomas Sulikwane, a native of the eastern districts, and one of those luckless and yet lucky individuals who fate allows to be carried along and bumped about by the abilities and decisions of their more consistent and capable peers.

Thomas Sulikwane was unlucky enough to be attending school at a Catholic mission when the 'boys in the bush' appeared, and after threatening the girl and the nun who ran the small school, abducted seven of the larger students and took them back across the border into Mozambique for training as freedom fighters. All the freedom Thomas wanted was the freedom to get a good job when he left school – which meant finishing school. He told this to the commissar at the training camp and got a rifle butt across his head for his enthusiasm.

The training was rudimentary, and by this stage of the war all that was required was cannon-fodder. The command set-up was in place, and areas of the lowveld were, in fact, considered liberated, with security force presence during the daylight hours, though at night everyone was left to themselves.

Thomas hoped and prayed he would be sent there rather than someplace where Rhodesian soldiers were commonplace and hostile. Like most soldiers, all the wanted was to survive the war and then get out of the army at the end. He actually did three forays across the border. The first two were brief and terrifying. Within four days of entering on both expeditions, which they called 'marches for freedom', something nasty happened. The first time, they had been in a village in a so-called liberated area with their troop commander and commissar ranting slogans to a crowd of locals after dark, when a shot rang out from the back of the throng. It was followed by a short burst of fire, and Thomas, wisely considering discretion to be the better part of valour, dropped his gun and ran for the bush. The shot had taken the commissar between the eyes, and only Rhodesians shot like that – Selous Scouts, for example – and so it was only a matter of time until Thomas would be the target, so his thinking had gone. He was right.

The second time after only two days in Rhodesia, they walked straight into a group of Rhodesian soldiers dressed like them, the 'boys in the bush'. Thomas's commander suspected something was up instantly, and challenged them verbally while raising his gun. He died in a swift volley of bullets, as did the man behind him. Again, Thomas dropped his gun and ran. Guns are heavy when you want to move like the wind, he reasoned. Again, he was right.

The third occasion lead to him being dubbed with his chimurenga – liberation – name, and a reputation for being a hard man. Most men selected a name they thought dashing. There were the inevitable choices, such as James Bond and Wyatt Earp. They had two uses. One was that their real identity would remain known only to the soldier, and therefore confuse efforts to identify them, their networks, families and homes, and the second was purely bravado. Surely a name like Rocky was that of a brave man?

The other type of names were simple nicknames, issued after some kind of occurrence of some kind or another. Thomas 'Bata' Sulikwane got his after chasing two terrified boys out of a village. He had run after them to tell them not to be so stupid, running away was dangerous and would provoke the wrong kind of reaction, and he wasn't going to hurt anyone, but as he caught the boys he had an accidental discharge and severely injured them both. Now he was in trouble, he thought. Accidental discharges were frowned up on in any military organisation, even the roughest militia, as they put the lives of their own men at risk. Panicking, Thomas told his superior that the boys were informers for the Rhodesian security forces, and gained much respect from the others in his unit as a ruthless, shoot-from-the-hip type who was totally committed to their cause. He was called 'Bata' after the chase's success, which one of his compatriots thought was due to the handsome white tennis shoes he was wearing.

The two youngsters? Fortunes of war, Thomas tried to tell himself. At least he was in the clear... for the moment. What happened next, after the ceasefire, was that 'Bata', with his reputation as a hard man, was deemed suitable for the elite Sixth Brigade, to which he was transferred without ceremony. Now, two years later and still in the army he disliked so much, he was crossing the river to search the other side for a maniac on the loose. Shoot to kill was the order.

Immediately in front of him as they crossed the river was Lazarus Munchedzi, perhaps his oldest friend in the army. Lazarus was a wily individual who, realising that no education whatsoever was a handicap in civvy street, volunteered for the Brigade. He was, as Zimbabwe African National Liberation Army (ZANLA) troops went, reasonably well-trained and therefore reasonably effective, and had been in the same unit as Thomas since Thomas joined. Together they had witnessed both the debacles that had marked Thomas's early military days. Even then Lazarus, as the quicker of the two, had been the first to run from the contacts, although he had taken his gun with him.

The two men in front of Thomas and Lazarus who formed the rest of the patrol as they crossed the river were virtual strangers. The one with the radio seemed a real hard-core bastard. As they stepped up the far bank, Thomas, as was his way, sighed and paced along. The only decent thing about the Brigade was that while you were with them, they were with you. As a civvy, any deviation from the party's progressive march towards socialism could mean you had to answer to the Brigade. Joining them was, for the moment, if not the safest option then certainly the path of least resistance.

They paused as one of the others, the corporal, looked over the terrain, and instructed Thomas and Lazarus to search the far side of the small hill a mile or so ahead. He and the radio operator would do this side and they would link up when the linked up.

'Yes,' answered Thomas to his orders, and headed off in the direction Lazarus was going.

*

It had gone noon, and it was very hot indeed. Max dripped sweat as he moved steadily parallel to the river. The straps of the pack cut into his shoulders and he was thirsty. He looked round to where Vicki trailed after him.

'You okay, my girl?' he asked.

She nodded and smiled weakly.

'We'll stop at that kopje there and rest a while,' Max said, pointing at the small hill ahead. He looked down at Sarah. 'You all right, squirrel?' She nodded, but Max thought it must be unbearably hot in the pack and so lifted hear clear and sat her on his shoulders before setting off again.

He had lost a few kilos of weight over the past few days and his skin was darker than ever, his arms, legs and face a rich mahogany colour. He seemed to Vicki to be very fit, and while sweating freely, the heat didn't seem to bother him.

They eventually stopped in the shade of Msasa trees, at the foot of the kopje. The ground was broken and interspersed with thorn bushes, and there Max dropped his packs, and sat against a tree. Vicki was opposite against a second tree, and Sarah wandered between them seeing whose water tasted better.

It was perhaps the heat that saved them, in that it was just too hot to talk so they were at their quietest since leaving the bridge when Max heard something.

He looked quickly at Vicki, signalling for silence with his finger across his lips. There, again. Coming closer, he thought. Voices of two men speaking in Shona, accents from the north east.

He silently indicated to Vicki, who picked up Sarah, and whispering to her settled back into the rocks beneath a thorn bush, taking her rifle with her. She forgot her pack and, looking back, saw Max put down his FN and silently draw the silenced .22 before throwing his packs behind a rock and settling against the bole of a tree, half-obscured by yet more thorn bush. He clambered around the tree very quietly, and then set the rifle at his shoulder, both eyes open absolutely still.

He was almost invisible, the green T-shirt and face veil blending with the background, and then Vicki could hear them as well, and her stomach turned to water.

Max remained crouched, frozen. All Andre's words came flooding back to him. No scratch, no blink, breathe slowly and evenly. Remember that they see movement or colour. Remove the colour, and that just leaves them movement. Remove that and you are invisible... oh shit... how many?... only two last time, maybe that's the standard search party number... here we go, close now, twenty feet, talking loudly, come on my friends, walk right past, don't look here, keep walking, let's keep this nice, let's all live through the next five minutes... keep walking, keep talking.

Now in view through the scrub, two men, leader and follower, follower with a radio on his back, leader with corporal stripes, both armed with 7.62 medium Sovbloc weapons, closer, keep talking, keep walking.

They were now only seven or eight feet from Max, who was partially concealed by the thorn, and those parts which were visible blended perfectly with the background. Had they been searching properly they would have seen him, but they were merely walking and talking.

Then something quite ordinary happened.

The radio carrier, walking behind the big, heavily-muscled corporal, dropped his cigarettes as he fumbled for them in his pocket. He called for his companion to stop and, hitching the radio more comfortably, stopped to bend down and retrieve the packet. As he did so, his companion turned to look, his eyes sweeping the scene. He almost didn't see it, but instinctively he knew somehow that a shape he had seen was alien, and he looked back to verify what it was. Yes, there it was. A pack or something, fifteen feet or so to their right, in the rocks. He slowly began to ease his thumb down across the safety on the weapon, all his animal instincts to the fore, and aware suddenly that he was being watched. The hairs on his neck began to rise. His companion felt the tension, the change in energy, and stopped talking.

Max, only six feet away and on the corporal's left, pulled the trigger.

The .22 hollow-point round entered the man's head an inch and a half below his left ear and began to spread and tumble and exited three times its original size above the man's right ear, having completely destroyed everything in its path.

The sound, the first time that Max had heard it too, was really no more than a muffled cough, and as the man began to crumble, his radio operator, bewildered, stepped back. He had been splattered by blood, bone and brain tissue, and even though his reaction time was slowed by the complete surprise, he was still bringing his own weapon to bear, the cigarette packet falling to the ground, when Max's second round slammed into his lower jaw. He dropped the gun and reeled from the blow like a boxer, and then displaying enormous reserves of strength, began to stagger then run away from whatever was in that bush, his lower jaw destroyed.

The second round was solid and did not have the incredibly damaging capacity of a hollow-nosed round, and Max, realising his mistake on the loading, dropped the rifle and pulling his knife, began to chase the fleeing man into the thick scrub. He still needed silence, so he couldn't use the awesome firepower of the FN. He would have to catch this man quietly. And then kill him.

Kill him before he could raise the alarm.

The knife held in his right hand, Max ran into the scrub and dog-legged left where he had seen the man run. The chase was drawn out, considering the condition of the soldier. His jaw was spurting blood from the entry hole and the pain was unbelievable. The soldier had always thought bullet wounds didn't hurt at first. He ran zig-zagging through the bush, trying to escape the maniac and the pain. Now it was following him, he could hear it. The maniac, running behind him. Long, measured strides. He turned again.

Max was half following the blood trail and half following the movement ahead through the sparse scrub. He stopped frequently to watch for the flickers of movement, then running again, closing all the time and hoping the man wasn't carrying a sidearm, hoping he was too hurt to think of that.

Suddenly they were in the open on patch of grass, and the soldier was thirty yards in front and to the right and running hard.

Max veered right and lengthened his stride, gaining ground rapidly, his hair and the tails of the face veil streaming out behind him as he ran the man into the ground.

Eventually the soldier tripped and fell forward, and as he rose to his feet Max was on him. The knife flashed beneath the shattered jaw, and the man fell, twitched, and lay still.

Max knelt, his chest hearing, and rolled the man over. He stripped the radio from his back, noting the frequency as he did so. He pressed the handset and it hissed into life.

That was exactly before the lucky but luckless Thomas Silukwane ran out of luck forever.

He was walking round the base of the hill as instructed, with Lazarus, explaining how his cousin worked as a clerk in the Matabanadza Bus Company, and was not without influence in securing jobs for relatives.

Vicki had heard them talking, just as Max had heard the first pair, and she settled herself lower in the rocks. Sarah murmured something and Vicki silenced her with a quick, 'Ssh!', and looked down to the selector switch on her file. She moved it to full automatic and then, as Max had done, raised it to her eye. It was heavy, and she could smell the oil. Sweat dripped into her eyes, but she held on and then they were visible, twenty yards away, and ten from the body.

'Furthermore,' said Thomas in English, 'no money ever needed for the bus again. Transport for staff is free.'

He stopped and looked. Immediately in front of them was a body.

'Oh my God,' he muttered, and as he began to unsling his rifle – many armies don't allow their men to have slings on their rifles because they make it so hard to get at the weapon, taking so long to unsling when you need it the most – Vicki opened fire with one short burst.

She aimed quite sensible for the largest target she could see – the centre of his torso – and three of the four rounds found their target. The first into his chest, the second into his throat, and the third into his head. The fourth and last round went over the top of his head. As short bursts go, it was extraordinarily effective, considering the experience of the person pulling the trigger, because round number two, after exiting Thomas's neck and shattering the vertebrae, clipped the earlobe of Lazarus Munchedzi, who in the time-honoured traditions of his ilk, dropped to the ground and rolled into cover, and then immediately rolled back to his feet and began to run for it.

Vicki, surprised by the recoil and the deafening muzzle blast of the Kalashnikov, was momentarily stunned, and then, realising that one man was down and the other running away, dropped the gun like it was poisonous.

Max's warnings came flooding back, and as she bent to retrieve it, she burned her hand on the barrel. Rifle back in hand, she settled back in the rocks, and as Sarah began to cry behind her, she focused for the first time on the corpse of Thomas Silukwane, and she wanted to be sick.

Three hundred yards away Max heard the burst, and still clutching the radio began to run as fast as he could back to the spot where he had left his friends. Please God, let them be okay, he thought. Please God, keep them safe!

As the ran, he reasoned. A single burst was unlikely to have come from troops. No return fire meant that whoever started it also finished it. Vicki had a 7.62 medium, and she was in cover, and a very capable young woman, and hoping she had fired and not been fired upon, Max ran harder than he ever had.

Just over a minute later he burst into the clearing. He didn't intend to. What he intended to do was enter it quietly in case his worst fears were confirmed, but in the rush he confused himself over its exact location, and came across it fifty yards earlier than he'd expected.

He saw the second body immediately, and as he looked about him, taking in the scene, Vicki struggled from under the edges of the thorn bushes beneath which she and Sarah had hidden. She held the tearful Sarah in one arm and the rifle in the other.

'He just came along,' she said, breathless. 'He saw the body... there was another one, but he ran away... I'm sorry, Max.'

She was visibly upset. 'It's okay, Vicki,' Max said. 'You did well. You're both safe and that's the most important thing. But the other one will bring the rest, so we have to go now. Give Sarah to me and get your pack.' He was speaking quickly and softly, trying to get her to think of something other than the man she had killed, whose face was already covered in blue flies, one eye staring from its socket.

'Get your pack,' he said. 'Hurry now.'

Still holding Sarah, who had settled since he had taken her, Max moved to his own gear and put her down and began to sling his two packs.

Suddenly he had a thought and, turning up the volume on the radio he had taken, he immediately picked up traffic. It was call signs calling in and the command station asking urgently who had fired and at what. Max was initially surprised at how close the command base was. If they were close enough to have heard the sound of the burst of fire then they were within a couple of miles. He listened to the agitated voice which was now demanding who had fired and at what. He shrugged and said to himself, 'Fuck it,' and looking at the handset of the radio saw a Dymo label reading 2-6.

'Two-six... two-six... very sorry comrade, accidental discharge. Over.'

A stream of abuse came his way, followed by instructions to put the offender in his report. Max finished the transmission with a sloppy 'All right, over', which received more abuse.

Within hours they would know he had the radio, but he would carry it and maybe get further with a 'we are lost' report later, giving them more time to get clear, until the last man linked up with someone and spilled the beans.

Vicki arrived back where he was standing, pack on.

'Can't we go after him?' she asked.

'No. I'm no tracker and he has at least two minutes' start. We go for the river, fast and quiet,' Max said.

He scooped up Sarah and set off at a jog, stopping abruptly when he realised Vicki would not be able to jog and carry both pack and weapon.

Only a minute later the first visitor to the carnage arrived, and within seconds read the scene. He quickly cast about and picked up the tracks of the two people leaving the area. He cast about a second time and finally found the tracks of the single lone man, and set off on the spoor, calling behind himself to alert his companions. He jogged at first, and then, as it became clearer, he picked up the pace.

The four moved fast, the leader and his big companion and twenty yards behind them the second pair.

Twenty minutes after that Lazarus Munchedzi slowed his pace and began to walk, still moving northwards, and looking for a patrol from the brigade. Never around when you want them, he thought, but light a smoke and that bastard commissar is there in a second. He thought about Thomas and the corporal back there and began to run again.

He was no match for his pursuers, and hadn't even heard them when he was almost knocked to the ground by a blow between his shoulders. He stared down and noticed something protruding from his chest. And then deep traumatic shock clouded his brain's impulses, and as he fell forward he was dead, which was just as well because the teeth that tore into his upper thigh and ground punctured his femoral artery, and he would have died soon anyway.

The excitement of the chase over, the large black animal sat back and awaited the leader. He had never actually bitten into a human before, and it wasn't particularly rewarding. No reaction from this one. No fight. Almost as if he was already dead.

The leader arrived, looked around and took something, and then they set off again, back to the first bodies and to start after the other two. This was much slower as the leader kept stopping and moving things on the ground, and once trailed something as they went. The large black animal hoped it was time to play but the leader ignored him, and soon the river was near. He could smell the water and he bounded ahead.

They crossed the road before dawn and were into the deep bush of the lower sloped by noon. They ate the last of the biltong and now overripe fruit, and Sarah wolfed down a whole tin of sweetcorn. Max noted this and hoped she would eat fresh corn just as enthusiastically. Called mealies locally, they formed the staple diet of the entire continent, and could be found anywhere there was habitation. Usually ground, the meal was boiled with water to make sudza porridge which had several advantages, being virtually tasteless means one does not tire of the flavour, it doesn't need refrigeration and, lastly, it contains large amounts of carbohydrates.

Max anticipated that they would need to start using mealie meal as their staple diet soon now. Sudza flavoured with anything you had to throw on the plate, like everyone else in Africa; except, of course, where there was no rain and the crops failed. In those places people didn't eat anything at all.

A favourite expression of his mother's had been, 'There by the grace of God go I.' Max, as a teenager, had once had an argument with his father, who had refused Max's request to borrow the family car. His mother had asked him what the matter was and, on hearing his reply, had driven them both down to the compound in the Land Rover. They visited the wife of the dip tank boy, who a year or two before had given birth to a baby with short appendages where his arms should have been. No one knew the reason. The child was now a toddler, and with the birth of another child since then, was very definitely taking second place.

They left, and on the drive home his mother said something that he remembered perfect years later. 'You are young and strong. You have the best education in the land and you are bright and intelligent. You speak two languages, one of which is spoken by most of the civilised world. You want for nothing. And you are white, which might not seem like a great benefit to you but certainly is. You are instantly accepted on first impressions for that reason alone, and you will have all the support your father and I can give. Now, young Max, you look at that poor little mite back there, and you said, "There by the grace of God go I," because right now your biggest problem is that your dad won't let you use his car. Grow up!'

Max had never forgotten it, and often when things weren't going as he'd planned or hoped, he would remember the child and his mother's words, and things would immediately take their proper perspective.

'Sudza,' he said. 'We are going to eat a ton of sudza on this trip,' and smiled. Hearing his words, Vicki thought he must like sudza.

12

In Harare life raced on, as much as life in a small city in Africa in the heat of the day can race on. The large, fashionable hotels were busy with casual guests, the bars full of loud, noisy crowds mostly beginning the pre-Christmas wind-up, of company drinks, and long lunches. The restaurants of the first floor of Meikles Hotel were far more sedate and elegant, its table reputable for four generations of Rhodesians. The smaller restaurant was the Bagatelle, its menu famous amongst those who could afford it, and who liked to think there was a real French chef in the kitchen. The executive chef really was French, but the men who did the work were all local Zimbabweans, proud of their culinary skills but especially proud of their garlic snails and rare fillets of Zimbabwe beef.

One diner who should have been gently picking his way through the snails and anticipating the succulent grilled *fillet de boeuf* was the Honourable Minister. But alas not today. The final snail on his plate disappeared into his mouth with no more anticipation and reverence than a cheap boiled sweet.

Minutes before, he had left a meeting with Heine Guttman and once again the German's intelligence sources had managed to embarrass him. Guttman hand known before the Minister that things had once again gone wrong in the search for Orpheus, or whoever was still out there.

'He has done it again,' Guttman said. 'Three men dead and one missing. At this rate he will decimate your Brigade by Christmas. One was killed with a light calibre. We don't know much of Orpheus, but we do know that his favourite weapon is a long-barrelled target pistol size. One was killed with an issue weapon. Excellent! Your people are excelling themselves. First they allow someone to walk off with one of their rifles, and then start killing with it. The last one, this is the best! He was killed with a knife. He had his throat cut! The autopsy was difficult with that one because something had eaten half his neck and head away.' The voice dropped to a whisper, and Guttman again reminded the Minister of a puff adder. 'If we lose this one, then it's all over. It must be him! Who else could kill three of your men? Put in more men! I have sent for two of mine from Lusaka. They will... advise on the search. It would be a pity for the Prime Minister to hear of your involvement in this matter, so do as I say. You are bought and paid for. Remember that!'

Even the hours spent with the French whore were now being affected. Last night, he had completely failed to become aroused. Lucky for her she hadn't laughed at him, or the mood he was in, it would have been the last sound she made.

*

The big black animal had led them across the river at dawn, the leader hanging back with the smaller tow. They have moved fast, still moving things as they went, and stopped briefly at the spot where the quarry had spent the night. Several miles into the bush they stopped moving things as they went, and the leader, looking above at the high ground, set off at a run. They were fit and had eaten well the night before, the big one having finished most of the forequarter of the buck the leader had killed. Late in the afternoon, the great red sun setting in the west, they had stopped, the leader resting and breathing easily as he sat on a rock overlooking the track

Soon now, their quarry would pass below.

*

Max, again with Sarah on his shoulders, led them higher up the indistinct game trail that ran round the side of the ridge. Still an hour from sunset, he wanted all the miles he could get between them and the killing ground of yesterday. He had dropped the radio at dawn into an antbear hole. The bodies would have been found by now, either by troops or tribesmen, or the last man would have made contact with his command. The radio was compromised, and it was too heavy to carry on the off chance they might gain useful intelligence from it. It was too easy to change codes.

Vicki had accepted the actions of yesterday as inevitable and had therefore accepted her part in it. She had pleased Max enormously when she asked him if she should change the magazine for a full one. He asked her to count the remaining rounds, and she said, 'No.'

He replied, with a smile, 'Ordinarily you would have topped that up with loose rounds. But don't change it. Better you have three full ones in reserve. Now where's the bra?'

'Don't be familiar,' she retorted. 'If that's what you call that webbing arrangement it's in my pack.'

'From now on wear it. Those mags are no good to us in your pack.'

Earlier in the day Sarah had walked for a while holding Vicki's hand and had begun asking questions. Max had been surprised but Vicki had assured him that all little kids ask questions constantly.

The first had been predictable.

'Where are we going?' She asked brightly.

Max looked down. 'Up there.'

'Why?'

'Because we can see more.' He surprised himself with such a clever answer.

'See what?' Oh shit. Now what?

'The world, squirrel. We will see the whole world from up there.'

Hours later, Sarah was tired and her talking had petered out to the odd grumble or request for a drink, which she had just made. Max stopped and, moving the sling of the FN, took a bottle of water from the webbing belt.

It was as he squatted down to her that he felt it. Nothing tangible, but it was there. It was too quiet. They were being watched, and the hackles began to rise along the back of his neck in the most primeval manner. He eased his hand down and across the mechanism of the rifle, and slipped his finger through the trigger guard, in what he hoped was a nonchalant motion.

Vicki moved nearer and eased off her own pack straps before she felt the tension. As soon as she did, she stiffened. Max said, 'The rock to my right. As soon as you se me move, get behind it as quick as you can. There's something here. Something watching us... NOW!'

He swept Sarah up, and as Vicki dodged behind the rock, Max went straight over the top and slithered down the back of it on his side, child under the arm whose hand was holding his weapon, the other hand breaking his fall as he went.

He crashed to a halt. It had been further than he planned and the last three feet were sheer. He literally threw Sarah to Vicki, dropped the large pack from his back, swung the heavy barrel of the FN around, then looked at her.

'Good girl,' he said. 'Now stay here. I'm going to hot foot it round the back and take a look.'

'Don't leave us again, Max,' Vicki pleaded softly. 'Please don't go again.'

Then they both heard it. The clear tune being whistled, strongly and resolutely.

They looked at each other. Max's immediate conception was that it wasn't the sort of tune that an African would whistle. Not out here. It was familiar and classical. Sarah began to cry. She had taken a bump on the way down the rock and now it was sore and the poor little thing didn't understand any of this.

The whistling stopped, then started again, then stopped.

Vicki's face was intense. There was something about the whistle. Something she knew.

Then her face lit up with a smile and she shouted, 'Tchaikovsky!' and began to laugh. Max was stunned.

'What the fuck are you doing?' He hissed.

'It's Jannie!'

Vicki put Sarah gently on the ground and ran around the rocks, giggling as she went.

Max thought she had slipped a cog.

'Seager, get up here man!' A voice bellowed.

Max began to laugh and stood up. He rescued Sarah from confusion with a big kiss, picked her up and made his way round the rock, this time at ground level.

Vicki was hugging Jannie and laughing and talking all at once as Max cleared the boulder.

He seemed taller than before, but that was the effect of the very short shorts he wore. Training shoes without socks and an old khaki shirt completed the kit. His hair was tied with a rubber band and a small pack hung from his shoulders. The walnut butt of a sports rifle protruded from a scabbard behind his right shoulder, and as he put out his hand to Max, his grin spread like a pool of oil across his face.

'How are things?' Jannie asked.

'You arsehole, you scared the shit out of me,' Max replied, grinning.

'You're too quick with the gun for me to have stepped out on you. You'd have revved me!'

Vicki stopped hugging Jannie and stepped between the two men, taking an arm of either, smiling broadly.

Above them in the rocks, confused by the meeting, the big black animal watched. The two smaller ones moved with him and gazed down at the humans. The black one took a deep breath, and a huge sound burst forth from his lungs as he charged down the hill. It was a bark, technically, but in reality sounded more like a roar, and Jannie turned and bellowed, 'Dingaan, *voetsek*!' and the big black dog thundered into him, pink tongue lashing everything in sight. Behind him, the two bull terriers joined the game, and Sarah squealed, 'Doggy!' and struggled to get Max to put her down. Once there, the two bull terriers greeted her with wet tongues and grinning as only bull terriers can do. The black dog watched, and then leant forward and smelled her hair.

'What is that?' Max said admiringly.

'Dingaan is a bad-mannered, ill-disciplined but still young Rottweiler. He's great, eh?'

Max looked carefully. He had never seen the breed before, but had heard of them. Mature they would weigh in at seventy kilos, intelligent and strong, they were originally a cross-breed of the Doberman and the bull Mastiff and had the best traits of both. The Doberman's intelligence and loyalty, and the Mastiff's enormous, muscled shoulders and chest, and short nose.

Dingaan looked at Max and now seeing someone friendly, stood up, his front paws on Max's shoulders, and tried to lick his face. Max laughed and turned his head away, and Jannie pulled the dog down, chastising him as he did so.

'Are they normally this big?' Max asked.

'No. He is very, very big. Dingaan, sit!' The big dog immediately sat at Jannie's feet, looking adoringly up at his master.

Max and Jannie's eyes met, and Max asked in Shona, 'Why are you here?'

The saw the pain flash through Jannie's eyes, and counted the seconds in the pause. Max's chest suddenly felt heavy. No, my mate, he thought. Tell me I'm wrong. Tell me you're always up here at this time of year.

'Later,' said Jannie softly, also in Shona. 'We will talk later.' Then he said in English, 'Come, there's a place just not far away. Water as well.'

They collected their packs and made their way round the side of the ridge and within minutes the now enlarged group was settling in for the night, and Max watched with surprise as Jannie built a large fire in the rocks.

'Is that safe?' Max said, prepared to give the younger man the benefit of the doubt.

'Oh yes. Nothing above it to reflect the glow. No visual line of sight and nobody in the immediate area.'

'I'm not so sure Jannie. We were compromised yesterday. One of them got away.'

'I know. I was on your spoor. I followed up the last one so he is no problem. Also did some antitracking after that, so there is no spoor for them. They will think we are still on the other side of the Sabi.'

The 'we' didn't go unnoticed by Max, who was no more positive than ever that the Van Heerdens had been visited.

Jannie broke open his pack, and threw meat to the dogs, who wolfed it down, and then, getting to his feet holding a water bottle, said he was off to water the dogs at the stream. He pulled the hunting rifle from its scabbard and set off down the hill, the three animals scrabbling behind him.

'Something happened at the farm, didn't it,' said Vicki when Jannie was far enough away to be out of earshot. 'I can tell'

'I don't know. I suppose he will tell us when he's ready.' With that, Max collected Sarah, and after taking a clean shirt, soap and underwear for her out of the pack, walked down the hill after Jannie.

It was later, after they had eaten, that they began to talk. Sarah was sitting with the bigger of the bull terriers, Aggro, on her sleeping back, her back against his wide flank. The dog was asleep and Sarah soon followed, her eyelids drooping steadily. Her clean hair shone in the firelight, the golden waves in contrast to the short, rough white fur of Aggro's back. Beauty and the beast, Max thought.

Vicki, too, was luxuriating in the feeling of being clean, and she sat contentedly, blowing gently into a cup of coffee to help it cool.

Max, for the first time since they left the fam, felt he was secure enough to strip and clean his weapon. That was one of the rifle's few foibles. Unlike Vicki's Kalashnikov, the FN needed to be kept clean to function properly, but he had never felt safe enough to completely strip it down. Now with Jannie in the camp, the dogs and the distance between them and the last scene, he could afford the time for this essential task.

'You too, Vicki,' he instructed. 'Strip and clean your rifle.'

She made a token complaint, and Jannie gallantly took it from her, stripping it down in six seconds flat. Then, after bringing his own rifle closer, he began work on it.

As they worked they began talking softly, the way people do in the dark, as Vicki sipped her coffee. Eventually Max, wiping the excess oil from the action, inserted the magazine, cocked the weapon and put it aside before looking across the flames at Jannie.

'What brings you?' He said in Shona.

The pause was long, and Jannie picked up a stick and prodded the embers as he gazed into the fire, and then began assembling the rifle. Finally he began.

'They came to Canaan, the farm. The afternoon of the day we left. Troops in a couple of trucks. I got the story from old Joshua. They took him and beat him. Then they started on his younger wife and new son. Eventually he told them that there had been visitors at the house the night before. Lots of dishes in the sink but he didn't see anyone. The troops went up to the house. Oupa was in the lands, but one of the boys ran for him. When he got back...' He gazed into the flames again, his eyes wet '. . . Ouma was on the ground outside the kitchen door. She was old and they hit her too hard. Oupa ran inside for his gun and Joshua said he almost got to it. That would have been a sight,' he said proudly. 'Oupa with his rifle. This is it.'

He held the weapon up in the light. The walnut stock glistened with years of loving linseed oil applications.

'Anyway, they shot him in the hallway.' Vicki had her hands to her face and was crying softly, crying for Johannes and Marta Van Heerden.

'I got back mid-morning the next day. Joshua sent one of his sons to meet me on the road. They were still at the farm, drinking the brandy and searching and... one of them actually had a shit on Ouma's dressing table. I waited, then went back down to my place and got some kit and Dingaan, and went through the bush back to the house, then into the bedroom and got some more kit, then back down the road to wait.

'When they left it was very late. I put a claymore mine in the bush at the bend in the road and as they came round I hit the driver of the first truck, then the officer. He was the one who did those things to Joshua's wife. And then... then as they leapt clear of the truck they went straight into the tripwire of the mine, and I took the gap. And now I'm here.'

Vicki got up, crossed to Jannie, knelt beside him and silently put her arms around him.

After a few moments, Max spoke. 'I'm so sorry, Jannie. I'm so sorry. I'm sorry I ever got your people into this mess.'

'It was Oupa's choice, Max. He knew the risks. He knew they would come, but for these two –' he indicated Vicki and Sarah

'– he would take whatever risks were necessary. As soon as we left he drove into town and posted your letters. Joshua went with him but didn't tell the terrs they had been.'

Max immediately felt better. If the letters had got through then Jannie's grandparents had not died for nothing. He wondered if the old man had perhaps realised the importance of the contents of the envelopes. No, he couldn't. Max wasn't even sure he did.

That night, as they slept, Vicki moved her bag alongside Jannie, and set a precedent for the remainder of the trip. Sarah woke wanting a drink, and as Max held the heavy bottle for her, he watched the big black shape of Dingaan the Rottweiler lope soundlessly through the camp, and he smiled to himself in the dark. His little group had become three hundred per cent more effective. The man sleeping lightly beneath a blanked was the answer to a prayer. Ex-Special Air Service, and then into the Selous Scouts, his training and abilities here in the bush were unparalleled except perhaps by another Scout. A modern, laughing warrior of the likes not seen on this continent since Shaka's impis. They were also legends for their innovative thinking and applied courage. If Max had doubts about making the border safely with a child and a young English girl, the events of the previous forty-eight hours had begun to dispel them. Vicki's initiation into survival and the arrival of Jannie Meyer left Max very confident indeed.

13

Pretoria in the Republic of South Africa is one of those compromises where nobody won. Like Australia's Canberra and America's Washington D.C., the petty rivalries over whose town would be the nation's capital had little to do with the final choice. At the time that South Africa was seeking respectability and the right to determine its own destiny, Johannesburg was a sprawling, brawling gold town, and while much of the nation's commercial and financial decisions were made there, the choice of capital went to a smaller, more genteel and staunchly conservative town to the north. A town called Pretoria. Capetown, already old and established, and Durban, the predominantly English speaking east coast port, were both bypassed in favour of Pretoria.

The reasons were simple. While Johannesburg was noisy and vulgar it was the seat of the nation's wealth and was important. But to the largely Afrikaans men who would make the policy decisions it was completely unacceptable. They were religious, family men, conservative and Calvinistic in outlook, and Jo'burg, as it was soon known, was a den of sin. They needed an alternative, nearby and of good, solid folk, god-fearing and not given to wild excesses. Pretoria was the solution. Other than its fame as the nation's capital, Pretoria became known for its beautiful gardens and avenues of blooms.

*

In a dusty old government building hidden amongst so many, there is a department without names on doors. Even the traditional numbers have long since been removed. It is the operational control centre for the Bureau of State Security's external operations.

Down in Johannesburg, twenty-two floors up in a glass skyscraper, lies the public front of B.O.S.S. There is a reception desk where a very polite bi-lingual lady will direct you to the person you want to see. It is more like the reception of a large multinational company. But in the dusty Pretoria offices with grey filing cabinets and linoleum floors, the real work is done.

It's not all grey filing cabinets. There is a room with a very big IBM computer, beige in colour. There are computerised film processing facilities and electronic monitoring systems with satellite access which, as we arrive there in the late 1970s, are state-of-the-art. There is a section of people who prepare ciphers and codes individually because computer selection was never as good. The section head still writes the bi-lingual crossword in the country's biggest daily paper, and still is infuriated when his wife does it in under ten minutes. He has wanted to employ her for years, but she thinks he runs the accounting section of the Transvaal Water Board.

Down the hall from that office lies the Panic Room. Called that since the trouble times in the sixties, it has three grey desks pushed into a centre island and a camp bed in one corner. A coffee machine replaced Thermos flasks last year.

A man stood at the machine and swore as the vent poured hot water all over his hand, missing the proffered cup completely. The man was Koos Lodevicus Smit and he was the joint senior controller on the African desk. As the department's largest sphere of operations it enjoyed the luxury of two controllers at that level, and superficially it worked well. Both men had rare talents and both applied their own styles to the task. Smit raised his burnt hand to his mouth and licked at the pain like an animal.

He was of medium height and stockily built, and in his student days at Stellenbosch University had achieved some fame as a wrestler. His angry red hair had given rise to the nickname 'Rooineik' but people were careful not to call him that to his face. In reality he disliked the English and thought them to be liberal weaklings. Rooineik Smit was no great fan of his country's Blacks either. To observers he seemed to have mellowed in recent years and applied himself to his job running agents the same way he wrestled – to win. Now in his mid-thirties he didn't look like a spymaster. His face was the pallid colour that those with red hair are often cursed with. In the sun he burnt bright red and blistered painfully, and his wife would rub on a salve. He was bright, cunning and on his way to the top. He also had red hairs that protruded from his nostrils like sea urchin spines from a head of white coral, which annoyed the room's second occupant intensely.

Richard Vickery was everything Rooineik Smit wasn't. He was urbane, sophisticated, and subtle. He was also as cold as ice and had a reputation for nerves of steel after telling the General commanding the department to mind his own business after the wheels had come off one operation. Vickery had calmly and professionally set about retrieving the personnel and to his credit the operation worked, with no more than some ruffled feathers in the country concerned. True, they were blown, but no one was hurt or left behind. After that he was allowed to operate very much to his own standards, the reason being they were higher than everyone else's, and the department could only benefit. He wore tailored three-piece suits, hand-made shirts and silk ties. His family, wealthy importers based in Natal, indulged their youngest son with a considerable allowance and thought he spent his time frittering it away on the Johannesburg stock exchange. Recruited from the Witwaterstrand University as a history scholar, his careful grooming had now resulted in his being the other senior controller on the African desk.

The two men worked well together, which surprised everyone. They complimented each other's failures and foibles, and in the last three years had produced astonishing results. Each had their own networks, and each left the other alone, but their reason for being here now was not their networks.

It was a person neither of them had ever heard of. The person had no name and no file that was accessible. The person was a deep sleeper agent that had been in the Salisbury administration for an astonishing twenty years, and even more astonishing was that the person had survived the post-independence purges of the departments. Now all these years later he had surfaced – with a vengeance.

In the last seven months his reports had stunned his masters with their completeness. He had access to the highest offices in the land and had developed his own networks. Then, three weeks ago, the agent had surpassed everyone's wildest dreams and cracked a series of coded sequences moving between the clandestine section of the Zimbabwe Prime Minister's Department and a foreign embassy. Without the aid of a controller, the agent pieced it together, and without the aid of the normal intelligence analysts, he analysed it all. The material and his conclusions were altogether too sweeping to commit to normal channels. It was enough to justify him presenting the data personally. Like a character from a le Carré novel, he was coming in from the cold.

Trouble was, neither Smit nor Vickery knew who he was. He had been recruited so long ago that contemporary controllers assumed that like so many other sleepers he was no longer considered active. No longer willing. No longer available for use. His original file had been destroyed in the great two-bar heater fire of 1966, when large sections of the building had been gutted. His initial communications with Pretoria had been by a long disused system, considered so unreliable it was dangerous.

Alexander Bell invented it and the next day, so sources said, someone started eavesdropping. The telephone was not one of the department's more modern methods of communication. But years ago someone had said to the person, 'If you find anything useful, give us a ring, old chap. Otherwise, sit tight and we will contact you.'

After many years, he rang, and kept ringing, until he was the hottest property in African intelligence, and now he was coming in with the big one.

And they didn't even know his name. Orpheus, he called himself, and all they knew was that he had once qualified with handguns, preference for a long-barrelled .22.

They also knew he hadn't turned up, and they also knew he was booked on a flight that had crashed killing all survivors in the thick bush of Zimbabwe. But had they? There were indications of military activity around the crash site, and a soldier had been killed. That they knew. Had Orpheus got away? Had he survived?

Vickery and Smit were there to discuss the prospect of that having happened.

'Puerile,' said Vickery.

'What?' said Smit.

'Orpheus. The legendary mentor of societies. Overcomes intrinsic evil... it's puerile, but cute. Come on my little Greek myth, come to daddy.' Vickery smiled his icy smile.

Smit walked from the table towards the window and then back again. Pacing. Vickery was mildly amused. He loved baiting his colleague. Smit usually rose to the bait magnificently, but today he didn't. When an operation was on the tension was there 'like a smell in the air', as Mrs Van Wyk once said. Mrs Van Wyk was their joint secretary and kept people from them. She made sandwiches and had once brought them small biscuits she had called 'custard kisses' when they had sat in the Panic

Room for three days awaiting news of an operator held by the Zambian police. Now whenever they had a problem it was their own code. Custard kisses was their term for a bad one, and this had all the looks of a custard kisses operation.

Smit, his angry red hair clashing with the orange baize-covered pinboard, paced back to Vickery. 'Fact,' he said. 'Seventy odd people on the plane. Fact: local authorities claim all survivors dead. Fact: one soldier dead. Conjecture: someone killed him. Conjecture: the killer is a survivor. Ergo, it could be Orpheus.' He stopped and ran a hand down his face. 'But the chances of that, the chances of that single individual surviving, are remote. Seventy to one... or less than that because we know he is resourceful and talented. Let's say thirty-five to one. And every day the military activity continues, the chances increase that it's our man because of the random chance that of seventy people on an aeroplane, one is that good. One is a survivor.' He finished, looking at Vickery.

Vickery rose and walked elegantly to the window, his hands in his pockets. He watched a woman trying to reverse an aging Peugeot out of a parking space until she stopped and got out to look. Her crimplene dress had risen up over the expanse of her hips, and the sweat stains under her arms were dark against the striped fabric. He thought she looked like a deckchair. He turned and walked back to the table.

'I don't like it, Koos. The odds are too long. If it is him, if Orpheus is in the bush and running, we will need to help. Eventually. But what do we know of this man? I assume it's a man! Let's find out. We have people in Harare. This man must have been senior. He must have time in. Pension records, something must indicate his identity. Who hasn't been to work for four or five days? Some high government official with access like that? There can't be so many. Someone hasn't arrived at work. We will check leave records, retirement, sick leave, absenteeism, and we will pinpoint our elusive little chap. Then when we know more, we can help more. Okay?'

Smit nodded.

'So, we look for a European male adult, aged between forty and sixty, civil servant, senior or trusted, or both, someone who survived the changes of the years, the accent is educated English. Let's work from there.'

They did. Various people within Zimbabwe were asked to establish a list of names of men who fitted the description.

And there was the error.

It was so basic that they overlooked it. Like so many Whites on the continent, they assumed that every Black was on the other team, either covertly or overtly. They did now allow for the possibility that any one of the group could be considered a friendly. In a way it was understandable. Anyone who had assisted a regime through that through legislation separated races, and graded them, would assume that only their little group were loyal to that concept, and as a rule they were right. Without debating the politics of the issue, that would be a fair assumption. Twenty green apples sitting atop a barrel of one hundred other varieties of mixed fruit, all wanting sunlight and fresh air, would naturally trust another Granny Smith above all others, and even then only after establishing its lineage and right to be up there at the top of the barrel.

Not that Richard Vickery was a racist. He was a perfectionist. His job was running men to achieve a set series of aims. He was the ultimate choice. Totally dispassionate, and totally applied to the challenge. In fact, if anything the challenge appealed to him more than the tasks set. The more his opponents tried to upset the system that Vickery was maintaining, the more the ice in his veins cooled, and the more he applied himself to defeating those opponents. The opponent didn't matter. The challenge did.

But years of conditioning and structured thinking, years of just living there and absorbing the thinking of others by osmosis had its price. A description that read Male Adult would have given the clue. And Rooineik Smit wasn't the man to correct the misconception.

Orpheus was Black.

In July of 1961 the rapidly expanding B.O.S.S. had seven recruiters at work. One of them was strangely enough a lay preacher working as a schoolteacher in Salisbury's St George's College. Conrad Hugo had noticed the winds of change sweeping the continent. In a short time the school's first African children arrived. African Rhodesians rather than Europeans. One very bright youngster immediately came to his notice and in the next three years the two spent many hours discussing theology, politics and the future of the continent they both loved. At the time the boy left for an English University, he had accepted the principle that Africa was for Africans, White, Brown or Black – but for Africans. He was a tenuous recruit on that basis: that whatever problems there were, were for Africans to sort out. With deep misgivings he accepted the telephone contact system and some basic training, thinking he would never use it.

His university degree finished, he headed home, but not without some contact with the fledgeling independence movements that had their disciples. The years rolled by and as a man with considerable education in a land with seventy per cent illiteracy he was quickly noticed by the nationalists and absorbed into the party. As hostilities increased, so did his involvement, and with that his disillusionment.

A brief visit to Tanzania and encounters with odd communist advisers through the war left him in no doubt of the Left's plans for his country. They would simply trade one master for another. After independence in 1965, the socialist utopia wouldn't exist. The happy meeting in the middle of White Rhodesians and Black Zimbabweans into one little country didn't happen, and what angered him more than anything was that the problem lay largely with his own people. Tribal affiliations, something he had never bothered with, and the corruption which inevitably followed, were more rampant than ever. With commerce and farming in the middle, the country had been driven to its knees in two short years.

Eventually, he made a decision. If there was to be outside involvement in the future, then let it be Africans. The South Africans were not perfect, but they were Africans, and offered, he thought, far better prospects than impossible geographical, political and ideological links to Beijing or Moscow. They could offer money, transport access to ports, technical assistance and the means to develop. They would offer that in exchange for a secure border.

And so he began to plan his action, soon deciding that credibility was important, as was unsettling the current regime and its ties to the Eastern Bloc. Kill two birds with one stone – provide the South Africans with the means to bolster their own defences by giving them something they needed. Intelligence. That done, his credibility established and the little puppets of Beijing unsettled, he could move again.

He picked up the phone one day, from his office, and set the train in motion, giving only the very best, and waiting for the *pièce de résistance* that would establish him as a man serious in his intents. Africa for the Africans, Russia for the Russians, and China for the Chinese.

Orpheus awoke.

Old Conrad Hugo, the teacher who recognised the potential in the young Orpheus, had died on his small vineyard up in the Cape Province two years before, a gentle, ambling man who finished his days pruning his vines and listening to his grandchildren laugh and play. With Conrad gone, there was now no one who could identify Orpheus.

Had the B.O.S.S. system been more sophisticated then Orpheus would have been nurtured over the years and by now considered more valuable than ever due to deep cover within ZANLA.

But no. In the sixties the bureau had been staffed by dour ex-policemen who were concerned with internal subversion, and many of the potentially useful people recruited by Hugo and his teammates were forgotten, then erased from the records forever by the great two-bar heater fire.

Until they awoke.

14

Just over eight hundred kilometres to the north east as the crow flies, many things had changed in the camp, including the order of march and the morale of the little group.

Jannie's arrival had evenly shared the burden of tactical decision making. Deep within his own element, at home as any animal, Jannie's experience, strength and humour gave Max time to rest and think.

Even the little things mattered to Jannie. The first morning he had made tea for everyone, and then silently indicated to Vicki to do the clearing up. She had been about to launch into her female/male role play argument when he quietly said, 'In the bush, everyone pulls their weight,' and smiled his disarming smile. No one was exempt except for little Sarah, and he silently admonished Max who had forgotten to give her clean knickers. The look was enough, and Max remembered Mrs Van Heerden's warning about infections.

When they moved out, Jannie remained behind, antitracking, removing the tracks of a night's stay, and for an hour would be invisible, behind them clearing any signs of their passing through. Then he would reappear, and take point, out ahead by thirty or forty yards. The two bull terriers walked with Sarah until she rode in the pack, and then they would move up to be either side of Jannie, like escorts. Only the big Rottweiler ranged out in front, running constantly, in through the bush ahead and then appearing behind and galloping past them, his great pink tongue out. He impressed Max immensely because he had heard the breed didn't like excessive exercise. But this young dog revelled in it. In the afternoon on the first day a routine began for the dog. As they walked he would be schooled. He would sit and heel on command, and as they went the commands became more demanding. Just when he saw something interesting he would have to heel and walk by his master's side.

Vicki asked why, and Max told her it was important that the animal obeyed when something happened. She appreciated the reasoning immediately. If they contacted, then they didn't want him bounding out into the field of fire or compromising any hiding place. The other lesson was silence. No barking or baying, like a pointer he was encouraged just to look and smell. No noise. He wasn't impressed. At his age of fifteen months one of his life's great pleasures was barking at chongololos, the millipedes that always appeared after rain, but he would please his master with silence and the little pieces of biltong he received as a reward were nectar for a dog.

Late the first day he was with them, Jannie stopped and opened his pack, and pulled out a small bright blue nylon bag from the side wall. He assembled the parts and eventually stood with a long bow and arrows. The bow was in two parts, joined at the centre by pushing both the fibreglass and pieces into a hollow aluminium handle. Max noticed one arrow was soiled, its head and shaft mildly discoloured by something brown. Max immediately knew how the last soldier had died but was surprised at the meticulous Jannie not having cleaned his equipment. He picked it out and looked at it, and then replaced it.

'Unlike you,' said Max, pleased at Jannie's mortality.

'The bushmen,' Jannie replied. 'They say the blood of the last will find the next.' Jannie grinned, embarrassed at his superstitiousness. 'We will need meat tonight, us and the dogs,' he finished, and loke at the Rottweiler, whose short, stubby tail was wagging furiously at the thought of the hunt. Already he recognised the bow. 'All right,' Jannie said. 'Come... heel.' Turning to the others, he finished, 'See you in a while. Keep going towards the hill there.' And with that and a shy smile at Vicki he moved off, his long legs eating up the distance.

Max looked at Vicki, who was watching the departure with a little half-smile. He smiled. 'Oi, this is not a Wilbur Smith novel and you are not Ruth Courtney watching Sean about to conquer a rebellion. Let's go.'

As he walked away, her reply was muffled but defiant. 'Max, I'm in love.'

He laughed, and quickly a small stone hit his pack.

'You're so coarse, Max. You used to be my favourite man, but no more. Anyway, I only read those books with orange spines. Penguin Classics.'

'Oh, like *Lady Chatterley's Lover*?' He turned. 'You think I'm coarse?'

'Enough of your glib chat. Just lead me to safety!' She replied.

By then Sarah wanted to walk again, and the two bull terriers, who had watched Jannie's departure with complete disinterest, immediately edged up beside her.

Her firm favourite was Aggro, and he seemed to respond with a similar sentiment. At any opportunity his great nose would be snuffling her ears, hair and face. She would giggle and walk along holding one of his shredded ears. Had Max tired that the dog would probably have had considerably less patience, but because it was a child he didn't seem to mind at all. If anything, he liked someone at his level, and when she sang to herself he would watch with interest. Her only really recognisable number was a French son with a name that Max remembered from his own childhood as 'Pharaoh Shaka'. He had always wondered what the paramount King of the Zulu had to do with long-dead Egyptians. It was years later that he would learn the correct name of the song. But even with that knowledge, it would always be 'Pharaoh Shaka' to Max.

Just before dusk Dingaan came galloping onto the track, followed a minute later by Jannie, a Grants Gazelle over his shoulder.

Vicki all but sighed, and Max suppressed a chuckle.

Late in the evening they sat, the three of them, the fire throwing flickering shadows onto the rock wall. Max watched them with fascination, the scene almost prehistoric, the shadows over a fire in the wilderness as adult humans take comfort from its light and warmth in the dark of the night, the young one asleep off to the side. Vicki now sat between Jannie's knees, leaning back against his chest and having overcome his embarrassment, he ran his hands though her hair.

He began to hum a tune, and she smiled. 'Tchaikovsky again?'

'His piano concerto in B flat minor,' he said.

'Max,' Vicki said, looking across the fire, 'said taking you into my world would be like taking Genghis Khan to a tea party.'

'Max,' said Jannie, mimicking her accent, 'is a man of great perception, if no musical taste.'

'Don't take his side, you're with me!' She warned, snuggling back into him.

There was a lengthy pause, and Sarah stirred briefly in her bag.

'I can hum the Dance of the Sugar Plum Fairy,' said Max hopefully, grinning then adding, 'but my style is Nat King Cole. I had a collection of his stuff. Gave it to a friend...' He trailed off and Vicki knew who the friend was by the way he stared into the flames.

'She will look after them for you,' Vicki said, her smile saying more than her words did.

'Ouma was the one,' said Jannie. 'She had a barrel of stuff. All the classics, all the jazz you can think of, Cole Porter, Louis Armstrong, those guys. Sunday lunch used to be classics and then by the evening it was Patsy Cline. But she hated bagpipes.

Oupa bought her a record once of some Scottish band marching through a fog. She used it to keep the plant post from staining the table.'

Vicki stroked his leg as he spoke, trying to ease the pain caused by the fresh memories.

Jannie paused, sipped his tea, and then looked up. 'Tomorrow we push hard for Chisumbanje area. With luck we are to meet someone at dawn the following day.'

He left it there and Max didn't ask who.

In the night Sarah snuggled up close again, Aggro snoring on the other side of her, dreaming his doggy dreams, while across the camp Vicki and Jannie were one lump lying in the darkness.

Twice in the night Max got up to do a sweep and listen for a while. The second time, Jannie said, 'Sleep, man. Dingaan is out there. If they come, he will hear it. Sleep. We have a long way to go tomorrow.'

They moved fast the following morning, Jannie the point man leading them down the valley floor parallel to the Sabi but twenty miles west. Max, watching the route, thought they could be no more than the same distance to the border with Mozambique. But there was no real refuge in that country. Frelimo, the current administration in what was Portuguese territory, were very closely tied to Zimbabwe's ruling ZANU-PF. Even now they may have had requests to step up patrols on their side of the border, and to short on sight the dissidents, or rebels or murderer, or whatever they had been labelled.

Max was also curious as to where those orders were coming from. Not from the Prime Minister, he thought. Robert Mugabe, who came to power the previous year, 1980, was a pragmatist and devoutly believed in his people's plight. He was an ardent socialist, if naïve about its possible applications on the African continent. He was not a mass murderer. He would not sanction such an act. But there were others in his administration who would. Certifiable madmen. That was the shame of it all.

Mugabe surrounded by competent, clear-thinking administrators could have made a staggering success of this whole episode in the history of their country. But no. He had two, maybe three men who were up to the job. The rest were jobs for the boys. Like everywhere else on the continent.

That was when Max decided that when they were clear and the girls were safe he would find out who had given the orders to bring the aeroplane down and wipe out any survivors, and who was behind it all. He was, after all, a policeman only a few short months ago and hunting bad bastards can be like a drug to some men.

He tousled Sarah's hair, and when she looked up from Aggro's level, the dog did likewise.

'You two all right?' He asked.

Sarah nodded and went into a long series of questions about why Aggro had scarred ears. She couldn't actually say Aggro. She called him Ungo. Fair enough, thought Max.

'There's a very long story about Ungo's ears,' he said, 'which I will tell you one night before bed. Okay?'

'No. Wanna hear story now,' she complained, looking up at him as she walked. Aggro was nice, but stories were even nicer.

'I'll tell you later. How about a drink?'

She nodded, distracted and happy.

Shit, he thought, forgot the malaria tablet. No time like the present.

'How would you like to go a yucky yellow colour and be very sick?' He asked, giving her his canteen. It was empty enough for her to be able to hold on her own. Phrased like that, what could she say?

'Oh no!'

'Okay, no problem. But you have to take this pill. All right?'

She took a bit of time to think about that, but eventually agreed. Max realised she hadn't asked for her mother for two days now.

He improved the offer with a boiled sweet from their rapidly depleting stock. Sand had got into the pocket and he blew the grains off the wrapper before giving it to her.

'Red one?' she said.

'Don't you like green?'

He gave her a yellow one and she ate that. He then wondered if she didn't know what red was, or if she liked yellow ones just as well. He decided against asking her. Let sleeping dogs lie. They walked on.

Vicki swung up beside them from her position trailing the field. Max watched her out of the corner of his eye. She was looking very fit, and was now a nut brown colour. Her hair, tied back with a leather rein, was dusty, and at the scalp sweat began to trickle down her face and neck. She looked how Max imagined the Israeli Sabras looked. Fit, strong, vibrant and no need of makeup to look wholesomely attractive.

This was a different girl to the one he'd met at the wreck site. Was it only a few days ago? She hefted the automatic weapon like it was part of her, but if one looked closely it was incongruous in her delicate, long-fingered hand.

She took her canteen and sipped from it, then offered it to him.

'*Mvura?*' Water.

'Very good, Miss Waters, very good,' he praised.

'Jannie said I couldn't go through life speaking only English. Learn the language and then you begin to understand the person. That's what he said.'

Max nodded his approval and they walked on in silence.

Vicki broke it. 'I know who we're meeting,' she said.

'Oh? Who might that be?' Max had been thinking about this.

Someone obviously contacted after the scene at the farm, so someone who could be of use to them. Maybe with supplies, or news, or maybe a vehicle. He had avoided getting his hopes too high.

'Some chap called Solomon something-or-other,' she said. 'The last name sounded African. Jannie said he was a Shangaan.' She hurried ahead towards Jannie.

Shangaan, Max thought. Now that's interesting. Their track through to the border would eventually take them into the Shangaan homelands. They were a Zulu offshoot before even the Matabele had swung north with their rebel chief, and inhabited the southeasternmost corner of the country. The nation's smallest minority, they were left very much to their own devices. Their language was not dissimilar to Ndebele or Zulu, so communicating would be no problem. Fiercely proud and independent, they had no real political loyalties to anyone other than their own and just went about life at their own pace. They crossed the border into Mozambique through the bush as they wished, and only the mighty Limpopo prevented them from doing the same into South Africa.

Fierce fighters, the legend was that even Mzilikazi, the chief who defied Shaka and swung his impis north, turned west to avoid having to do battle with them. The Shangaan had received the right to leave the traditional Zulu homelands before Mzilikazi, and they did, travelling north to establish their own homes among the rich hunting and cattle grazing areas of the lowveld. Upon arrival pestilence set in amongst the herds and they took to farming and hunting instead of complete reliance on cattle. It was not a difficult transition. The Nguni clans, welded by Shaka into the Zulu nation, had a communal cropping programme second to none in the world. He needed tons of grain and maize to feed his massive armies and to supplement his feed requirements for the royal herds of cattle.

When the Shangaan swung north, the decision to become farmers was easy. They had the skills and they had the seed grain. They stayed and the generations went by, and then they had a separate identity. They were no longer of the Zulu. They were Shangaan and proud of it. They bowed to no one and as long as they were left alone, they gave trouble to no one, except of course the wildlife people and the District Commissioners in the old days. But that was good sport.

If Jannie had sent word for someone to meet them, he would be worth the effort.

Vicki arrived back. 'I'm not allowed on the point,' she complained.

'It's now longer a point if you are there. It's the main body, with me and Sarah in the rear. Leave him out there. He can smell things before you and I would even see them. You distract him,' consoled Max.

'Do I?' Vicki said, pleased.

It was after the noon break when the hot sun was beating down and even the animals found shade that Jannie said he was going to swing west and look at the road. Max took the point with the two terriers, Vicki and Sarah, and no one in the main body.

In the Panic Room Vickery was lounging elegantly in a hard-backed chair, if that's possible. His trousers with their perfect creases irritated Smit, whose own wrinkled pair always seemed creased and tired even after being cleaned. It was noon and the sun's glare burned through the window with a harshness that hurt his eyes. He could almost feel the skin on his face peeling in sympathy.

The phone rang, with its cricket warble shattering the dusty hot silence.

Smit crossed the floor and picked it up, a sausage roll from the canteen in his hand, and as he said, 'Yes,' he bit into it. It burst, spreading dry flakes of pastry all over his front like shrapnel.

'Nice one, Koos,' Vickery said languidly, and stretched and stood and walked to the window.

Smit put the phone down and then picked it up again and dialled an internal number. He spoke rapidly in Afrikaans and replaced it without ceremony. Vickery raised an eyebrow.

'Not much,' said Smith. 'Jan Smuts. A couple of East German hard men just transiting through from Lusaka into Salisbury.' He still used the old Rhodesian name for the town. 'Strydom will make sure they contact no one while they are here...' he trailed off in thought.

Vickery looked back out of the window. Where are you Orpheus, my son? Who are you? And what do you have to tell us? If you are alive out there, keep moving. Keep moving. They will be looking for you. They will want to kill you. They might even bring someone in to...

He spun around, crossed to the phone and dialled. It was answered.

'I want the files on the two Germans at the airport quickly,' he said.

He put the phone down and looked at Smit. 'I wonder if they are looking for our friend, if they are going into the bush... yes, I wonder.' His smile was ice, and he walked back to the window. 'Curiouser and curiouser,' he mused.

Smit shook his head and removed his jacket. When Vickery said that, it usually meant a long night ahead.

'If they are,' Vickery said, 'they will be survival specialists. They will have spent time in Tanzania, or maybe Angola. Who do we have in Lusaka?'

Smit smiled. 'Good people. The files will be accurate. Lusaka was his patch.

Vickery looked down at the island table. On it was spread a large relief map of Zimbabwe. The last surveys had been done by the Rhodesians, and nothing had been added. No roads built, no dams, no progress whatsoever.

He leant forward over the bottom right hand corner of the table and spread below him was the section covering the lowveld area, the southern edge being the long blue line of the Limpopo river.

'A fit man, Koos. A fit man running from someone… what sort of distance in a day?'

Smit looked out the window and then back as he calculated.

'Thirty, maybe thirty-five miles a day. No more in that country, or as little as one if they are close and he is moving at night and quietly.'

It was as Vickery expected.

'Now say a man in his fifties or early sixties, and maybe not as fit as he could be, but very smart, very cunning?'

Smit was quicker this time.

'Twenty, maybe. Dead maybe, by now. A man of that age they will run into the ground as soon as they have his location pinpointed. But a smart chap? One who knows the bush? Maybe they will never find him.'

A polite knock interrupted their thoughts.

'Yes,' Smit bellowed.

The door opened and a timid little mousy girl edged forward with two buff files. She had never been in the Panic Room before. She had just heard the stories and the rumours in the canteen. This was where everything with capital letters happened, and the two senior controllers of the Africa Desk were held in more reverence by her than the Old Testament in Ouma's Bible. She had worked in the department for them for three years and had only ever seen Smit once. They had their own door and usually their secretary stopped anyone seeing then, but she had recently been cleared to Grade Six and was allowed to do little chores involving the Panic Room.

She neared the desk and Vickery looked up, then smiled. My God, he smiled at her!

'You're Janet, aren't you?' He said.

She just nodded, stunned that he would even recognise her, let alone know her name.

He smiled again, said, 'Thank you,' and took the files form her, and as Janet de Kock left the room she thought she might be in love.

Smit took the files and went straight to the section tabbed with blued highlighting pen towards the back of the index. It was 'Movements C&UC'. The 'C&UC' meant confirmed sightings and the unconfirmed but suspected movements.

'Yes,' Smit paused, 'Horst Polanski... sounds Polish. Sighted four times August '79 in Angola, twice the following year in Lubumbashi. Disappeared until June this year, turned up in Lusaka.'

He paused and flicked through to the yellow section titled 'M&ST'. This was Military and/or Subversive Training. It was brief but maintaining files on every Sovbloc man on the continent was a major task, and they had done well with the twelve odd lines of typed script.

'Two years in Cuba, basic training as infantry officers, slipped into the nasty stuff in '71. Suspected special forces training... Ah, here we go. Suspected involvement in Uganda in the early seventies... confirmed responsible for death of opposition politician in Rwanda... I agree, they're not going to Salisbury for Christmas with relatives.'

Vickery was looking down at the map, and then began to run his finger down the possible path of a fugitive. He flicked a few pastry crumbs from the map with annoyance as Smit added, 'Other one is the same. Name of Krieger. Willi Krieger. I would say he is the junior of the two. Takes orders from Polanski.'

Vickery stood straight and walked to the coffee machine.

'I think we would be doing everyone a favour if we culled these two.' He wait for the coffee, and for Smit's reaction.

'Jesus, Vickery. No, man. I'm not going to the Director to get the all-clear for that.' Smit sounded scared.

'Fear not. I shall go into the breach,' Vickery replied flippantly.

He didn't. Not even the Director would sanction that. Not without more proof than they had. But he did issue instructions for an accident to take place and told Smit he had been turned down. He wanted to ease the odds a little, and Richard Vickery was quite capable of breaking the rules to achieve that which he wished done.

Jannie had long since disappeared up the steep sides of the ridge that provided the geographical barrier between them and the road. On the western slope it fell gently down into the Sabi River Valley, with the river itself just over twenty miles away in the hot yellow haze.

Max slowed the pace down, unslung the rifle, and with Sarah tired and grumpy in the pack they move down along the smaller tributary. He wasn't sure of its name, but the map showed that it eventually met the Sabi where it swung east and flowed lazily into Mozambique and then out to the sea.

Late in the afternoon he saw the dust of a vehicle on the road rise high into the still air and then get collected by a warm breeze and dispersed. He pushed on and as the dusk became the dark they stopped and selected a place to spend the night.

Jannie arrived a few minutes later, breathing hard and jogging up the track with the Rottweiler trailing him, and panting. He stopped at the point where the tracks left the trail, and casting about, moved off into the trees until joining up with the group.

There was already a small fire burning, and after he dropped his pack he looked at it, saying, 'No larger than that tonight. They're on the other side of the ridge doing a sweep all the way to the road. We should be okay but I haven't been antitracking so if they cross the ridge and if they have a tracker they will pick up spoor sooner or later.'

Max stood and walked a helpless little circle, then swore violently. 'Fuck! All the way to the road? Shit, Jannie, how many men is that? Fucking hundreds!' He stopped and looked. 'From the ridge to the road, or parallel to the ridge and down the valley?'

'Parallel. They have a man every forty yards or so, of the klick I watched.' Jannie sipped at his canteen, the sweat on his face shiny in the flicker of the flames across his face.

Max did some quick mental calculations.

'That's a thousand men! Christ, they must have the whole brigade down there. How many in that unit? Any idea?'

Jannie shook his head and sipped again. He was tired. Vicki, who had remained silent, handed him a cup of tea. They had run out of coffee. She sat down beside him and looked over at Max, who was still standing with Sarah tugging at his shorts.

'She wanted the loo,' said Vicki, and she gave a bitter little laugh. 'It's ironic. Only today I was thinking about how to break the news to my family that I'm alive. They will think I'm dead like everyone else. I thought I might just phone and say, "Hello, Mummy, it's me," but now I might be spared that task.' She paused, then said very quietly. 'I thought we were clear. I thought we just had a long walk ahead.' Finishing, she began to cry.

Jannie put his arm around her shoulders and awkwardly tried to comfort her in a traditional manner. It didn't work, so he tried a more Meyer-ish method.

'Vicki, listen now. Those men out there are lazy and badly motivated for this task. They don't want to be here any more than we do. The more of them, the better. They will be confusing each other in the dark. We will get through here. Tomorrow we meet Chimkuyu, and we go deep bush, into Gonarezhou. We will be there in two or three days and then for them it will be needle in a haystack time. Okay? Between Max and me, we are the mean team. We will have Chimkuyu on the point, and the firepower here with us. We will get through. Now please stop crying, because you scare Sarah. Let's go and wash. It will be the last time I can guarantee you washing water until the reserve.' He stood, took her hand and pulled her up.

Later that night Max finally could contain his curiosity no longer and asked Jannie who Solomon/Chimkuyu was.

'It's a long story,' Jannie said. 'He's an old Shangaan bloke. Well, not old, maybe forty. When I left school I spent time down in this area and then again in any time I had off from the army. When I went into the Scouts we began ops down here. First was just pseudo, but you know all that. After we had worked that, I stayed behind with a couple of Shona troopers. After a while I began to hear stories of a Shangaan hunter who would hunt in the park, in Mozambique, wherever he wanted to go. He was supposedly a legendary tracker and my boys reckoned we should try to recruit him because his bushcraft was so good. Well, my boys were good and if they reckoned this other one was good, that was enough for me. I phoned the boss next time I was in Chiredzi and he said go ahead. But we never did get him on our side. He was completely apathetic bout politics or who was in power. But bit by bit he became more useful. It began more as a backlash against the ZANLA thugs than being pro us. They wanted him to chant slogans one night in a village somewhere. He told the commissar to fuck off. He took a round through the calf and one through the thigh. We found him and patched him up. I wanted to get him out to a hospital but he shot through one night, wounds and all. I thought that was that. But a few weeks later he walks into our camp. This camp was very well concealed by the way – ZANLA wanted to find us. After dark it was pretty much a liberated area. We were the only good guys around. Well, in he walks. Turns out he has tracked the ones who shot him and he wants to take them out, but sixteen is too many for one man. He actually said that. Four or five he could do, but not sixteen. So perhaps it was time to join forces. He said he had heard of a young murungu who tracked as good as he did, and this was lies, because no one tracks like him, but maybe the young beardless one showed promise and could help him. In return he would help the murungu when he could.

'I jumped at it. We had been looking for those buggers for months. So we went in. The four of us. Solomon, as was his name, had pinpointed everything in their camp. My blokes were good men, so without calling any extra fire we hit them just before dawn one morning. We got seven of the sixteen, including the commissar.

'As the weeks went by, he began to pay his debt to us. He wasn't really aware of how much we owed him for leading us in. He would leave signs for us, little notes in Mission English about things he had seen. We did very well. I spent as much time as I could with him. He taught me much. He can track over anything. Find water when others like me would die of thirst. He is an old-time Shangaan who if he agrees to help will do so on a point of honour, and because he likes us. Simple as that... but when we go into Gonarezhou we will need him. We have women with us, they will need water, shelter and escort when you and I have other things to do.'

Jannie lapsed into silence and began stripping his rifle. Only then did Max notice that the walnut stock had been covered by strips of fabric breaking the outline and colour with drab green. The blue of the barrel was also made matte by smears of mud, allowing no glint or reflection. Jannie Meyer was gearing up, and Max liked that, because he was getting tired of running.

When you and I have other things to do meant that Jannie was not ready to start hitting back, and that meant Max would not have to talk him into it.

'We will have to take out a couple,' Max said. 'Get you an automatic weapon.'

Jannie looked up and smiled his lazy smile. 'All taken care of. I know where there is a cache. We get to that and we can really make their eyes water.'

'You two,' admonished Vicki, 'are talking about attacking a regiment. Even my father wouldn't do that and he is crazier than either of you!'

'Ring him up,' said Max. 'Invite him along. Honestly, Vicki, it's sound policy. Hit them wherever you are not, and then where you are. It would be easy to just hunt us. More difficult if they are defensive the whole time. Trust me.'

Sarah and Aggro were sleeping on top of the bag. It was hot, and Max for the first time covered her with a mosquito net. The dog was included by virtue of his proximity. Bovver, far more independent, lay asleep on his back, all four feet in the air and whimpered as he dreamed. Jannie prodded him and he rolled over, giving a big sigh, while Dingaan was out in the night.

Krieger and Polanski were met at the airport in Harare by the Embassy driver in a civilian-registered Peugeot 504 and driven into town. They were met by Heine Guttman and briefed on what they had to do. Meet the officer commanding and 'advise' on a search in progress in the bush to the southeast. They knew what that meant: assume command and get the job done. They had done jobs for Guttman before and had never seen him this nervous.

'You will take the car outside,' Guttman said. 'The one you

came into town in. When you get to Nandi contact this man.' He handed them a slip of paper. 'He will take you into the area. The imbecile commanding this catastrophe is Colonel Chabegwa. He is expecting you. Now get on your way.'

Guttman left the room and walked to his car. If he had been looking carefully he would have seen the woman who looked like a housewife pushing the pram up the quiet suburban street. She watched the man leave, and then the pair followed in the blue 1981 Peugeot. She left and made a phone call, and finally fed the baby.

Seventy miles outside Harare on the road to Fort Victoria, the Peugeot rounded a bend and careered into the back of a parked bus. The driver from the embassy was killed outright, and the other front seat occupant, Willi Krieger, was taken to hospital with spinal injuries and compound fractures of both legs. Polanski, sitting in the back, suffered no more than a broken wrist and some lacerations to his face.

The driver of the bus was never found. Quite often in Africa, when a situation like that occurred, the driver would simply run off into the bush and make his way home to the tribal areas rather than risk the police and all the associated problems. That's what this one did. With a thousand dollars in his wallet. If the murungus want to kill each other, why not?

It was, however, a genuine tragedy that a second car hit the wreck of the Peugeot. The driver, a salesman from Harare visiting his parents-in-law in Fort Victoria, walked away from the crash. His wife didn't. She died after going through the windscreen, over the top of the wreckage of the first car and into the bus.

Polanski flew the following day into Chiredzi on a scheduled flight, his arm in a sling and his mission already plagued by trouble.

Vickery had evened the odds a little.

15

In spite of the optimism of the night before, Max still had deep misgivings about their ability to survive the coming days.

While Jannie's willingness to become capable of belligerence was tactically useful the odds were still badly in favour of the hunters. To have the capacity to hit back was merely the lesser of two evils. To simply run would be too easy for the troops. One man can hide indefinitely, two can do so with ease, but three people, with one inexperienced in the bush and another a child, would be nearly impossible to conceal for any length of time. Now four, along with three animals, they were visible and eventually one of a thousand searching men would find spoor or see a movement. Right now it would be useful, though undoubtedly dangerous, to divert attention from the main body and its course. By the same action, if that diversion could throw the hunters onto the defensive each individual's priority would change. Men looking for an ambush look in different places to those looking for another in hiding.

As a tactic it was fraught with danger. But then drastic events needed extraordinary tactics, and things were getting drastic.

They were now sitting in the shade of a stand of trees. It was hot and humid and Max sat with his back to a tree, sipping from a canteen. In front of him was the circular stone arrangement of an old fire. Men had stopped here before. Below them and six or seven miles away was the Sabi River. It had eventually swung east and through the heat haze Max could see the ground rise up on the far side. Where the hills began so did Gonarezhou National Park. It seemed close, but it was in reality nearer forty miles away by the route they would take. Three days moving slowly, because somewhere down in there was a small brigade, looking for them.

Max's thoughts were interrupted by a soft giggle from Sarah. Jannie was making animal noises to her, placing his hands over his mouth and perfectly imitating the grunt of a hippopotamus, then the bark of a zebra and finally the haunting cry of the fish eagle. To each she giggled delighted, no understanding or identifying the noises but marvelling at the variety of sounds coming from one mouth. He finished and she ran to Vicki only four or five feet away to tell her all about it.

Jannie looked across at Max. 'He's late.' His tone betrayed his fears.

'If he's as good as you say he is then he will get here,' said Max.

Jannie nodded, saying nothing, and eventually stood and, cradling his rifle in the crook of his left arm, leant against a tree trunk, one leg bent at the knee, one foot resting on the other.

It was twenty minutes later when he suddenly grinned and dropped to the ground, and from his pack extracted a small, black enamelled telescope. He stood again and scanned a piece of bush down the valley.

'That's him,' he said.

Max stood and looked, then borrowed the telescope. 'What's he doing? Sneaking up on us?'

Below them, moving carefully from cover to cover was a figure. Dressed only in bold khaki shorts he was tall and ebony black against the bush.

'Shit, no,' said Jannie, laughing softly. 'If he was sneaking up on us we would never have seen him. He always moves like that.'

He was tall, sinewy and his skin had a healthy sheen of sweat. Broad-shouldered, the fine cords of muscle that ribbed his chest and biceps lay just beneath his skin, and he moved with a natural grace that seemed to conserve energy and remain fluid all at once.

As the entered the camp his eyes seemed to see everything,

and as Sarah and Vicki stopped their game he settled onto his haunches like a coiled spring, his calves taking the weight of the backs of his thighs.

He placed a plastic Woolworths shopping bag at his feet, reached into it and produced a tin of snuff. He carefully placed a wad into his mouth, before his eyes slowly came to rest on Jannie. With that, Jannie spoke. It was a mixture of Shona, Ndebele and pure Shangaan, and Max was able to follow the conversation with ease.

'Greetings old one,' began Jannie. 'How are you?'

'I am well. How are you Pungwe?'

'Pungwe' means that which moves at night, but many dialects used it to describe a leopard, and was obviously Solomon's name for Jannie. It was apt. Greetings over, they spoke of crops and rain and each other's families, skirting everything of importance for the sake of protocol. Jannie handed him a water bottle and Solomon drank sparingly.

When it was appropriate, Jannie got down to business.

Gesturing towards Max, Vicki and Sarah, he said, 'These people, Chimkuyu, march south. There are those that would seek them.'

Solomon looked about himself, as if to notice the others for the first time. That was good manners for an old-fashioned type. Not for them the effusive hand shaking of everyone present. With strangers, be strange.

'The woman, is she yours?' He asked.

Jannie nodded.

'She has the look of one who will not work well,' he remarked paternally. Max stifled a laugh, thankful that Vicki didn't understand the language.

'Well enough. She is of high blood,' Jannie said firmly.

A twinkle ran through the Black man's eyes, and they continued.

'The bearded one,' said Jannie, referring to Max's growth, 'takes the child. Already they-who-seek have killed the mother. In the Hondo he was Mambo of ma-Special Branch at Kariba.'

Solomon looked at Max and spoke. 'I heard talk of such a one, who used the power of the *svikiros* to hung the *gandangas*.' A man who used the power of the spirits to hunt terrorists.

Here Max joined in, pleased at the geographical distance covered by his reputation.

'What think you of this talk, since I am the one of which they speak?' he asked.

Solomon added more snuff to the lump in his bottom lip, and then looked up. 'It is only fit to frighten small children and old women,' he replied, his eyes flecked with mischief again. 'But then, those you seek only attack old women and children so perhaps it is fitting.'

He looked back at Jannie. 'And you, Pungwe. You march with them? You have your rifle?'

Jannie nodded, and Solomon continued.

'On my journey I heard talk of such a search. I also heard talk of a farm where two died in a fire that was not a fire.' He finished and looked at Jannie.

So that was the cover-up, thought Max. A fire.

The young man nodded twice, his eyes betraying no emotion, before asking, 'Will you march with us, Chimkuyu?'

Solomon said nothing, adjusting the snuff with his tongue. The heat shimmered and the bush was quiet, the only sound in the air was the cooing of emerald doves away in the trees. Sarah and Vicki had begun playing again, this game involving hands clapped in the right sequence.

Max simply watched the two men. They were so alike and yet so different. They were men who could tell when it would rain by the way the game moves and read stories from pebbles moved by a passing foot, or hoof or claw. They were both at home here in the wilderness, yet one knew classical music, was fair of hair and blue of eye. The other knew better the musical call of the wild and took his pleasure from the feel of the wind in the grass and having eaten well after the hunt. Ebony black and from a culture far removed from the others, all they had in common was the bushveld. The hundreds of thousands of square miles of savannah that was their home.

Solomon produced from the bag a handful of nuts and offering them around he caught Sarah's eye. She looked at Max, who nodded and smiled, and she edged forwards towards the man's outstretched hand. He showed her how to crack the nut with her teeth and she settled at his feet with the handful between her knees, picking at them one by one, her face a picture of concentration.

'Well?' Asked Jannie, his impatience cutting through the required protocol.

Another pause.

'Pungwe, you ask me to journey with you. There are those who would seek you, therefore there will be fighting and men will die. It is indecent to decide these things so quickly,' he rebuked gently, and then continued. 'But yes, I shall march with you. He was your father. Also, you are still as a baby in the bush and cannot be left on your own.' He began a chuckle that was a deep bass rumble that began in his belly and grew upwards.

'It is good to see you, Pungwe,' Solomon said.

'And you, Chimkuyu,' smiled Jannie. 'And you.'

Again the order of march changed for the group. Now as often as not it was Solomon who walked the point, and Jannie who moved sometimes in the main body and sometimes in the rear, antitracking and confusing spoor for anyone who may stumble across it.

If Jannie Meyer was good in the bush then the Shangaan was

in a class all of his own. He would appear from the trees alongside them and disappear again like a puff of smoke. He was absolutely silent in everything he did and frowned like a disapproving old woman when someone sneezed or talked.

Jannie had given him the single-shot .22 until they reached the cache and he accepted it like it was diseased. Initially he had complete disdain for its light calibre and considered it a child's gun. He quickly retracted his dislike when Jannie demonstrated its silenced capability, and the hunter and poacher in Solomon immediately saw its potential. He fell in love with it.

On the first night they stopped just short of the river and made plans to cross the following day. Solomon disappeared before dark and was back an hour later with three chickens he had stolen from a village somewhere, but it was the next day at dawn that he displayed his full abilities.

He had set out long before first light. Max had watched him go, and held onto Bovver who didn't like anything that wasn't white in colour and was still suspicious of him. Three hours later Solomon was back with news of the searchers, breathing hard and sweating. He squatted and few on the ground with a stick the complete deployment of the troops between their little group and the river, and the deployments on the other side. He had obviously crossed and looked at the other bank and the foothills, and covered about fifteen miles in secrecy.

His news, drawn onto the ground, was not good. Deployments on both sides, and with vehicles, and with a camp at one place. Max was fascinated with the comprehensive intelligence gained and watched as Jannie conferred in fast Shangaan with Solomon.

'How many men at the tents?' Max interrupted. Jannie stopped and looked at Solomon.

'Maybe ten. I only saw three but there were four small cloth shelters that two men could sleep under. There was one large tent and a truck.'

Max calculated and agreed with the figure.

'Was there at the truck or the tent a wire line, like for washing, or a small wire tree from the roof of the truck?' Max asked.

Solomon nodded. 'Three small metal trees,' he said.

'Ariels,' Max said. 'Three would mean a big comms truck with VHF, SSB and crap. That's the command centre.'

Jannie nodded, grinned, and joined the session of passive interrogation. He looked at Solomon and spoke. 'Any officers?' He asked, putting his fingers to his shoulders. 'Any men with small pieces of cloth like bird droppings on their shoulders?'

Solomon thought for a moment and then shook his head. 'There was coming and going from the truck, but I could not see into it. There may have been. I saw no one with that mark.'

'You did well, madoda. Very well,' said Max.

'Which way? Chimkuyu, would you lead us?' Asked Jannie. 'What is the way through them?'

Solomon reached for his snuff and Sarah walked over to watch this operation. She was disgusted and fascinated all at once, especially when Solomon spat out the thick brown juice at regular intervals.

'Would the young lion walk through a herd of buffalo? It would seem to be much the same.' Solomon paused, enjoying the suspense he had created.

Africans are great story tellers and have incredible memories for words and tales. Their history passed from generation to generation by word of mouth and demanded this for accuracy's sake. They are masters of timing and of drawing out a tale with proverbs and anecdotes.

'Would the leopard walk into a badly set trap?' He paused again. 'They are many and we are few. Let us disappoint them. Let us go east and cross below their lines. Let this Pungwe walk around this trap with all the honour and the dignity of an old tom. Then let us piss against it!'

He laughed with delight at his mischief and Jannie shook his head incredulously. But the idea appealed to Max.

'Chimkuyu, how would you piss against this trap?' He asked.

Solomon's eyes twinkled and he spat onto the ground, causing Sarah to leap back and out of range in case the brown saliva moved again. She prodded it with a stick. Vicki muttered something under her breath and then said to Sarah, 'Don't touch that.'

Solomon ignored the exchange. Although he understood basic English, he had no idea that he had been insulted.

'It would seem that the small trees are of importance.' Solomon paused yet again and sipped from a canteen. 'If we were to tie them to a truck then when the truck left it would pull the trees down.'

'A good idea, but it will show them that we know they are there,' said Max. 'We may want to do that in a more warlike fashion at another time. Let us leave it for now.' He spoke carefully as he was still unsure of exactly what Solomon would consider suggestions and what would be considered orders from one who was not yet in a position to give them.

Solomon looked at Jannie, who nodded at him. He looked back at Max and nodded too.

'What would you suggest?' Solomon asked.

'Let us remain as the leopard,' Max said. 'Quiet and invisible and never seen by any other than the best hunters. Then when we wish to, we will strike, but till then let them look in vain and we can move south into the deep bush where a man such as you is like the chimera.' His words were designed to appeal outrageously to Solomon's vanity. Jannie stifled a grin, and remembered that Max Seager hadn't been the country's most effective counter-insurgency investigator for nothing. He had used the same techniques used by all effective man managers. The use of vanity, pride, fear, morality, love, hate, grief and revenge channelled to suit one's purpose.

With Solomon the words were aimed at his vanity, and the words worked.

The man nodded, accepting the wisdom of the decision, and then spoke. 'Then let us swing east with the river and cross where the hills fall and the river widens.'

They broke camp immediately and with Solomon on the point moved slowly and quietly downstream, and by mid-morning swung east parallel to the Sabi. Max had Sarah in the pack and trained the group. Ahead of him Vicki and Jannie walked side by side, the dogs padding quietly and feeling the change of pace and tension.

Max was impressed with the new discipline on display. For the first time they were moving into a search pattern. Before, all they had done was run from it. Now they were heading into it.

It was just before lunch that Sarah presented her first real problem of the trip.

It began innocuously enough. Bovva and Dingaan, who spent the day running beside Jannie, were joined this morning by Aggro, until now Sarah's constant companion. The dog had become bored with Sarah in the pack and had moved forward to be with his four-legged brethren. Sarah had wanted to walk, and Max had refused her. She had accepted that. If she had to ride, she had to ride.

The problem manifested itself when Max wanted her to ride with Vicki. It was important to them that Sarah be equally at home with any of the other three as circumstances may require, such as that moment.

Max wanted to move his gun forward with Jannie and to have Vicki and Sarah bring up the rear. With the child in the pack on his chest or back, his manoeuvrability was severely hampered, and therefore compromised his ability to unleash the awesome power of the heavy-barrelled rifle.

Now, as they moved into a search pattern, he wanted to change the march order, and Sarah protested.

He chuckled softly at what he initially thought was simple crabbiness from a tired child and went to lift her clear. She clung on with both little fists and as he attempted again, she burst into tears, and followed that with a petulant scream. Jannie stopped dead in his tracks and sank to the ground, and Solomon appeared back from the point, both of them glowering at the source of the noise.

'It's all right,' said Max, and then he looked down at Sarah, who was sobbing in depe little breaths.

'Don't you want to ride with Vicki? She wants you to.'

Sarah shook her little head venomously.

'Why not?'

'Wanna,' she took a big gulp of air, 'wide wif you.'

'You can't, baby, I'm going to run in front,' consoled Max. 'Come on now, go with Vicki.'

'No,' she muttered. Max lifted her and she squealed again.

Max, driven by exhaustion and fear that all their good work at hiding their trail was being undone by Sarah's demands, forgot for a moment that he was dealing with a small child and barked an order at her. 'Stop crying about nothing and go to Vicki!' He snapped.

Sarah stopped, stunned, unable to believe what had happened. And then the real tears began, slow, quiet ones. Max immediately felt guilty and was about to put her back in the pack when Vicki came to the rescue.

'Come along, madam. I'll tell you a story. Don't whinge about Max. He loves you very much, but you must do as you're told. Okay?' She took the pack from Max, slipped it on and picked Sarah up.

Max watched them walk away, the moved forward and past them, turning to wink at the child. She ignored him so obviously he was tempted to laugh.

Solomon went to the rear and began antitracking and Max and Jannie went to the point. There Jannie began a crash course on incursions into hostile territory.

'You are here for a variety of reasons, but primarily to establish the presence of an ambush, or a patrol or compromising situation as soon as possible. Look for...' And so it began.

By mid-afternoon Solomon was back on the point having completed several miles of antitracking. Spoor would be virtually impossible to follow for that section and could hold up a chase for days until they picked it up again. It was very hot and very humid, and storm clouds were building in the east. The wind was freshening and it was Jannie who put a time on the storm's arrival.

'Rain before dark,' he said.

They picked up the pace because crossing the river after it was swollen might be impossible. They were three miles short of the northern bank and moving fast when they were compromised.

It all happened very fast indeed and began with Solomon running back down the track. As he appeared round the bend, Jannie closed the bolt home on his rifle and dropped to one knee. Turning back, he waved Vicki into the bushes with Sarah. Max, his weapon cocked, flicked off the safety and tried to remember the drills.

'Four men coming this way,' Solomon said in fast Shangaan. 'maybe one minute.'

'Shit. Okay,' said Jannie. 'Solomon, take the women to the river, cross and wait for us at the trees on the other side. Good luck!'

Solomon nodded once and jogged back to Vicki. He pulled the pack clear and bundled it, child included, under his arm, and pulling Vicki up, made to go. Vicki looked at Jannie and he nodded quickly.

'Solomon,' said Max, 'guard them with your life.'

'Go,' said Jannie in an urgent whisper.

They disappeared into the bush and Jannie turned back to Max.

'It will be more than four, my friend. We culled four last time. They will have doubled the patrol size. Eight minimum, maybe even twelve-men sections. Ever used that weapon in an ambush?'

'No,' said Max.

'Okay. Fire on my command. Hit the main body. I'll bonk the point and radio operator, then we go in fast and shoot anything that moves. Bushes, anything. Okay?'

Max nodded and breathed out slowly. He was frightened.

'They will break and run, but none must clear the area. Use the scope and lead a running man. Sshh now.'

They moved into cover and froze.

This is fucking madness, thought Max. Two of us are about to ambush a force of uncertain size with unknown firepower. But we have no choice.

They settled and lay still.

The bush seemed very quiet, and that was always an omen. When the birds stopped, look about you. Something is there.

Only nine miles away, Horst Polanski walked to the door of the command truck and threw a plate of food out onto the ground.

'Corporal,' he barked. 'I'm not going to eat this sudza shit. Bring me grilled meat, not fucking boiled. All right?' His arm was giving him trouble and since arriving at the camp he had witnessed nothing but poor leadership and sloppy procedures. An ex-special forces man, he found whole set-up intolerably amateurish. No wonder they hadn't caught one man, he thought. These idiots couldn't catch a cold. Their man in charge was a fucking idiot who wasn't competent enough to command a platoon, let alone a brigade.

He walked back to the table below the big radio and began to study the map again. Losing Willie Krieger was a severe blow to the operation. He now had to decide which way to go. He couldn't split his team as he had no team to split. He was it.

East into Mozambique, or south? South was further, but infinitely preferable in the long run to a shorter dash into a marginally safer Mozambique. Yes, south it would be. He picked up a pencil and began making notes on a sheet of cheap newsprint. Fucking country, can't even make decent paper, he thought.

The corporal arrived back at the door with some virtually raw meat on a metal issue plate and sullenly offered it to the German.

'Put it there, thank you,' said Polanski without looking up. The man dropped the plate and slouched from the door.

Polanski watched him go and then called for the young captain who lay in the tent, sleeping after a night patrol. The youngster showed promise and was willing to learn and take orders.

He appeared at the door a minute later, saluted and straightened his belt.

'Captain,' Polanski said, 'that corporal on the cook detail. I want him in my section when we go out. He is about to learn soldiering the hard way.'

'Yes, sir,' said the captain. 'It will be a pleasure, sir.'

'I think,' said Smit, 'that it's time to use the Americans.'

'What for?' Said Vickery.

'They were mouthing off one day, about some bloody satellite or other. Takes pictures of anything and uses scanning devices. Let's call in some bonds and find out what they can see for us from up there,' finished Smit.

'It's all bullshit,' said Vickery. 'How's a camera going to find someone in the bush? It will take pictures of crops, installations, roads, not bits of bush. They'll never do it for us.'

'We know roughly where they are, right? Well, let's lean on them and get some pics anyway. It can't hurt. Jesus, man, we need help now!'

'Okay,' said Vickery, knowing when to stop fighting his colleague. 'Try them. They'll only say no.'

Smit pulled on his jacket and walked from the room, straightening his stained tie as he went.

Vickery looked at the map again and then walked to the phone.

'Mrs Van Wyk, please get me an external line at the Defence Force... yes, Mr Whatshisname... ask him to have lunch with me tomorrow... at the Rosebank... thank you... yes, one o'clock... thank you.'

He walked back to the window and reminded himself that the place needed painting.

Looking out but not seeing, he was willing Orpheus to keep moving.

Just raise your head, my friend, and for you I will send in ground support and hard men and aeroplanes that drop things that expand rapidly. You will be safe with me.

Come in, sport, whoever you are.

16

It was so quiet that Max could hear his heart beating. He looked across at Jannie Meyer. The young man lay absolutely still in the grass six feet to his left, the rifle to his shoulder as he looked with both eyes open over the top of the scope. A fly landed on his nose, its proboscis deep in a large drop of sweat. It drank undisturbed.

After what seemed like an hour, Max watched Jannie's blonde head slowly drop and peer through the sight. He looked back through his own, and there they were.

Max found himself counting them into sight. Their point was useless, because only three or four yards behind him was the main body. One, two, three, four, five... must be more. Come on you bastards, where are you? Yes, six, then a gap... any more? Wait for it, Jannie boy, Max thought.

The fear was going. This patrol they could handle. There was no automatic heavy-barrelled gun, and no radio visible. The men's backpacks were swung casually and would hamper their return fire. The last man was doing up his fly buttons as he walked. They had stopped for a leak, and that was why Solomon had only seen four.

Wait for it, Jannie, Max thought, and then the unbelievable blast of Jannie's rifle shattered the silence. Max squeezed his own trigger and he saw the point man thrown backwards, jack-knifed by the force of the round hitting his body. He actually hit the next man as Max's opening burst tore into the tight group. The FN FAL 7.62mm round leaves the muzzle with a velocity of approximately 2,700 feet per second. The thirty round burst left the barrel in just under four seconds and in that time every man except the last, frozen for a millisecond on the third and trickiest button of his fly, died or was mortally wounded. At a range of twenty feet the ambush was classically initiated and finished by the same man. The last soldier had only run two paces when Jannie's second round blew a half-inch hole in his cranium and exited an inch above his left eye, leaving a hole of a similar size. The round would travel another five hundred and seventy yards until it finally came to rest four inches into the bole of a mopani tree.

Jannie slung the rifle over his shoulder and stepping into the path, scooped up the nearest dropped weapon. It was an A.K.M. with folding stock and he checked the load before advancing into the shocked and crying survivors.

Max changed magazines and slowly joined him.

He watched Jannie pause beside one man, who was gasping for breath like a fish as blood bubbled from holes into his chest. Max joined him and the two men walked into the mass of bodies, some moving, some not, and finished the job.

'Let's go,' Max said, less than a minute later. A look passed between the two men, a silent acknowledgement of the horrors they had just witnessed and committed. Quickly, though, they moved beyond the moment. There were urgent matters to attend to.

'Not yet,' said Jannie. 'We will need two rifles and mags.'

They quickly stripped the bodies and Max looked at the enormous wound which killed the first man. 'Hell of a gun, Jannie. What on earth is it?'

'Weatherby,' Jannie said. 'It's meant for big game. Elephant, buffalo... it's too much for this. I was hoping they would walk past but that one was a tracker. Did you see him reading the path? He would have picked up the spoor right here.'

'I was wondering what a point man was doing so close. Time to go, I think. Which way?'

'There,' said Jannie, 'the opposite to the girls and Solomon. We leave good spoor for a few miles then go for the river. The rain will obscure tracks and we want them to have plenty going that way.'

He settled the increased load on his back and set off at a jog, heading for thick bush. Max immediately wondered how long he would be able to run with his pack and extra weapons – he was carrying his share – and keep up with Jannie Meyer. Probably not very long, he concluded.

Five hundred yards away, Solomon put Sarah into the pack, took Vicki's hand and set off, pushing her to the front and clearing spoor as he went. Max and Jannie were running a course at forty-five degrees and blazing a lovely trail for the worst tracker to follow with ease.

It would be seventeen hours until they were safe across the river and a further four before they were reunited with the other half of the group. In that time they would cover nearly fifty miles and survive two further contacts with their pursuers. On both occasions Jannie's path took them took them well clear of likely trouble spots, always leading the chasers away from Vicki and Sarah. However, on both occasions they were spotted running, and from several hundred yards Jannie's formidable marksmanship with the Weatherby prevented the small groups of searchers taking too much advantage. One dead man in each stick was enough to dampen their enthusiasm for the chase, at least until others arrived. Both times saw the pursuers halt as Jannie and Max jogged further away, each time into very thick bush, where the pursuers' instincts told them an ambush might take place.

They forded the river in the pre-dawn darkness, both concerned about the girls and Solomon. The river was high, and

Solomon's task would not have been easy. As far as Jannie could recollect he couldn't swim. They pushed on, the dogs easily keeping pace.

Three miles short of the rendezvous, as they walked in silence, Jannie said, 'Tough work, back there. Most of mine has been done from a distance. Up close like that, it's…'

'I know,' said Max. 'You have more experience than me, except for one thing. I watched them at the crash and I watched them with Helen, so I will never regret what we just did. I'm a realist.' He paused, feeling responsibility perhaps because of his age compared to Jannie. Eventually Max found some words which seemed to fit. 'It's hard because we're human,' he said, 'and we must stay that way, even if we have to fight.'

When they walked into the camp at the mbizi trees both girls began to cry. Vicki with relief and release of tension, and Sarah, who had been bottling up her fear, saw Max, ran to him and let it all out.

There were brief words with Solomon, who immediately left the camp to see where the searchers had progressed to. He was equally relieved to see the two men, if for nothing else to cover his share of the childcare.

Max sat patiently while Sarah told him all about their river crossing, taking big breaths as she spoke. When she was finished, Vicki added more. 'We went under a couple of times,' she said, 'and she was very, very good, weren't you darling.' She smiled at Sarah.

After this, Sarah would not allow Max out of her sight and later asked for her mother. Max held her tightly.

They ate over a small fire before dusk. The meat was fresh and produced by Solomon with no more ceremony than if he had bought it at from the butcher. The dogs, all asleep, lay scattered about the camp as they swapped news of the chase. Max was very pleased with the outcome. They had proved they could separate and cover ground effectively. His muscles ached from trying to keep pace with the super-fit young Jannie and he was tired, dog tired. They had also arrived at the arms cache and tomorrow they would dig it out and re-arm.

That night Max dreamed of the men he had finished off. They were looking at him with hate in their eyes, and his sleep was fitful and restless. Solomon sat high in the trees watching the approach to the camp. He alone seemed unaffected by the pace they had set. Perhaps, Max thought, he always moved that fast.

They were just over halfway to safety.

*

'The tracker says they were here when they fired. Two men, same size. Went that way,' the captain pointed into the bush.

Polanski looked at the site. Not chosen carefully, forced by circumstances more likely. So there were two now. Good, easier to find two than one, he thought.

'Can he follow?' Polanski asked.

'Yes, sir,' said the captain. 'But can we follow from the last sighting?'

'Yes. I want maps. They are heading into the Game Reserve. I want to see where there is water. They will need water. Give my compliments to the colonel. Tell Chabegwa I want all the men into the top end of the park. Go.' He turned and walked to the Land Rover, shouting back, 'I want a helicopter, too!'

He was not looking forward to the prospect of having to find two men in the vastness of the Gonarezhou. Outside the reserve there would be fleeting sightings by his people and by the locals interested in the reward he had placed on the two murderers. They would need to cross dirt roads and areas where the bush wasn't too thick. But once in the reserve the odds would leap in the murderers' favour. Thirty miles wide and almost eight long, the park was in inhospitable in the extreme in the heat of summer, with water and cover scarce. But now with the rains the grass was high and the vegetation thick. There was ground water and streams that were dry eight months of the year now flowed.

Polanski would cover the water holes and the streams, and hope they walked into a trap.

Then there were the animals. Polanski didn't like animals, especially wild ones. They ate people and trampled on them. They gored them with horns and raked them with claws and in National Parks they weren't afraid of men. He knew that from his time in Zambia. He had been with a group of men on an exercise when one had been killed by a buffalo. It had come round the side of some thorn bush like a terrible black shadow, the size of a Spanish fighting bull and twice as agile and with a cunning and a malevolence that no animal that strong and fast should have. The warden had said later that she had a calf, and no, he was not going to shoot her. They should not have been there anyway. Polanski understood and respected that, but now he was going back into a place full of animals. Men, he understood and never feared. But wild animals? They were different. So he would ride around in a helicopter.

Helicopters were about to become part of a conversation several hundred kilometres to the south, on the elegant veranda of the Rosebank Hotel in Johannesburg.

The waiter approached Vickery's table and he smiled at the man. Vickery made a point of always being courteous to staff. He found that one got better service that way. This was South Africa and the waiter was Black but that was no excuse for Vickery or anyone frequenting the place to be rude, which was something he abhorred in many of his countrymen.

'A long gin and tonic, please,' he asked pleasantly, and as the waiter walked away he saw the man he was meeting threading his way through the noisy throng of lunchtime drinkers. Salesmen who wouldn't be going back to the office, wives allowing their diet-trim bodies a little indulgence, lovers meeting for illicit assignations and a fair smattering of students sitting shirtless in the sun, their green Amstel bottles piling up faster than the waiters could get rid of them.

Meetings of this kind generally took place somewhere more private but Vickery had liked the Rosebank since his student days and besides, he couldn't be bothered with cloak-and-dagger tactics just for the sake of it.

The man arrived. Vickery stood and shook hands.

'John, nice to see you again. What's your pleasure?' He said.

'Cane and orange, thanks. What's all this about? Whenever of you blokes buys me lunch there's a horrendous price to pay,' he replied.

The man was with the planning section of Defence Force External Ops and had occasional contact with the B.O.S.S. people. Most of them he disliked but Richard Vickery was on the level and usually returned favours. Vickery smoothed his way past the question and they talked amiably. The waiter, urged on with a five-rand tip, quickly produced the second drink.

'I would recommend the braai,' said Vickery. 'The rump is usually bloody good but give the coleslaw a miss. It usually has a fly or something in it by now.'

They were well into their steaks when Vickery began, almost off-handedly. 'How easy would it be to get an extraction done?'

'I was afraid you were going to ask something like that. Where is your man?'

'We're not sure. That's the problem.'

'No way. It's difficult enough when you know where they are.

These things need exact pick-up points and the right support depending on who is after who and who has nicked the silver.'

Undeterred, Vickery continued. 'I think it will be within a couple of weeks or so and it will be very close to the border.'

'Which border?'

'Tell you nearer the time.'

'Fuck off, Vickery. You'll need orders from the top before my people will plan that sort of thing.'

'No problem, son,' Vickery said icily, adding, 'The cheesecake is usually good. We will need a few hard men on the ground, too.'

All this assumes we can find him before they do, he thought.

'Helicopters should do it. You know the sort of thing.' Vickery smiled charmingly as the waiter began to clear plates. When he left, Vickery continued, 'Be a good boy and sort out the people and logistics. You will get orders and have to move at an hour or so's notice. So be ready.'

'You must want this one badly,' said the other man.

'Oh we do. How is the cheesecake?'

Jannie pointed at a tree and sipped from the cup.

'Under that branch.'

They began digging and had gone three feet down and under a large rock when Max hit the first oilcloth-wrapped bundle. Within in an hour they were laying out an arsenal between the trees' shady canopy. The air was hot and still and the haze obscured the horizon.

'Let's take this stuff and leave the rest,' said Jannie.

Max looked disbelievingly at what he'd selected. 'Christ,' he said softly.

'Good, eh?' Chuckled Jannie.

In the pile which would be added to their own weapons was the queen of the battle. Complete with tri-pod and four steel boxes of belt ammunition was a general purpose machine gun (GPMG). It was fitted with a sling and a spare barrel lay with webbing and packs to carry the steel ammo boxes. Jannie had also selected a rocket-propelled grenade (RPG) launcher and had laid out five rockets. A matched pair of pump-action shotguns with shortened barrels completed the selection.

'Solomon, do you want that gun with the short barrel,' asked Jannie, 'or that one?' He pointed to an FN FAL in the other pile. Solomon shook his head. He would stay with the Kalashnikov they had carried back from the ambush.

'Okay,' said Max, 'everyone top up mags.' He looked back at the pile. 'I'll carry a claymore too.'

As they left, Solomon took the brunt of the new load, with two ammunition boxes and the RPG and rockets in addition to his own rifle.

Jannie carefully slid the Weatherby into a scabbard he pulled from his pack and hefted the FN FAL onto his shoulder. He also carried a steel ammo box, as did Max. Vicki took ten extra magazines for her rifle and they were clear of the area and moving by mid-afternoon. Jannie stripped the FN as they walked and cleaned moving parts. It was rudimentary but would have to do until they stopped for the night. At dusk they crossed into the park and pushed by the moonlight for the Chiredzi tributary.

It was December 15th and they had been on the run for two weeks and were getting stronger and better equipped by the day. Morale was high and Solomon's dry sense of humour and jibes at all of them brought fun and a sense of occasion. In spite of this, discipline was good and now they never spoke in anything but whispers and did everything as quietly as possible. Even Sarah spoke *sotto voce* and entered into the spirit.

From now on, whenever possible, they would only move and night and rest and eat in daylight, hidden from view.

With the added firepower, and now in the park, where Jannie

and Solomon's talents could be utilised, they were a formidable band, an as long as they could avoid direct contact with a very large group they would be all right.

They covered ground the next four nights at a pace Max would not have thought possible. It was cooler at night and with Sarah asleep the silence was easy. Solomon was always on the point with Max and Vicki in the main body while Jannie either with them, ranging ahead or behind them antitracking. At one stage max moved up right behind Solomon and watched the tall man move through the bush like a big silent cat, seeing everything and being seen by nothing. Whenever Solomon felt the need, he let the others catch up and swung them around whatever was ahead. The first night was five adult elephants and a calf, standing swaying in the moonlight and feeding from the trees overhead with their trunks. One night they moved around the side of a herd of zebra. The animals were wary in the dark, but not skittish as they were in daylight.

Considering their location they had surprisingly few incidents with animals and this was entirely due to Solomon and Jannie and their knowledge.

The first incident was on the third morning. They were laid up in the shade overlooking a wide *vlei*, a shallow pool of water. There had been small buck grazing there at dawn and Jannie had watched an old kudu bull move across it later in the morning. They had been asleep when Sarah had left the camp against instructions, while Vicki was on watch. The laid down her rifle and wandered after the little girl, who was more intent on a vivid butterfly than staying in the trees.

Neither had seen the elephant.

It was camouflaged against the trees along the far side well enough to be virtually invisible to the non-expert eye. It was young and male and rather bad-tempered. It had only recently been evicted from the herd by one of the matriarchal females and had not yet teamed up with any other young displaced bulls big enough and strong enough to take females of their own. The rest of his late herd were only four or five hundred yards away when Sarah walked into his limited range of vision. He wasn't very sure what she was, so she was a threat, as was the bigger animal behind her. Vicki.

He wheeled to face them and let out an excited trumpet, more to himself than them, and began the traditional threatening gestures. Ears flapping, advancing a few steps, trunk curling up clear of his small tusks and breathing like bellows, dust rising from his agitated flanks.

Vicki grabbed Sarah, who turned and ran back into her, and froze, unsure of what to do next.

In the camp, Solomon and Jannie both heard the young bull's squeal and Jannie immediately sat up. Not seeing Vicki anywhere, he jumped to his feet, pulled the Weatherby clear of its scabbard and ran towards the noise.

He was in the clearing in seconds and instantly summed up the scene. There ahead of him, forty yards away, was Vicki with Sarah, and forty yards beyond them was the elephant. Not the best short with the girls in line of fire. He called softly to them.

'Nice and slowly. Move backwards. Give him room. Slowly now...'

As he was talking he was edging sideways to give himself a clearer field of fire.

Vicki was terrified but had the presence of mind to do just as he said. She began taking steps backwards, unsure if even to reassure Sarah or just keep absolutely silent.

By then Max had arrived and Jannie heard him cock his rifle, and said softly, 'No... it might be a bluff,' and then louder to Vicki, 'Nice and slow, keep coming.'

Then everything happened at once. The elephant took more

than its usual three or four paces forward, Vicki turned and ran and Jannie slide the bolt home on the Weatherby and lifted it to his shoulder.

Max watched the whole episode as if in slow motion and saw from the corner of his eye Solomon appear running from behind him and throw a rock at the elephant.

The young bull stopped dead in his tracks, startled by the sharp rock, span and ran off into the trees the way he had come.

Jannie burst out laughing, closely followed by Max.

Vicki, still scared, asked indignantly what the hell they were laughing at.

'All the guns we have,' said Max, 'and old Chimkuyu does it with a rock.'

'It wasn't funny, you bastard,' snapped Vicki.

That set Jannie off again.

'Don't you start,' she said. 'You'll be on rations!'

Jannie laughed even harder and eventually she smiled a little. Max sat and explained the situation to Sarah, who wasn't sure what was funny about being told she mustn't ever walk away from camp again and that some animals were dangerous.

'Like lines?' She said to Max.

'Yes,' he said. 'Like *lions*.'

The second incident was to be more tragic, but that was still three days away. Also significant was the fact that they had been seen. A lone Black man high on a kopje, with a large, tripod-mounted Zeiss telescope had seen them and recorded the details in his notebook.

An hour later, back at the camp Jannie was still explaining to Vicki that she was in no real danger.

'He was young and just as scared as you... most elephant charges are mock. They are really very gentle. I promise.'

'All right for you. You weren't there,' she said.

'No, I was right behind you with a Weatherby, four rounds in the magazine and watching. A round from that rifle would have stopped him dead in his tracks, literally. It would knock four thousand pounds of jumbo back on his bum. You were safe.'

Solomon was sitting smiling to himself. Max suspected, not for the first time, that he understood more than he let on.

Vicki folded her arms. 'Well,' she said, 'there aren't any of them in England!'

Jannie looked across at her and smiled, the corners of his eyes creasing up. He ran a hand across his brow and round the edge of his hairline, wiping away the sweat. His hair was tied back in a ponytail and except for the blue of his eyes, his face was a deep brown.

'I've been thinking about that,' he said quietly. His voice had a sad tone to it, and Vicki immediately looked up. He was serious.

'Tell me,' she said.

A long moment passed before he replied.

'I'm not sure I can live in a country with sixty million other people which is the same size as this place. It rains there, Vicki, all the time. It's cold. I went there once with a mate. Everything was grey. The sky, the buildings, the people. All they wanted was my money. I need to feel the sun on my face and the wind clean against my skin. I need...' He broke off.

'Silence,' she offered, remembering a conversation with Max. 'You need silence.'

'Yes,' he smiled. 'Silence.'

'Well, we can't come back here,' Vicki said.

'No, the natives are hostile now. This is one white Rhodie on a one-way ticket out.' Jannie smiled but his regret was obvious.

Max, who had given this exact problem a great deal of thought, knew exactly how Jannie felt and immediately offered a solution.

'Aussie,' he said, slicing off a piece of biltong with his knife and sliding it into his mouth using the same hand that held the blade.

'Pardon?' Jannie said politely.

'Aussie,' Max said through the biltong.

'Yes?'

'They're a lot like us and so is the land. It's hot and big. Lots of space. They grow cattle, tobacco, wheat, some mealies, heaps of sheep. Good people. A bit basic, sometimes, but so are we. They're decent people.'

'Will they take Rhodies?' Jannie asked, clearly interested.

'Sure. Perth is full of bloody Rhodies,' Max said. 'But the place for you is Queensland. Better for crops than Western Australia and politically they're a little to the right of Attila the Hun.'

'That would suit both of you nicely,' said Vicki.

'I shall ignore that,' said Max, offering biltong to Sarah who loved its salty flavour. She loved watching him cut it, too, and stared as the silver foil rolled back like a wood shaving.

'There's a place you would love, Jannie. Magnetic Island. No tropical jungle shit. It's like this and the centre of the island rises to a hill with big granite boulders like Matopos. There's just a few locals there and it's not a quiet. Take the ferry into Townsville for graze once a week. Three pubs or so, general store, white beaches. Fucking great, I tell you.'

He glanced down at Sarah to see if she'd noticed his bad language. But she seemed absorbed in the biltong.

'Peasant,' said Vicki, shaking her head.

'Sounds nice,' said Jannie. 'I think we would like it there.' He smiled questioningly at Vicki, who had come to a point where she didn't care where they went as long as she was there with him.

Max had visited Magnetic Island on a whim several years before on a trip to Australia and loved it. It was where he would have taken Svea to try to make a new life it that had been fate's way. He thought about her often now. More than when in the bush at Kariba. It was, of course, accentuated by the proximity of Jannie and Vicki, and sometimes when he watched them looking at each other the pain returned and he missed her terribly. He didn't want to admit to himself that he still loved her. He looked back at the other pair across the small fire, Sarah sat beside him. He was still amused by that basic law of sex appeal and the emotional attachment which followed. These two were the complete opposites of each other and yet they were as one. Vicki Waters, society darling and wealthy English debutante, and Jannie Meyer, bushman, farmer, naturalist and soldier.

'Genghis Khan and Lady Di,' he said. 'Look at you two, cooing like lovebirds over there. It's almost indecent.'

Jannie blushed and Vicki retaliated with all the breeding she could muster.

'Bollocks to you,' she said, embarrassed and pleased all at once.

It was two days later that the second incident involving animals took place. Reptiles, to be more precise.

They had skirted several small groups of soldiers that day. The chase was definitely becoming more localised and Max was beginning to wonder if they had changed commanders. The whole tactic had changed. Solomon had reported several waterholes ambushed and led them to water that only he and the monkeys knew of.

Max was half-hoping Solomon would report finding the truck and tents again. They had heard a helicopter early that day as they laid up in the shade again so the new forward command wasn't too far away.

It was just into the afternoon and they were asleep, all except for Jannie who was taking his turn on the watch.

The two bull terriers had been sniffing around in the bushes when one began snarling and Jannie heard the slavering, agitated growl of a dog locked onto something. He arrived too late.

The pair had torn a large puff-adder to pieces, the bottom section still twitching in its death throes.

He put down his rifle as Max and Solomon arrived at the source of the disturbance, both armed, and began searching the flanks of both dogs for puncture wounds that would indicate bites from the snake.

On Bovver he found three sets of wounds high on the shoulders and by the time he returned to Aggro the older was licking his lower flank. He too had been bitten before the snake had died.

'They've both been bitten,' Jannie said. 'Quick, get the first aid box. We'll try some anti-venom.'

Max ran the twenty yards back to his pack and pulled the silver box clear. Vicki ran with him and watched as Jannie injected a massive dose into each dog.

'Fucking dogs,' Jannie said, nearly frantic. 'You know about snakes. You know about them... oh, shit, man...'

The big blonde man was close to tears as Solomon put down his silenced .22 rifle beside him.

Max bent to take the rifle.

'I'll do it,' Jannie said. 'They were Oupa's dogs. I'll do it,' and wiped his eyes.

Bovver was whimpering as the venom took effect and Jannie ran his hand over the dog's back in a vain attempt to comfort him.

Max took Vicki by the hand and whispered, 'Leave him alone. Just for a while.'

'But the injection?'

'No good,' Max said. 'The puff-adder injects a hemotoxin. It attacks local tissue. Most anti-venoms are for neurotoxin bites.

Those dogs will die in great pain over the next ten or twelve hours. In a human even with immediate hospitalisation a bit from a puffy often means the area eventually being amputated as gangrene sets in. Better this way.'

Vicki was crying now. 'Oh poor Jannie. He loves those dogs.'

Now Max had to wipe tears from his own eyes. For the dogs, for Jannie, for Sarah, for all of them.

The man wore khaki shorts and an old, pale green shirt and desert boots locally called *veldskoen*. He was short and wiry and sported a neatly trimmed beard. The beard was stained with tobacco after thirty years of the habit and the Tanganyika meerschaum pipe was as much part of his authority as was the uniform he wore so badly.

He was Robert Chapping, Chief Warden of the Gonarezhou National Park. He was unusually crabby today. His wife was visiting friends in England over the holiday period and he missed her around the house and in his bed. He was also disturbed by a report from one of his rangers. The man, a likeable, bright youngster by the name of Simon had been on a count patrol way north of the main admin camp and claimed he had seen two men, a woman and a child on foot in the park.

'Did you approach?' Chapping asked Simon.

'No.'

'Did you report them to Visitor Control?' The park was closed during the rainy season. The roads were all but impassable and the grass was too high. There should be no visitors in the park at all, let alone on foot.

'No.'

'Why not? You know the regulations about hunters!'

'They were armed. Not hunting! The guns were like the army carries. My brother was in the army. He brought home a gun like that once, with some other men. It is called a machine gun.'

'Murungus?' The question was not racist. Asking if they were white was merely confirming his conception. Four locals moving across the park would have been unremarkable to the warden. They had to be whites for the ranger to come to him.

'Yes, sir.'

'Which way were they moving?' Chapping asked.

'South. Boss, I did not report them to Visitor Control because Luke is there.' Luke was their pro-government man, operating strictly by the rules and always quoting the party.

'And I recognised one man,' Simon continued.

'Who was he?' Asked Chapping.

'It was the Pungwe,' he said, with considerable awe.

'Pungwe? You are sure? Boss Jannie?' Chapping was incredulous.

'Sure, Boss. The Pungwe is back!'

'Right then,' said Chapping softly. 'All right. Simon, tell no one about this. I must think.'

17

Chapping sat back in his old government-issued chair and lit the old pipe, puffing thoughtfully.

Jannie Meyer back in the park, with another man, a woman and a child. What the devil were they doing there? He knew Jannie. Knew him quite well, in fact. They had met when the youngster was in high school and passionately interested in wildlife. He had spent holidays with the staff at the camp. Time went by and he proved a quick learner with all things natural. By the time he went into the Parks Service he was teaching rangers and wardens things. From there the war halted what would have been an exemplary career with the Parks and Wildlife Department.

Jannie had operated in the area during the war and had gone out of his way to provide the rangers with bits of information that saved them from many attacks. Chapping's own wife Ruth had been saved by Jannie's boys, who knew where ambushes would be, where mines were laid and who would be the next target. The Pungwe became a legend amongst the superstitious Blacks, one who could track anywhere and move like the leopard that gave him his nickname. He eventually teamed up with an old Shangaan poacher who taught him even more. The poacher was never a serious problem. He only killed what he needed to eat and he was never really pursued like the serious commercial operators were.

Together they were like the guardian angels of the park. Now the Pungwe was back, armed and moving south. Why? There wasn't even a courtesy call to say he would be in the park, which Chapping would have expected from him.

It was the next day that one of Chapping's rangers advised that the army were in the park and shooting game. He spent a frustrating hour on the phone to Harare trying to get someone he could talk to, but to no avail. He eventually slammed the instrument down with a 'Damn and blast!' and stormed to the door.

'Chiseri,' he called to the old-timer. 'I'm going up to that army camp tomorrow. Put petrol in my Land Rover please, and my kit. We go at dawn.'

The old chap waved and got on with the job he was doing.

Robert Chapping hated the army. They came into his park and shot his animals. He was a passionate conservationist and regarded every animal as his, by God, and it was his responsibility to protect them and by Christ he would do it! Chapping went back into his office and tried to phone his daughter but couldn't get through.

'Damn and blast!' He shouted, and bit into his pipe. The staff smiled. He was always like this when his wife was away. Sore like an old lion.

'That's beginning to piss me off,' Jannie said.

He raised the now grubby telescope back to his eye and watched the lone helicopter clatter its way across the trees a mile away below him. They were sitting high on the slope of a hill deep in the shade of a leafy overhang.

'If we hit it, they will just send more,' replied Max.

'Nah, they don't have that many. Anyway, let's hit it on the ground and rev everyone else along with it. What do you think?'

Max remained silent, deep in thought.

Jannie began again. 'Look, it's probably based with the radio truck and command tents that Solomon found. Let's hit it with a rocket or two, a couple of bursts from the gun and then take the gap?'

Max was still silent.

'I'm getting stick of running, Max. Let's take out the command and these guys will be fucked... trust me!' He finished with a plea.

'Trust you?' Max raised an eyebrow. 'You're bloody crazy.' He was worried about compromising their position while safe deep within the park. He was worried for Sarah, for Vicki and for everything else. 'They don't know we're here,' Max said. 'I'd like to keep it that way.'

'Don't be a waste of air, man,' Jannie said. 'Why do you think they keep flying over patches of bush? Why at dusk or dawn? They have infrared gear. They pick up a heat source. In a bush it's easy. Animals will run away. If the source doesn't run, they rev it. They'll get round to our bush sooner or later.'

'Infrared?' Max was incredulous. 'Where did they get gear like that?'

Jannie shrugged. 'Dunno. Russians, maybe. That's why I want to rev it on the ground. Well?'

Jannie put the telescope down as the helicopter disappeared into the low haze and looked at Max. The older man's eyes were rimmed with dust and as he turned to look at Jannie his eyes seemed to glitter.

'Okay, let's do it,' he said. 'If we can find it.'

Jannie whooped with delight. 'Don't worry,' he grinned. 'Solomon will find it.' Seeing the look on Max's face, he added, 'Trust me!'

His grin was infectious and Max smiled and shook his head, wondering what he had let himself in for.

Dawn that day found Robert Chapping and the now old Chuseri on the rough track heading northeast from the main camp. Chuseri was the park's longest serving employee and the senior scout. His written English wasn't good enough to pass the exams for promotion to ranger so there he remained, teaching the younger men what the courses and universities didn't. He often accompanied Chapping on patrol and the two spent days travelling together, often in silence the whole time. What is there to say when men have worked together for thirty years?

The Land Rover edged its way slowly northwards on the fist leg, Chapping's quick brown eyes under salt and pepper hair taking in everything around him, unconsciously counting herds, evaluating grass growth and absorbing the beauty of the wilderness as if it was the first time he'd seen it.

Mid-morning, they stopped for tea and during the course of their drinking session, Chuseri began a tale. It was about a man's son who returned and was young and foolish and wasn't aware that he needed the help of his father, so he never asked. Chapping, initially surprised by the normally quiet man's eloquent delivery, was, however, an expert on the African habit of circumlocution. They all talked around the subject. But he knew what the old man wanted.

'No, Chuseri, you may not leave. Forget the talk of the Pungwe.'

They finished the tea, but Chuseri still managed to have the last word with a patient and drawn-out sigh. He had made his point.

It was mid-afternoon by the time they located the camp. It was evident by the column of cooking smoke high over the spot and Chapping turned the vehicle and moved in its direction.

A kilometre from the camp Max and Jannie were making preparations for their arrogant little assault and once again Jannie had managed to surprise Max. Jannie had cleaned the gun and made all the preparations he could. He now turned to the 'better idea' and ferreted around in his pack before producing four test tubes, two plastic bottles and a roll of toilet paper.

'And?' Max asked.

'A short and informal incendiary device,' Jannie said.

'How?' Max asked disbelievingly.

'Watch and learn. Nasty little number, this. A bit basic but always works. First, into the bottom of the tube... pool chlorine. About half full, see? Then the crap wrap. The longer the delay you want, the more paper you use. Lastly...' He stopped speaking and held up the last bottle '. . . brake fluid. It eats through the paper, contacts the chlorine and you have a chemical reaction that gives off flame.'

'How long is that one good for?' Asked Max, indicating the test tube waiting fluid and cork.

'Dunno,' said Jannie. 'Never done this before.'

Max put his head into his hands and rubbed his eyes patiently before looking up. 'Sorry,' Max said. 'I must have misheard you. Thought you said you'd never done it before.'

'I did,' said the smiling Jannie.

'Fuck me gently,' said Max, a trace of despair in his voice.

'Seen the boys do it, though... a wad the size of a cigarette will give us about an hour's delay. Trust me, Max!'

'I know,' said Max. 'I'll try.'

'I'll just sneak down there and put these into a couple of gas tanks and one under the trailer,' he explained cheerfully.

'Jannie. See that big yellow ball up there? It's called the fucking sun. It lights up the place so much it's called sunlight. It's so much light it's got its own frigging name! You won't get near the place.'

'Yes I will,' Jannie said. 'I'm going pseudo. Let's grab one of them going for a piss and I'll wear his kit, walk in, drop the stuff and walk out. All you need to pull off this kind of thing is the nerve to do it.'

'What if they see you?' Max asked.

'I'll be all right. You're nearby with enough weapons to win a war on your own.'

Max shook his head slowly.

As plans went, it was audacious and would require nerves of steel from its executors. Luckily, they had nerves of steel as well as the other crucial element – luck. Within fifteen minutes of Max and Jannie getting into position on the smelly piece of scrub being used as a toilet by the soldiers, a candidate appeared. He was also tall enough and a few minutes later ex-Sergeant Meyer was once again in the uniform of the ruling body's army.

He spent a very nervous forty minutes waiting for four o'clock and then stepped out into the camp clearing, blacked-up and floppy hat pulled low. He walked straight to the generator and after making sure no one was watching, dropped a freshly corked test tube into the petrol tank. He followed that with the towing truck, luckily a petrol Chevrolet, and as he walked past the trailer towards the helicopter he threw one under the trailer as well.

Max watched all this from two hundred yards across the clearing, bent over the gunsight and with Jannie's telescope in hand.

The helicopter was done with nonchalance bordering on comedy. Max watched Jannie walk towards the aircraft without a hint of hurry and, upon arriving, calmly start cleaning the plexiglass canopy with a rag. Max cursed, thinking it a crewman, until the telescope confirmed Jannie's tall frame.

Out of the corner of his eye Max saw dust rise and he swung the glass to watch a vehicle pull into the camp. When he looked back, Jannie had gone, and he spent the next twenty minutes in an agonising wait for the safe return of his comrade-in-arms.

Robert Chapping clambered from the Land Rover like a gamecock bristling for a fight. His pipe twitched in his mouth and his lithe frame shook with anticipation.

'Who's in charge here?' He addressed the nearest man. Chapping was directed to the command tent and launched into his attack. 'Now look here,' he said. 'Your chaps are hunting here. Perhaps I should say poaching because this is a National Park and there is no hunting allowed. Bad enough you enter without informing me, but no hunting! Understood? Or do I have to contact the Ministry of Parks and Wildlife? Eh? What do you say?'

He was stabbing the man in the chest with the stub of his pipe.

The big Black man in the uniform of a full Colonel was about to burst a blood vessel when Polanski arrived. He had heard the outburst and come running. Guttman had said expressly, no outsiders. No one beyond the brigade must know.

'Good morning,' Polanski said. 'Yes, I know why you are here. I am very sorry, a complete breach of discipline. Does happen at times, I'm afraid. It won't happen again, I assure you.'

Polanski smiled charmingly at the little fellow.

'Ah,' said Chapping. 'All right then. But you must assure me of that.'

He was instantly placated and felt almost guilty for his outburst and tried to make up for it by being over-friendly. 'German, yes?' He said. 'I can tell by the accent. *Guten tag*! Ha ha ha! Yes, right. How long will you be here?'

'A few days more. Anti-insurgency operations. Tell me, Mr...'

'Chapping,' he said through the pipe.

'Mr Chapping. I'm told that nothing moves in the park which your men don't know about?'

'Correct,' again through the pipe.

'I'd appreciate any news of anyone who shouldn't be here... if you know what I mean. In return I'll assure you no more game will be taken.'

'We do a standard report to the local police for that sort of thing. I'll get you copies made if necessary. However,' Chapping began to bristle again. 'Herr Sturmbannführer or whatever you are, any of your men harm any of my animals and I'll have your balls! No deals! Keep your men off my game regardless, and if any of my chaps spot anything you'll know about it.'

He turned on his heel and walked back to his Land Rover.

Back at the vehicle, Chuseri spotted a face he recognised and winked at the man, smothering a grin.

As the pair drove away, the German walked to his vehicle and also left on a routine check of observation points he had at waterholes. He was becoming worried. Still no sign of them.

He didn't have long to wait.

Jannie slid back into the depression, back in his own kit and breathing hard.

'That's how it's done,' he said.

'Who's in the Landy?' Max asked.

'Old Bob Chapping. The warden. Giving them shit about shooting. Overheard most of it. Old Bob, eh? A good guy for sure, and I think his ranger recognised me. Gave me a wink. Chuseri, another good bloke. But that was easy! Like taking candy from a baby. Those blokes are shit. Never had got that close in the war. Victory has made them careless.' He took the lass and looked into the camp. 'There's a white man down there,' serious now.

'Yeah, the pilot,' said Max.'

'No. Another one. East German, high ranking too,' said Jannie.

'That's why the style of their operation changed. A decent officer took charge.'

'We're going to miss him. He just drove off. Fuck it!' He looked through the glass again, turned and said, 'Should be going up in about ten minutes. You use the GPMG. Give me the FN. It's got the scope.'

The sun was dropping quickly and the clearing was bathed in deep shadow, as if anticipating the darkness of death. It was about to become a killing ground.

18

Ten minutes went by.

Twenty minutes went by.

Twenty-five minutes went by.

'Well?' Said Max.

'Dunno,' replied Jannie. 'Too much bog paper, I should think. Give it a few more minutes.'

'It's getting dark,' Max informed him unnecessarily.

Jannie grunted, then said, 'When it starts, chop the shit out of the command truck and then the big tent. I'll do the men.'

'If it starts,' said Max.

It did. Right then. The generator went first followed immediately by the helicopter. A great sheet of bright orange gasoline flame blew upwards with a deafening roar and the dusk became like day. Men tumbled out of the tents and as Max opened fire with the big automatic gun the Chevy went. They never saw the blaze begin under the truck with the command radios as it was completely dwarfed by the spectacular blast of the other charges.

Max's gun was the deciding factor in the short battle. The GPMG has a rate of fire of between 600 and 1000 rounds per minute, and even with the short, measured bursts Jannie had told him to fire in, the effect was as intended by its makers. It cut the running and panicking figures down like wheat and as Jannie began with the slower, scope-fitted FN FAL, the battle was won. In eleven sections men lay dead or dying and seventeen others had run terrified for the bush. The whole camp was ablaze and the expensive communications set-up, aircraft and all the vehicles were burnt beyond salvage. Within two minutes of the first blast Max and Jannie were running into the thick, welcoming bush westward of the camp.

Twenty kilometres away by road, but only seven as the crow flies, Robert Chapping was inching his way up the slippery side of a grassy slope, taking a shorter route through to the main track south. The Land Rover in low ratio was whining its way steadily when the blast lit up the sky to the east. He stopped and climbed from the vehicle and pulled the old binoculars from the leather case behind the seat. By the time he had them to his eyes the second blasting column of bright orange flame shot forty feet skywards and he knew the camp he had left so recently was under attack. As the angry ripping bam-bam-bam-bam of Max's gun entered the fray and echoed around the low hills, he climbed back into the cab.

'Army business, Chuseri,' he said and started the motor.

'Yes, boss,' the older man replied as he watched the fire out of his window. Army business with Pungwe, and the army coming second, he thought. He started to chuckle to himself, proud of the boy he had watched grow up in the park. *Pamberi ro Pungwe*, he said to himself. Forward the Leopard!

'Tomorrow come back with three men,' Chapping said. 'Check on the fire. Make sure it doesn't move too far westward.'

'Yes, boss,' said Chuseri and as he looked across the cab he could have sworn he saw the Chief Warden with a little smile on his face. He knows, thought Chuseri. He knows it is Boss Jannie down there.

Polanski, heading the other way, never saw the sky light up as his command was razed. He only discovered its demise the next day, mid-morning, and walked around it in stunned disbelief. This Orpheus was good. Very good.

His anger and hurt pride was quickly tempered by the realisation that this was the best thing that could have happened. He was close. Very, very close, so must follow now. He began yelling instructions and within twenty minutes what troops that had come back from their mad, panic-stricken run for the trees were assembled and ready for a forced march.

By dusk he was angrier than any of them had ever seen. The spoor had disappeared completely. The tracker was beaten and the pursuit was lost... for the moment. It was like trying to follow an animal.

He began to formulate a new plan. Five flying columns in the park to chase his man and his friend into a series of stop groups along the southern border. He would use the Rhodesians' favourite tactic on themselves. He would also make the same mistake of stringing them too widely. Trying to cover too much ground with too few men.

The reasons for Polanski's tired feet turned up at their meeting point a day and a half after the assault. Their route had been east then south and finally west, and they had covered almost seventy miles. Both men were exhausted upon arrival and slept for most of the following day.

Mid-morning on the next day, they were laid up in the same high kopje of granite boulders, the flat top acacia thorns spread below them through the veld like green picnic tables on a lawn of faun.

'We can move out tonight,' Solomon said to Jannie. It was a question.

'Yes, old one. Pick a safe path. How far do you see to the fence?' answered Jannie.

Solomon looked at him fondly. 'Three days march... if we march and do not run off on fool's errands.' The rebuke was gentle. 'However if any more errands need doing... allow a man to join you, instead of watching over those who can hide like rabbits in the rocks until our return and allow another rifle into the fight!'

'And to the river?' Jannie accepted the rebuke as it was intended, half concerned father and half frustrated warrior eager for the fray.

'Direct, a day and a half fast march, but to skirt the kraal lines and roads, two days, maybe two and a half.'

A hundred miles, thought Jannie. He knew that he and Solomon, or even he and Max, could do it in two days with light packs. But that was a killing pace and would run even fit people to exhaustion.

'They are like angry bees out there,' said Solomon. 'But to catch the Pungwe and me... they will need better men!'

'Take six days, Chimkuyu. Pick a safe path. The girl, Vicki, she will bear my sons,' Jannie said.

Solomon nodded and stood, and without looking back meandered down the hill to scout the trail ahead. He thought he had seen a watcher the day before. Someone following them.

Sitting back in his chair and looking at the enormous relief map on the wall, Chapping sucked determinedly at his dead pipe, the ashes long cold. Somewhere in there was Jannie Meyer, and he was in trouble of some kind. Chapping had no doubt the young man was behind the attack on the army camp, so that meant they were looking for him. A nice lad like Jannie wouldn't do that without good reason and the army these days were a rabble, even the famous Sixth Brigade.

Ruth, Chapping's wife, would never forgive him if he didn't help the boy. They had never had a son and from the first day of the gawky, gangling fourteen-year-old's stay in the park, Ruth had a soft spot for him. His impeccable manners at the table had been almost embarrassing and as the years went by, Ruth secretly hoped her daughter Helen would appeal to the lad. That had never transpired, but he had remained part of the family. When news of his operating presence in the area during the war reached them, Ruth was both worried and pleased. With Jannie out there, the park was safe.

But now he was in trouble.

As Chief Warden of the park and a man who wanted to stay in the country, he could not help overtly, or be seen to. But if he disappeared off for a few days on patrol, with enough food and ammunition for an army, who would be any the wiser? Link up and re-supply and then hope for the best.

He sat up and tapped at his pipe. 'Simon!' He called. It was Simon's day in the office.

'Yes, sir,' Simon appeared in the doorway and saluted.

'No need to salute. This isn't the army! Tell Chuseri to pack kit for a four-day patrol... ahem... the big tent, mess table, portable fridge... the usual stuff as if... erm...'

'As if you were taking Mrs Chapping and Miss Helen?' Simon interrupted.

'Ah, yes,' said Chapping a touch guiltily.

'Yes, sir,' said Simon, before saluting and walking from the office.

Simon wasn't fooled for a moment. He had a grin a mile wide and he walked to the secretaries' office and quickly and expertly forged Chapping's signature on Luke's leave form, thinking rightly that it would be a good thing to get the pro-government man out of the way. 'Effective today,' he wrote, with a flourish at the bottom. Luke, delighted, left the camp three hours later for two weeks' Christmas leave he couldn't even remember applying for.

Chapping walked past, out the door and headed for the house, where a cold lunch would be laid out for him.

Simon began to whistle 'Jingle Bells'. It was going to be a good Christmas.

By three the following morning, when dawn was only an hour away, Chapping was ready to leave the camp on his 'patrol'. The big five-tonner was loaded and the lightweight short-wheelbase Land Rover was fuelled up. Chuseri sat in the cab of the truck before dropping to the ground and standing with a group of five or six rangers and scouts awaiting Chapping's appearance from the house.

He finally stepped from the door and saw the group of men, instantly aware that mischief was in the air.

One stepped forward. It was Simon and he respectfully began what he had been rehearsing all night.

'Boss... it seems to us... ah...' he began to falter. Composing himself, he continued, 'Sir, with the army in the park, we think we should be watching them... in case they begin poaching again... especially around the place of the elephant kill last Easter.' He paused for a moment. 'Furthermore,' he went on, 'if we were to see any... cause for concern we could inform the main camp on channel twenty-two.'

Chapping looked at Simon and his staff and suddenly felt very proud. They had told him where to find Jannie and that while he went to see him they would advise him of any movements of the army searchers.

'Luke...' he began, warning them of the party man.

'He went on leave yesterday,' said Simon.

'Who authorised that?' Chapping asked.

'You did, sir,' said Simon. 'You signed his paper as a reward for good work.'

'Did I?' Frowned Chapping, before suddenly realising. 'Oh yes, I did. How forgetful of me!'

He walked towards his Land Rover and then turned back to the men.

'*Tatenda shamwaris.*' Thank you, my friends.

19

Again that night, Solomon lead the group further south by the minute. His load lightened by the abandonment of the rocket launcher, he had slung both the assault rifle and the silenced .22 over his shoulder and walked with a spear made of a bayonet lashed with wet rawhide reins to an ironwood haft.

The march was uneventful and dawn found them only thirty miles away from the fence that made up the southern border of the park.

Solomon had been increasingly worried by sightings of a watcher, or rather the lack of sightings. He knew they were being watched but could not spot the eyes. He knew it by instinct – and he was right.

The eyes made themselves apparent just after six that morning, when a figure moved up the shallow slope towards the camp where all but the tireless Solomon were preparing for sleep after a night's march.

A man, in his thirties, Black and in the uniform of the National Parks and Wildlife Service moved gingerly up the incline. Halfway up he began to whistle, the way one does at night to reassure oneself on a dark path, or the way one does when one wants to appear obvious.

He had only gone a few feet, whistling, when Solomon appeared from the trees to his right.

'Strange, is it not, that in all the bush here, you a mere counter of what I hunt, happen to walk up my path... or could it be that you follow? Speak, young boy –' He indicated the spear so recently made '– or shall I loosen your tongue for you?'

The younger man looked and then finally recognised the speaker.

'Chimkuyu they call you!' Replied the scout. 'That is apt. You are thin like biltong and thin in the head. I have been on your spoor for three days. I could have had you any time! I have a message for the Pungwe... it would be in your interest to take me to him.'

Solomon's eyes twinkled. He had worthy adversary here. No lily-livered Shona, like most of them.

'And if not?' He asked.

'Try me and see,' said the scout, hefting his rifle.

Solomon laughed out loud.

'Come, young one. I shall take you,' he said.

He walked to Jannie, came to attention and saluted. As his hand dropped he broke into a broad grin.

'*Kanjani, Pungwe?*' How are you, he greeted Jannie.

'Jacob,' said a startled Jannie. 'Why are you here?'

'I bring a message from Mr Chapping,' he said.

They reached the spot just before midnight. Jannie had moved to the point where he was watching for signs left by Chapping that there was a trap. Chapping was no fool and if he had been coerced then he would have left some indication. It would be subtle, a hat on the ground, a lamp lit and hanging in the wrong place or maybe the camp laid out all wrong. But Jannie found no such sign and returned to the group.

'Right, Vicki, you and Sarah stay here for the moment. Max, you cover me and Chimkuyu... if it starts, hit the road. Don't hang about. If Solomon and I can't hack it, then one more rifle won't make the difference.'

Max looked up. 'Something wrong?' He asked.

Jannie smiled and in the darkness Max could see the white of this teeth. 'No, not as far as I can see. But I'm not taking chances this close to the fence.'

Thirty minutes later, thirty minutes spent watching Chapping smoking his pipe in a fold-up chair in the flickering light of a fire, seemingly alone, Jannie sat up in the darkness and perfectly imitated the night bark of a zebra stallion, twice.

Chapping sat up in his chair and immediately repeated the call, once.

Jannie walked warily into the clearing, Solomon guarding his back. He looked about and then approached the fire.

Chapping rose to his feet, a grin across his face, and held out his hand. 'Hello, Jannie. How's your grandfather? Nice to see you.'

The younger man went forward and took the warden's hand. 'Mr Chapping, good to see you. I'm find, thanks. How's Mrs C?'

'She's well... you can call your group in. There's no one for fifteen miles in either direction and those on the limit are being watched by my chaps. Your people are quite safe here for the night.'

Solomon went out for the girls and Max entered last from the darkness on the far side of the camp. He looked particularly aggressive with the array of weaponry and covered with the dust of the days.

Introductions were made and Chapping finally looked at his watch. 'Right,' he said. 'Let's celebrate.'

'Celebrate what?' Asked Max. 'We aren't clear yet.'

'You can tell me what you're running from in a minute's time.' He looked at Max, who was looking around the camp. Big tents, cooking fire and one social fire in front of a big mess tent laid out for a meal, and with a hurricane lamp burning brightly, moths committing suicide against its glass. 'But right now it's the day most of the Christian world celebrates. It's Christmas Day, so Merry Christmas!'

He handed Max a bottle. He and Jannie laughed at once and Vicki squealed with delight. 'Merry Christmas,' she cried and leapt at Jannie, smothering him with a hug.

They had been on the run for over three weeks.

Max looked at the bottle. It was brown, with a familiar label and in the warmth of the evening its chilly contents were condensing in the moist air outside to form dewdrops on the bottle.

'My God... a cold beer,' he said with such solemnity that Vicki started laughing and the mood was set.

Chuseri came from the darkness and after greeting Jannie drew a bath in the canvas folding arrangement that Chapping had bought in Kenya years before. They used the water in turn, feeling cleanish for the first time in days and eventually sat in chairs around the fire with drinks and waited for the food that Chuseri was preparing on the fire.

Vicki was slowly savouring a gin and tonic complete with ice, a marvel of the big American cooler unit hitched to the bank of batteries on the tray of the truck.

'Feeling better?' Asked Chapping. They all nodded.

'Right,' he continued. 'What the hell are you playing at, Jannie? Shooting at people in my park? The place is crawling with people who are hunting you and they're disturbing my animals!'

Max started to laugh and Jannie shot him a quick look to shut him up.

'Mr Chapping,' Jannie began, 'it's a long story.'

'It's a long night. Pray continue,' Chapping said dryly.

Jannie spoke of the plane and the arrival of the troops and the escape and eventually finished with a 'and here we are'.

Chapping said nothing for a while and finally as Chuseri arrived to call them to the table he looked at Jannie.

'Sorry about all that. I liked your grandfather very much. Let's eat and later we can consider the plan.'

Chapping's raid on his wife's larder was not so much a raid as a complete victory. Their table was spread with a vast amount of food and even Sarah, who habitually slept at night, was awake and agog with the sight.

There was a small turkey, cold rare beef, salads, bread, biscuits, milk and in the centre a Christmas pudding in a white bowl covered with foil. Chuseri, who had no real conception of what came first, served everything at once, which appealed greatly to Sarah.

Chapping watched and said, 'My chaps said you had a child with you. Small treat...' he walked to the truck and came back with a plastic bowl and gave it to Max, who had Sarah on his lap. He looked up at the standing Chapping and got a lump in his throat.

'Thanks, Bob,' and looked at Sarah. 'You got your wish.' He pulled the lid off the bowl and held it out to her.

'Ice cweem!' She squealed and in less than a minute had it all over her face.

Solomon stepped into the light and waited respectfully.

'Invite him to sit down.' Vicki nudged Jannie as she spoke.

'He won't,' said Jannie softly. He continued louder, 'Chimkuyu, come forward into the light, my friend. Meet the man whose game you have been hunting all these years.'

Solomon grinned and walked forward. 'Pungwe, it is as they say. The bush is quiet and no one waits.' He had been having a look around while the others were drinking. Jannie immediately felt guilty.

'Solomon, this is Mr Chapping, warden of the park, and seeker of the man called Chimkuyu who hunts like it were all his own.

'Perhaps less time in camps like this and more time spent like the one he hunts and he would find him,' said Solomon solemnly.

Chapping doubled over as the smoke went down the wrong way and after a cough straightened up and looked at the man before him.

'Damn and blast! He's right! Cheeky but right!'

Chapping turned and walked back to the table, loaded a plate to the brim with beef, turkey and bread and took it to the man standing beside Jannie.

'Eat... Chuseri will have sudza if you wish it. We will talk later,' said Chapping.

Then Max had a brain wave and he took the ice cream that a very sleepy Sarah had abandoned.

'Chimkuyu, have you ever eaten milk frozen with sugar and the flavour of wild berries?'

Solomon shook his head.

'Try this, my friend.'

Solomon took the bowl and touched his finger into the melting contents and withdrew quickly, exclaiming, 'Ah!' at the cold. But as he put his finger to his lips he smiled. It was a great, beaming smile. Max knew that rural Africans had a very sweet tooth and for many sugar is a luxury. Hence the billion dollar sales of Coca-Cola on the continent.

'I have heard of such a thing,' he said. 'You can buy it in a store with a freeze machine.' With that, he walked delighted into the dark towards Chuseri's fire.

Max put Sarah to bed with her blanket on a camp bed in a tent and re-joined the others who were about to begin to lay waste to a large bottle of KWV brandy around the fire.

Later, before the dawn, Vicki Waters conceived a daughter and while that was going on Max was thinking about the promise he had made to Sarah's mother and checked the small pocket in his pack for its contents.

They spent the night at the base of a giant baobab tree, the grass tall around them. Sixty miles to the south was the Limpopo river and safety, and its proximity was obvious in the mood of the evening, although now dampened by no fire and virtual silence.

What whispering there was, was silly jokes and giggles and lots of what-I'm-going-to-do-when-we-cross.

Jannie and Max had decided to rest the night and do a hard push the next day and try to cover the bulk of the distance to the Bubye river. From there it was one day's hard slog.

Before first light they ate lightly of the food that Chapping had given them and were moving by the time the great red sun rose over the eastern bush.

'Ran later,' said Vicki to Sarah and together they chanted the rhyme, 'Rain, rain, go away, come again another day.'

They made their first mistake by splitting the firepower and the experienced eyes.

Mid-morning Jannie had decided to head westward on a reconnaissance and try to see what lay that way. If necessary they could swing west if compromised, but not until he had looked. The ranger reports would have put the troop formations far to the east but he wanted to confirm that.

'I want to come with you,' said Vicki.

'No. You stay with Max and Solomon. Okay?'

'I want to come. Please, Jannie. You said I was fit now.'

'Fit, yes, but not fit enough to keep up,' he said firmly.

She snuggled up beside him, slipped her arm through his and said, 'Please, Jannie? We never have any time together. Please?'

Jannie eventually relented and together they headed west after planning to meet the other three at the base of the Mateke Hills that afternoon.

He had grave doubts about the wisdom of taking Vicki with him and was to be proved correct.

It wasn't Vicki's fitness that was the problem. The problem was she didn't like walking through bush when not ten feet to the side there was nice short grass.

It was late in the afternoon only three hundred yards from the meeting point set up with Solomon that Vicki tired of walking behind her man, stepped to the side and into the grass. Like a meadow surrounded by trees and undergrowth it was a clearing some hundred yards in diameter.

She was tired, and tired people do break the rules. That's why airline pilots can only fly so many hours per month and that's why accident rates in industry soar along with the overtime paid out.

So she stepped out into the clear grass, only four feet from the protective cover of the trees, now deep in shadow. She was out there for only sixteen paces, but it was long enough.

The group lying tired and disheartened on the other side of the clearing were the last in the line of Polanski's stop groups and by pure mischance were miles away from where they should have been. The sergeant in charge wasn't very good with maps and had he trusted his own natural sense of direction they would have been better off. But no. He wanted to use the map and here they were, right in front of what could only be the Mateke Hills. That put them seven or eight miles to the west of where they should have been.

The men were discussing softly just how much trouble they were going to be in when one looked round and saw a figure moving on the other side of the clearing. He looked a second time and then silently nudged his companion. Soon all six were settling on their bellies, weapons to the fore. The sergeant looked down his sight and Vicki Waters, young, beautiful, pregnant and in love, had four seconds to live.

The irony of the whole occurrence was that the soldier who actually shot her had his eyes shut when he pulled the trigger of his AK47. The rest, who were braver and actually aimed, spread their rounds wildly through the trees and into the dusty sky.

Jannie swung back to look for Vicki and as he did so, saw her out to his right in the clearing, walking tiredly.

'Vicki,' he said softly but with urgency, 'don't walk out there. Come back in here.'

She looked back and smiled, as if remembering him and his rules fondly. She made a guilty face and said, 'Sorry.' As she turned to re-enter the treeline the first bullet hit her, then the second and finally as she began to go at the knees the third struck high between her shoulders.

Jannie watched the shock wave run through her body as the first bullet found her and as the second hit he saw the surprise in her eyes, her mouth open and the final realisation as she began to fall.

'Sorry,' she said in a little voice as her knees went and as she toppled forward Jannie caught her and staggered himself as if hit, and then lowered her to the ground.

The bullets were whizzing all around them and the angry gunshots from Polanski's ambush party were clear in the warm afternoon, easily reaching Solomon and Max three hundred yards away.

The men immediately broke into a run in the direction of the contact site. Dingaan raced to the front with Solomon while Max, with a heavier load, trailed by several yards.

As he ran his hair streamed out behind him and he slipped the FN onto full automatic, breathing hard and his feet pounding the ground as he took great long strides.

The three of them arrived almost together. Max and Solomon from the right flank ten yards apart and Jannie straight across the clearing. They heard him first, the blood-curdling scream of anguish and pain and anger, and then they heard it turn into the crazed yell of the berserker and then they heard the gun begin to fire across the clearing.

It was a deeper, faster note than the others of the ambush

party. As Max burst onto the side of the clearing he saw Jannie Meyer running, the GPMG on a sling firing on full automatic into the bush were the attackers lay shooting back.

It was a classic act of bravery under fire, often reclassified as stupid later. To Jan Henricks Meyer it was quite simply the fastest way to get in amongst and destroy the men who had taken the life of all he had left. Max himself opened fire at thirty yards and watched two men crumple who had stood to run away from the blonde madman charging them from the other side.

That Jannie was an expert with the GPMG was not a surprise. What Solomon did was. He dropped his rifle the moment he had fired his last magazine to completion and taking the bayonet spear he had fashioned three days before, he moved amongst the terrified remnants of the ambush party like a whole impi of Shaka's finest warriors, the blade dulled with blood again and again, and speaking the ancient chant 'I have eaten' in pure Zulu each time the blade withdrew.

The last man he literally ran into the ground and finished off with the spear the same way. Solomon finally got his action.

Jannie, his bloodlust and anger abated, ran back to where Vicki lay and Max moved amongst the bodies making sure.

By the time he joined Jannie who was cradling Vicki's body, the bush was unnaturally quiet. There seemed to be blood everywhere, on Jannie too. He stopped beside them and sank to one knee.

'Oh Jesus, no,' he said, agony in his voice. 'Not Vicki, not so close.'

It was only then that Max remembered little Sarah, who was terrified and shivering in the pack on his back.

'Leave us, please, Max,' whispered Jannie.

Max stood and backed away so as not to let Sarah see Vicki's blood-soaked body. His eyes glittered for a moment and he said to himself, 'You will pay for this, you bastard. I will kill you for this.'

They buried her at dusk, deep in a cleft in the rocks and piled other stones above her so the animals couldn't get to her.

Jannie was silent throughout and when they left the grave site he was pale beneath the tan and his bright blue eyes had lost their lustre.

21

They stopped two hours later at the base of a ridge overlooking the pass through the hills. Sarah had stopped shivering and lay asleep in Max's arms. She was restless and troubled and he occasionally stroked the matted blonde curls and the sweaty, grimy little forehead.

It was then that Jannie said, 'Is she asleep?'

Max nodded.

'Have a look at my back. I'm hit.'

Jannie pulled his pack clear and in the light of the small fire he exposed his lower back to Max. It was an ugly open wound, deep and bleeding heavily. Now Max knew why Jannie was so pale and slow on the move from the firefight. He lay the child to one side and looked closer.

'It's bad, Jannie. Lie down and let's do something for you.'

'Strap it up... clean, wet cloth over the hole... there's a drip in my pack... strap it tight, Max.'

Solomon looked at Max as he worked and caught his eye. He shook his head.

They spent the night there, Jannie lying prone with the drip in his arm and drinking frequently from the last water bottle they had. He woke several times in the night and once in great pain asked Max to clean the spare barrel for the GMPG and prep the last box of rounds for the gun. Max agreed and did both jobs while Solomon and Sarah slept. It was the first time Max had seen the Shangaan actually asleep. The pace was beginning to tell.

Two hours before dawn they were up and Jannie asked Max if he still had the claymore mine.

'I do. Why?'

'I can't run, my friend. Leave me the mine and the gun and let me get up that hill over there. Put chlorine bombs in the bush, it's a westerly so blow the fire into them... the mine in the pass and me above with the gun...' He was in great pain and very weak. 'And then you and Solomon go for it. I'll hold them for a few hours.'

'Jannie, don't be thick!' Max snapped.

'Do it!' Snarled Jannie. 'Just do it... for Vicki and for me, okay. Everything I ever loved is dead now. There's nothing left. In a few hours I'm with them. Until then, let me be of use.' He coughed and winced in pain.

'You stubborn bastard,' Max said quietly.

Jannie smiled weakly and slung an arm around Solomon's shoulder as they moved into the darkness.

'Give the firestarters three hours or so... that means three inches of paper.'

Jannie was lying down, the GPMG set up on a rock in front of him.

'See the trees there,' he pointed. 'Put the mine a hundred yards back and put the wire between the trees. Don't arm it until you're behind it.'

Max was back by the time the light was full on the valley. Solomon had filled water bottles somewhere and left one with the wounded man.

'Take the Weatherby, there's eight rounds left. Take a shotgun. Remember, shoot long...'

Jannie reached into his pack and as Max moved forward to shake his hand he pulled something out and pulled it onto his head. It was the brown beret of the Selous Scouts, its stylised osprey badge as clean as when it was issued. In it, although wounded, he looked every inch a soldier and every inch worthy of the legendary men who wore the beret.

'*Pamwe Chete*,' Max offered, reciting the Scouts' motto, 'Together only!'

'*Sterek*,' grinned Jannie. 'Now fuck off. Take the telescope too.'

Max shook his hand. *Sterek* was the Afrikaans word for 'strong' and, Max reflected, was typical of the man. 'Thanks, Jannie.'

Jannie gestured at Sarah. 'Get her clear, Max, or we all died for nothing.'

Max turned and walked down the southern slope of the hill, one hand on Dingaan's collar. Solomon remained for a few moments longer, just looking at the true friend he was leaving to die. The two men exchanged some words and then Solomon, too, walked down the hill.

I'll kill you for this, Max thought.

They heard the gun begin firing two hours later and the dull crump of the mine almost immediately. The fires began later still and by lunchtime the sky was black with smoke, a bush fire burning along a twelve-mile front between them and their pursuers.

'Max,' said Solomon as they walked, 'this morning when we left, the Pungwe gave me this.' He held up a small package wrapped in newspaper.'

'What is it?' Max asked. Solomon handed over the package and Max unwrapped it. Within the folds of the paper was a small gold cross with a red and gold ribbon. Across the centre was a lion's head and two words inscribed read, 'For Gallantry.' Max's hand gripped it tightly and he turned and looked back at the glow of the fires in the hills behind them. It was Rhodesia's highest award for valour, given out only three times in the entire war. One of the recipients was never named for security reasons. But now Max knew. So, Jannie my friend, he thought, you were one of the few. Goodbye, my friend.

He turned back to Solomon, handed him the medal and said, 'In the times of Shaka and Mzilikazi warriors who had proved themselves in battles above all others were given special shields, white ones. You have heard of this?'

Solomon nodded solemnly.

'This piece of gold is such a thing. In the war only three ever received this. A badge of bravery worn that all may know.'

Solomon turned and looked at the fires and said softly, 'He was a man.'

That phrase is the highest form of praise an old time Matabele can give. It is an abbreviated form of the famous quote used by King Lobengula at the demise of the Shangani Patrol in 1896, where he said, 'They were men of men and their fathers were men before them.' The Shangani Patrol, also known as Wilson's Patrol, were the thirty-four British South African troopers who took over four hundred of Lobengula's finest impi with them to their deaths. The term was much older but that was its most documented use.

Solomon looked up at the hills. 'If one must die, then this is a good place for it.'

Max nodded and as he felt Sarah move in the pack, he settled it more comfortably on his back.

Solomon held out the medal. 'Max, take this to that place of which you spoke and place it high in the rocks, so that all who see it may know.' Solomon refused to talk directly about Magnetic Island.

Max took the medal. 'It shall be done. Now, can you make tracks for two?'

'Am I not Chimkuyu, who taught the Pungwe?' Solomon said, raising himself to his full height and with great dignity said, 'I can make tracks for the devil himself.'

All right, go west, then go home and make tracks as far as the road. I shall go south.'

'You know how to send word if you need me?'

'Yes,' said Max. 'Go now. They follow. Travel carefully, old one.' The term was meant and received with the highest respect.

Solomon nodded and Max turned away at a jog. He looked back once and Solomon raised his rifle in salute, and then he too moved off.

Max stopped a mile further on and, ignoring Sarah's questions about the whereabouts of everyone else and why was he throwing away the tent and other things, he lightened his load the most effective way. He kept what they would need for the next forty-eight hours and discarded the rest.

He kept Sarah's blanket, a bowl for the dog's water, a cup and a small bag containing a few tines and cold food, some water and the weapons, and finally Jannie's telescope. The rest he stuffed down an antbear hole and finally turned to the south and began at a steady jog. He didn't maintain it for long. His load was well over fifty pounds and with the awkward shape of the weapons it was too much. He soon settled for a fast walk, the Rottweiler easily outpacing him, and every now and then ranging far to the front, almost as if in the absence of his master he would work the point.

It worked.

Twice in the afternoon Max came across the big dog standing still on the track watching the bush ahead. He had seen nothing but they were downwind and the dog had smelled the men ahead. Both times they skirted the group and Max never actually saw the men in question.

He slowed his pace and soon was moving very slowly indeed, discretion being the better part of valour, stopping often to watch and listen.

Nightfall found the three overlooking the floodplain of the Bubye river and, moving slower than ever, they spent the entire night edging their way south. The area was thick with troops and several times in the dark Max had his hand over Sarah's mouth while hoping that all Jannie's training of the dog would pay off. At one stage five men came within spitting distance and Dingaan, shivering with anticipation, stood firm under Max's comforting but firm hand.

The entire night gave them cover for only a few kilometres of travel and at dawn Max's despair was completed. Daylight showed they were in fact smack in the middle of an enormous troop formation that stretched a mile either way. He had walked them into a bivouac line and it was then that he really began to miss Jannie and Solomon, either of whom would have known what lay ahead.

Light drizzle began and together they sat deep in a thorn stand and watched the cooking fires of the followers preparing breakfast. They were there until late morning and when Max was sure they area was clear again they began their snail's pace movement southwards.

Sarah was damp and niggly and even the offer of baked beans did nothing to lighten her spirits. The dog drank water and ate biltong and at three they forded the Bubye, its narrow sandy course only fifty yards wide.

By this stage Max was more animal than man. His long hair was matted and filthy and the growth of his beard made him look like a pirate. His face and neck were tanned a deep brown and he was superbly fit, fitter than he had ever been in his life. His instincts were also sharper, which was what saved them from the next encounter.

The south bank of the Bubye at that point was steep and edging upwards, rifle and dog in hand, Max felt the hackles on the back of his neck begin to rise. He looked at the dog, but the animal was preoccupied with gaining a grip on the muddy clay surface of the bank.

Max stopped and looked around, and that instinctive feeling became more powerful. He scrambled upwards, desperately trying to get into cover and off the exposed bank. He was not a second too soon. As he pulled the scrabbling dog up the last few feet a burst of fire from the other bank stitched the ground where they had been, the dull thuds of the rounds hitting the bank audible over the reports from the muzzles sixty yards away.

He didn't bother to attempt to return fire. He had not seen the place it had come from and instead he began to run for the hills in the distance, south and east. There he would find rocks and cover, and would, if he could, dominate a battle until dark allowed him to escape. He had learned much from Jannie Meyer and use of a height and distance advantage was the most recent lesson.

Running, he heard the sound of engines nearby and for the first time began to doubt they would actually make the border. So near and yet so far. Thirty miles, maybe. Thirty-five at the most. Only a day's walk, but now they were within a few yards of him with vehicles, men and radios.

Max pounded the ground with long, powerful strides, breathing hard as the protective cover of the hills grew nearer with every step. Behind him he could hear the excited yelling of the followers. Like hounds after a fox, they smelled easy victory after such a long chase.

The dog, tireless, paced at his side and like some recent mythical tale, the man and beast ran before the hung. Whatever the outcome of the day, Max would die, of that he was certain.

22

Incredibly, weighted with pack, child and weapons, Max managed to gain ground and by dusk was deep in the rocks three-quarters of the way up the northern slope of the small, rocky hill.

Below him, six or seven hundred yards away, were the troops and from his vantage point the sight was not encouraging. There were probably three companies of men on foot an several trucks making slow progress from the east. They were spread in a line of skirmish groups and moving slowly, now confident they had won.

So this is where it is to end, thought Max. With the sheer mass of men below it would be easy to seal off the hillside from all directions. Escape from here seemed impossible and Max pulled the telescope from the narrow pocket on the side of Sarah's pack and watched the trucks edge their way round to the south of the hill, dropping men as they went.

Incredibly, Sarah was still asleep, and had been throughout the rough, bouncing ride on Max's back. He gently unslung the pack and watched her for a moment, her thumb firmly in her mouth. The long night had been too much. Sleep little one, he thought, because it starts any minute now. I know that because I'm going to start it. Dingaan nosed her gently, as if he'd heard Max's thoughts.

He pulled Jannie's beloved Weatherby from the scabbard and checked the loose rounds in his pockets. Four. In the magazine there were a further four. He cleared the dust from the scope and watched through the crosshairs for the first time. The powerful sight was the pride of the Bushnell scope company and below the first man he sighted on, six hundred yards away, leapt into view as clear as Max could possibly have hoped for. Good enough, he thought. He quickly checked the load in the cut-down shotgun and worked the pump action a couple of times, then reloaded. Lastly he changed the magazines on the FN and eased the rest into a webbing around his chest. Then, like the last part of a ritual, he woke the child.

'Wake up sleepy head,' Max whispered. She woke reluctantly and he continued, 'I'm going to start the thunder in a minute. Cover your ears, okay?'

Sarah immediately accepted the need to do so and with a frown covered her ears with her hands and settled lower in the pack as he swung it up and onto his back. He changed his mind and pulled it round to his front and then finally settled against the rock in front as far as he could, resting the rifle on a T-shirt on the rock's top face. The height was perfect.

Deep in the last shadows of dying daylight, beneath the bright blooms of a Karrif tree, Max Seager chambered a round into the breach of the Weatherby and began his last stand.

He carefully sighted on a non-com in front of his squad and in the time-honoured manner of a range shooter went through the drills. He held his breath, gently breathed out, squeezed very gently and said to himself *come and get it you bastards*, then went onto the second pressure.

The blast and recoil were awesome but in the curious way of most users of high-calibre rifles, Max didn't even feel it. But the man in his sights certainly did. He was plucked up and thrown backwards as though a mighty fist had hit him.

That .400 calibre round is enough to stop an elephant in full flight. And not just stop him – he would be knocked back onto his haunches. The bullet is just under half an inch across (1.2cm) and so that gives it about five tons per square inch of hitting power.

Max watched the man's body hit the ground, swung left and fired again. By all rights the second man should have been going for cover, but at that range they had only just heard the blast of the first shot when the second was fired. Max compensated for the fall in the heavy bullet by aiming very high for a downhill shot. The bullet took the second man in the head, which simply disappeared from his shoulders while the blast ripped open his chest.

By then the whole company was going for over and Max watched through the scope for the idiot every platoon has.

He didn't wait long, as not thirty seconds later a man stood up to look for his friends in the grass and this time Max's aim was true. The massive bullet his the man in the legs, smashing both femurs and miraculously missing his femoral artery. The man may well have wished it hadn't because as soon as he went down he began screaming.

It was what Max intended, cruel in the extreme but necessary to unnerve the man's comrades and to draw another into the trap. Sure enough, another stood to try to identify who had been hit and Max fired the last round in the magazine. It took the man in the pelvis and he too was thrown back into the grass.

Jannie, my friend, I wish you were here, he thought.

Darkness was falling quickly and he loaded the last four rounds into the rifle. They were the size of a small cigar and shiny amongst the mud and grime. With a few seconds' peace, Max lit a cigarette.

It was now too dark to shoot, but Max fired four rounds down the hill anyway. They were yet to see him miss and with luck they would assume that more of their group were down.

The dog whimpered at his feet and as Max felt Sarah stir in the pack he gave Dingaan a reassuring pat then reversed his grip on the rifle and, careful not to burn himself, smashed the stock twice against a rock until it was shattered and useless. The rifle had been built by a craftsman and Max knew Jannie would not have wanted it to fall into the hands of those below.

Sarah was strangely silent in the pack and when he stood still he could feel her shivering with terror. Not long now, my girl.

He lifted up the FN off the ground and began edging upwards. He knew the soldiers would be coming up the hill now it was dark. The first arrivals would be at the bottom of the slope and he wanted to gain all the height he could so he could cover his back and in one final, desperate try, probe the south slope.

Below Max something moved on the slope and in a fluid move, and glad of the flash eliminator, he double tapped the movement and kept going. He heard the shouts of the first brave ones, who were shielded by the night and urged on by their instructors and officers. They were no more than a hundred yards away now and for the last time Max let the big dog run free.

'Go, boy... home, boy,' he said softly. The dog just looked back at him, and as he pushed further round the slope, it padded at his heels, alert and tense.

A ragged volley began below him, the discipline of the troops pushed to such a limit they were now firing at shadows. Four or five rounds buzzed overhead of Max, the sound like a vast angry wasp. Ricochet, he thought, surprising himself with his lucid judgment, and then started to laugh. The laugh was that of a man with nothing more to lose and he turned and fired a long, sustained burst down the slope, his madness that of the man who has faced his fear and beaten it.

'Come on, I am here!' He bellowed at them and laughed at the answering volley of fire which missed him entirely and went off into the darkness.

Max moved further round the hill and in the darkness again saw movement, this time very close. He pulled the shotgun from his back, pumped a round into the breach and swore, because he'd dropped it. He fumbled around on the ground for the unused cartridge, no longer caring who heard him. He founded it and reloaded, and with that his blood cooled and his rational thought sequence took over.

Slow now, he thought. Very slow. They're here. One in there to the right...

He felt Sarah shivering in the pack and looked down. She was strangely silent, her wide eyes watching her little hands clutching the sides of the pack as it swung and jolted around. As his movement became slower and more predictable she changed grip and chanced a look up at Max. 'Sshh,' he mouthed quietly, and slowly began to move forward.

He had only taken three hesitant steps when Dingaan shot past him. Not bounding across the rocks like he had done earlier in the day but low and very fast, and absolutely silent. He went straight over a rock and disappeared from sight, and as Max froze and dropped to one knee he heard the dog attack something. There was a high-pitched scream which dropped into a low moan and then into a jabbering, terrified cry for help. Using the diversion, Max stood and moved on, and as he did so a burst of fire came from where the dog had gone in.

Still moving, Max hoped the dog hadn't been hit and then ran into trouble himself.

It was a group moving quickly up the western slope of the hill and Max virtually collided with them. Once again, his phenomenal reaction speed paid off and the first round he fired from the shotgun hit the lead man full in the chest.

One down, three to go.

Come on the rest of you, he thought, join your friend in hell. Come on, you oh-so-brave boys, there's only me and a little girl and doggy. Come on!

He fired again at a movement and then rolled into cover, the child in the pack rolling with him as he pulled off a kind of cartwheel move.

Two down, two to go.

Come on, the last of you, he thought. Come on! It's just me and a little girl and a dog who has already ripped the throat from one of you so come and fucking get it!

But where was Dingaan? Oh fuck, he wished Jannie was there.

Max scrambled to his feet and the shotgun ripped into the night as a shadow advanced and then fell.

One to go.

He turned and ran back the way he had come, hoping it was still clear, hoping they hadn't got that high yet.

A shape, low, looked out, moving fast. He swung the gun up, pressure on the trigger... no, it's the dog. Good boy, he thought. Come, boy. Come to my side.

Another shape in the darkness now, a burst of fire, the rounds coming very close, give the shotgun one more squeeze, missed, oh shit!

They were very close now. Dingaan launched himself at a movement then fire came from behind, faster, shorter bursts. Jesus, Max thought, they're behind us now.

Max turned and swung the barrel across his chest, protecting Sarah who was still in the pack, hands over her ears, the dog's mauling jaws audible only yards away and the victim beginning to scream... when night was transformed into day by a magnesium flare.

'DOWN, DOWN, DOWN!' screamed a command and as Max's racing brain comprehended that it was meant for him, a figure ran into the light and crashed into him, knocking him to the ground.

A withering burst of fire began chopping into the bush behind him and a voice inches away from his ear said, 'You bloody police are never any good in a contact,' and a hand pulled him out of the blinding light of the flare and into the cover of a welcome pool of darkness behind a coffee table-sized rock.

As the four-second flare began to die, figures raced past him, pulling night vision blackout goggles from their faces and began firing into the blinded, leaderless and decimated patrol of Sixth Brigade that had just finally failed their mission.

'Mind the dog!' Someone yelled as five of the eight-man section of the South African Defence Force's 38 Battalion Recce rolled past Max and his bodyguard and into the vicious close-quarters massacre with shotguns and Heckler & Koch machine pistols. It was brief and final for those with no night vision from the flare to help them spot the silent new comes. Fire arced up from positions further down the hill but it was ineffective and high.

Within a minute the men were back and Max, his mind still racing, began to realise what had happened.

Cuddling Sarah through the pack he began a barrage of questions as he was pulled to his feet. 'Who are you people? Where did you come from? How the fuck did you know we were here?'

'38 Bat, SADF... we have come to take you out,' said the closest man and then continued, 'now move up there and find the boss.' With that he turned to the group now settling into defensive positions. He looked back at Max, who was still on the same spot. 'Move!' The soldier snarled. 'We're not out of this yet!' As Max moved away, the man said quietly, 'Call your dog. He's down there. Now go!'

'I'm going,' said Max. 'Don't get your little knickers in a twist.' He was recovering rapidly from what he had been convinced was certain death.

'Dingaan,' he called. 'Come, boy.'

The dog moved like a shadow as far as the men and sniffed an extended hand suspiciously.

'Come, Dingaan,' called Max again, and the dog bounded over to him and Sarah, still terrified and silent.

Max moved up the hill and was met only twenty feet later by a man unmistakeably 'the boss'. He was short, lithe and the beret on his head distinguished him from the others, who all wore black wool ski masks. The man put out his hand and beckoned.

'I might have known it was you,' he said.

Looking into the darkness Max could only see the man's outline, but the voice was familiar.

'Get into the harness,' he said. 'Hot one in sixty seconds. Sergeant, help him.'

The big man from below came up. 'Step into this,' he said, spreading a harness on the ground, and then added, 'Do you want to do the dog or shall I?'

'The dog comes with us,' said Max. He's saved our lives three or four times today, so he comes. Please.'

'Pull it up that side,' said the man, pointing at the harness. 'Can't do the dog. Fine. I'll do it.'

'NO FUCKING WAY! That dog... he comes with us.'

The boss returned and the sergeant looked up. 'Okay, said the boss. Love me, love my dog. I get it. Sergeant, tell Cashton to get up here and dump the camo net. He takes the dog. Forty seconds.'

'Yes sir,' answered the sergeant, then turned to Max and said, 'I like dogs, really.'

A sustained burst of fire came from below and was returned by the men further down as Cashton arrived and began making preparations for the dog's extraction.

'Here, Fido,' he called uncertainly. Max, now in his own harness, helped the soldier load a struggling Dingaan into the pack.

'Right, let's go... move, move, move!' The officer was back. Max looked at him and the pieces began falling into place. The voice, the short walk, the commanding air. Pascoe. The RLI captain at the first and second missile attacks in Rhodesia. Max laughed at the irony.

'You're Pascoe,' he said.

'I am. I wondered if you would remember. Right, up here, now hurry. Ten seconds and then the choppers and the ground strikes.'

Pascoe knelt by a radio and spoke into the handset, and then pulled a pair of flares from his pack.

'Sergeant, are we ready?'

'Yes, sir.'

'Right. Here we fucking go then.' He pulled the lanyard at the base of the first flare. It shot skywards and burst high above them then hung suspended by parachute.

It swung below the miniscule silk canopy like a miniature sun and for a moment the fire from below stopped and then recommenced at the flare, thousands of rounds of tracer pouring upwards. Seconds later they heard the banshee screaming engines of three Buccaneers of the South African Air Force as they lined up their attack run on the flares.

Pascoe fired the second flare and the first jet commenced its run. Max, who had never seen a ground strike, stood mesmerised by the speed and ferocity of it all.

Withing seconds the entire grass flat below the hill erupted into flames as napalm and rockets blasted the area and cannon fire raked into the milling, running men exposed on the open, grassy killing ground.

Max, for all the fear and the hate of the last weeks could only feel pity, and Sarah, her blonde head clear of the pack's top, watched big-eyed as flames from the napalm canisters soared skywards.

'Choppers,' said Pascoe and as they watched two Bell 212s came in at max speed from the left flank, and bleeding airspeed as they dropped, Max felt someone grab his harness. Below the helicopters were cables hanging thirty feet and at the bottom of each was a 'T' bar.

The men ran into two groups of four, Max following Pascoe who had his harness loop. As the helicopters came closer, the 'T' bars swing into reach and as the men hooked themselves on, the helicopters, without ever actually stopping, clawed their way upwards and away from the ground fire they were now attracting. With the men hung below, the aircraft flew off into the blackness of the night.

A few miles away the helicopters settled briefly onto the ground and after the people on the 'T' bars climbed back into the aircraft and Cashton had given Max back his four-legged companion, now shivering and nervous, the 'T' bars and cables were jettisoned an the helicopters moved south, low and fast.

Twenty minutes later they were settling together onto the rolled asphalt surface of the perimeter of a camp and as the rotors ground to a halt, Pascoe looked up and flashed a thumbs up at Max.

The men began baling out and as Pascoe went to join them Max took his arm.

'Thanks,' he said, 'but why? That little sortie must have cost a fortune.'

'Dunno,' answered Pascoe. 'I just work here.'

He jumped grinning onto the ground and Max allowed Dingaan to jump down after him. The dog began sniffing the ground and then looked back as if to ask, 'Are you coming or not?' I know why, thought Max.

He looked down at Sarah. She was staring up at him and was beginning to stand up in the pack. He pulled her upwards and as she put her arms around his neck, he said, 'All finished, little one. No more thunder.'

Then, much to Max's relief, she began to cry. It was a slow, quiet cry, from deep insider her very soul, and he rocked her as it all came out. He was rather pleased with Sarah. The last few days had been bad – far worse than anything a child should experience – and he had feared for a while that she had forgotten how to cry at all.

Max barely noticed Pascoe return. 'You coming in?' He asked.

'No,' said Max. 'The lady and I will compose ourselves for a while, thanks. We'll be in shortly.'

Pascoe nodded and walked away into what must have been the ops room and left Max sitting in the now silent helicopter with the child.

Twenty minutes later Pascoe reappeared and patting the still sniffing dog on the head he approached the door of the aircraft. 'Got someone on the net from Joeys,' he said. 'Wants to know if you have a briefcase and how old you are.'

'Tell him to fuck off,' said Max.

'I did,' replied Pascoe. 'They're flying up at first light. Wankers.

23

We did it, Jannie, thought Max. We did it, my mate. Home and dry. Now just check the score cards and let's see about some bonus points.

Max entered the pre-fabricated hut after Pascoe and followed him down the narrow corridor.

'Don is away,' said Pascoe. 'You two can use his room.'

He led them to the end of the corridor and into what was obviously the mess, basic and spartan. Two club chairs and an old dining table were the only furniture and Max looked around as if seeing chairs and electric light for the first time.

'Sixpence!' Pascoe yelled. An old head appeared round the side of the door. 'Six beers. Cold ones. Then run a bath and make up Captain Collins' room.'

Max dropped the pack and with Sarah cradled on his hip stood in the centre of the room and eventually settled into a chair after Pasco had indicated to do so.

The beers arrived and together they drank silently, Max savouring the flavour and the sensation of the bubbles bursting against the roof of his mouth. He let Sarah sip the bottle and was rescued from refusing her when Sixpence came back with a Coke and a straw.

'He will bring food,' said Pascoe. 'I suggest you bath then put Sarah to bed and we can talk before the wankers get here.'

They bathed, the pair of them, Sarah playing with a shampoo bottle until the water was cold and then Max took her to the room. She was squeaky clean and dressed in a cut-down T-shirt, and as they entered Sixpence tactfully suggested that the little lady might like the bed with sheets. Max peeled back the mosquito net and there on the pillow was a teddy bear. Sarah squealed and demanded to be let down, and as Max turned to the door Pascoe appeared.

He didn't speak. He had a lump in his throat.

Eventually Pascoe said, 'Cashton went AWOL and drove a sixty-mile round trip that little bugger. Just had to roast him for it.'

Max settled Sarah down for the night, her first with Max in a bed since the night at the Van Heerden's farm. She snuggled into the pillow and said, 'Story?'

'Sounds reasonable,' said Max. 'Once upon a time there was a dog called Ungo...'

She giggled deliciously and he continued until the Sandman came.

Later, Pascoe queried the name and Max told him it was an in-joke.

They spoke late into the night. Max told Pascoe of the crash and the escape, the killing of Helen Johnson. He spoke of the run to the road and the kindness and subsequent deaths of the Van Heerdens, and Jannie's arrival. He spoke of the way that Jannie and Vicki looked at each other and Solomon's ways, of Robert Chapping, of the battle at the Mateke Hills and of the last desperate charge to the Bubye river. At times his eyes had that glitter and when he told Pascoe of the briefcase and the report and the massacre at the wreck his voice was soft and deadly dry. It worried Pascoe because for someone it bode ill and although he was convinced Max Seager was not the man he had been sent to extract, he was not sure the events were unrelated.

When Max eventually went to bed the moonbeams from the window lit Sarah's hair silver on the pillow. Her sleep was restless and at times she cried in her dreams and that was when Max decided to keep the promise he had made to her mother.

His own sleep was fitful and he was up long before the dawn.

Max was sifting through the few things they arrived with, answering Sarah's questions as he worked, when he heard the wump-wump-wump of a helicopter approaching.

Pascoe popped his head round the door. 'You're on report,' he said. 'In the ops room. Two of them. One bloodnut and one real smooth one. Don't take any shit. I'm off to Joeys.' He handed Max a piece of paper. 'I'll be on this number this afternoon if you need anything.'

Max followed him across the compound and stepped into the ops room. A tall, elegant man in a three-piece suit stood as he entered and held out his hand.

'Richard Vickery. Mr Seager, isn't it?'

Max nodded.

'I'm from Pretoria and we hoped... sorry, this is Mr Smit... we hoped that you might have something for us?' Vickery got straight to the point.

'Pascoe said you were asking about a briefcase,' said Max non-committally.

'Yes. Did you see it? It's very important we get that case.'

'I saw lots of people get shot,' Max said. 'I saw my friends die. And yes, I saw your briefcase.'

Vickery's face was slashed by an icy smile and Smit stood up from his pose against the window sill.

'Where?' Smit asked bluntly.

'At the wreck. The doctor had it. I think he hid it... he's dead too. Wants me to phone his wife.'

'Hid it where?' Vickery's smile vanished.

Max shrugged. 'I was going for the bush by then.'

'We didn't rescue for that, man. Tell us where you saw the case!' Smith snapped.

'I just told you I didn't see him hide it.'

'You'd better remember.' Smit's tone was threatening.

It was suddenly very quiet in the room and in the stillness the noise of a generator could be heard away in the distance.

Max's eyes glittered for a moment. 'Don't push your luck, Dutchman.' Max moved forward, daring Smit to repeat the threat.

Vickery stepped between them and urbanely simmered things down.

'Now, now, gentlemen. Mr Seager, would you like to collect your things and your little companion? You can fly back to Johannesburg with us. Press conference this afternoon. You may tell the world, as you requested.'

'It doesn't matter anymore,' Max said, and the room went quiet.

Old Chuseri knocked at Chapping's door and entered at the instructions mumbled from between pipe-clenching teeth.

Chapping looked up from the report he was reading.

'Sir, there is word from the south,' Chuseri said.

'Yes,' muttered Chapping. 'What is it?'

'There is talk of a battle in the Mateke Hills... where one with the markings of the Selous Scouts... where such a one killed many before he himself was taken... and the fires raged during the battle and blackened the sky... and while the fires burned another with a child fought south and was collected by helicopters and men from over the border...' The old man finished, his eyes blazing with the glory of the battle need to take the Pungwe.

'Thank you, Chuseri.' Chapping stood and went to the window and looked at the bush, red in the setting sun through the glass.

'Thank you.'

He would have to tell Ruth when she came home. Break it gently, the news about the son she never had.

'Chuseri?' He called after the figure walking out.

'Sir?' Answered the old scout.

'Any word of a girl... or the Shangaan?' Chapping asked.

Chuseri shook his head.

'Thank you,' finished Chapping and once again he turned to the window to watch the sun set over the bush.

The press conference was scheduled for the afternoon and after a two-hour interrogation Max was eventually allowed to go up to his room in the Carlton Hotel. He bathed with Sarah and then in clothes ordered from the shop in the foyer they went out, the two of them, rather like father and daughter.

He contacted a friend, a photographer and one of the recipients of the letters he wrote at the Van Heerdens' farm, Canaan, and visited the man immediately, and while there phoned a woman in Salisbury called Mrs Cochran. He made several other calls, one to a banker in Jersey, another to a firm of solicitors on the island. He went into a sports store and bought a Browning Hi-Power semi-automatic handgun against his Rhodesian Police warrant card and lastly went into a large department store. It was like an Aladdin's cave of treasures and several hundred rands later they were both equipped for a winter's day in London. Max put the overcoat on immediately. It was one of the variety you can put your hand through into the pockets.

He also put ribbons into Sarah's hair. It was too loose and the bow all wrong, and a woman helped him do it properly. She also surprised him by making a very obvious pass. He didn't think that women would do that to a man with a child. They then went into the tea shop and both made themselves almost ill eating cream cakes and chocolate bars and sugared almonds.

When they arrived back at the hotel the receptionist was all agog. She had read the function's notice board and seen 'Press Conference – M Seager' and wasn't sure if he was a movie star or what. He didn't look familiar but a press conference was something that only famous people gave, so he must be, surely?

By twelve they were both back in the double bed asleep and at four Max got up and dressed for the press conference. A babysitter arrived from the housekeeper's office and he walked downstairs into a packed seminar room. An hour later it was over and his eyes hurt from the batteries of camera lights, but he had done it. Now the shit would hit the fan, he thought, and now for the others. Now for the real ones.

24

They entered the room together, Smit and then Vickery. Smit had a smug look on his face.

'Don't you people knock?' Max said.

'Don't have to with this.' Smit waved a master key. 'Now just be a good boy and answer the questions.'

'Or what?'

'Or the kid is in a state welfare home within the hour and you have lots of trouble with your passport. Little things like that.'

'You have no grounds for putting her in custody, so fuck you, Smit.'

'The briefcase, Seager. Describe where it is again...'

There was a pause. The tension in the room mounted and to all in there it seemed hot in spite of the air conditioning. Vickery was sitting elegantly in a chair, one leg crossed over the other, and he spoke for the first time.

'Be reasonable, Seager. We need the briefcase and we can make it worth your while to go back for it. Lots of hard men, a fast terrain-radar chopper, everything. You'll be back in a day at the most.'

'Nothing personal, Vickery, but no way. I'm not going back. And you –' he looked at Smit '– listen carefully. You try anything with the child and I'll beat the shit out of you right here in the hotel. The one with all the reporters. Remember them from this afternoon? It won't wash, so fuck off out of my life.'

Vickery rose from the chair and moved towards the door. By now Smit was sweating and nervous. Jesus, thought Max, they must need the case badly. We know why, don't we.

They had reached the door before he said almost as an afterthought, 'Is it the case you need, or the film in the handle?'

Both men spun round. Smit had gone white and Vickery hurried back. 'Where is it?' He said.

'Safe,' said Max.

Vickery was quick. 'What do you want?'

'Well now, let me think. I reckon sixty-five people have died so far, because of that film. And that's just the good guys... the wreck...' Max was talking softly now and his eyes had that glitter again. 'Remember the wreck. All those dead people, all that pain, and that horror. Now there are just two of us left. It's time to pay the piper and the price is ten thousand per head, in Sterling. You're going to get off lightly. Imagine the insurance company if they knew this.'

Smit lunged forward. 'That's six hundred and fifty thousand,' he snarled, spittle flicking from his mouth, and his complexion an angry red like his hair.

'Shut up,' said Vickery and turned to Max. 'Where? And how? I'll get it cleared, no problem. We need that briefcase, Seager.'

Max handed him a piece of paper. 'It's on here. Jersey bank. Make the instructions. All very proper. It's a trust fund for an orphan.'

'You were pretty bloody sure we would pay,' Smit said bitterly.

'Oh I knew you would pay... once I had seen bits of the copy.'

Vickery, who by now was on the phone, looked up sharply.

'Sorry, didn't I tell you?' Max continued. 'Yes, had an old friend do some developing this morning. Most interesting. Oh yes, you will pay for that.'

'How much did you see?' Smit had gone white again.

'Oh, just bits, agent names, lots of odd things, a whole network really, about to come undone. Not worth sixty-five lives, I don't think. Your little cloak and dagger number got rumbled, so your man got scared and tried to run for it with the prize. Only you fucked up...'

'What would you know?' Interrupted Smit.

'I spent the last five years a counter-intelligence officer, you idiot. Read your files.'

Vickery had put down the phone now, and was listening intently as Max went on.

'But were the names of a few sympathisers worth all those lives? And the effort to get me out? Or the other crap in the last report? A few sleepers, a few surprising names? Were they fuck! It was the big one, wasn't it? The reason your man headed home instead of using the normal channels. What he had was too big for that. So big he risked his cover by breaking into the hotel room of the commission member who had the briefcase... so big he followed it to make sure, but he fucked up. They sussed him and then they shot down an aeroplane and killed all those people, and then they chased me and a small child for five hundred fucking miles!' He was shouting now. 'Why? What was the big one? They thought that agent was alive, and me. They thought I was your man. There was no altruism in that extraction. So what was the big one? Perhaps another agent?'

Smit was sweating and Vickery was leaning forward, his sharp eyes missing nothing.

'Perhaps,' Max said, 'another agent, someone in the government. I wondered how they always found our tracks again. They knew where to look! Someone with pictures or infrared, a satellite photo, but who had that access? Your people did, access to American satellite photos. You were covering the escape of what you thought was your agent. But someone else was seeing the pictures of us and telling the searchers where we were. So perhaps the name, the name everyone died for, is an agent in B.O.S.S., maybe East Germany's man embedded in South Africa's good old Bureau of State Security, or perhaps even the

Russians themselves own him. Someone deep in B.O.S.S., on their way up. Bright, successful and on their way to the top... worth protecting for the years to come.'

Smit gave a short laugh. 'This is ridiculous,' he said.

'Carry on,' said Vickery. 'I like this.'

'I would have walked away. Not my problem. But every time I did that some bastard kept shooting at me and they kept shooting at Sarah, and I started to get pissed off. I wanted to get that fucker. So I did.'

Max stopped and lit a cigarette, blew a stream of smoke into the tension-charged air and dropped his hand back into his pocket.

'Like they say in *The Sweeney*, Smit, you're fucking nicked.'

Vickery spun round, astonished, but in that millisecond an ugly black automatic had appeared in Smit's hand.

'Very clever... but not clever enough. You will both have to die now. Sad, but inevitable.'

'Why?' Seager asked. 'What was the payoff? Money?'

'You simpleton,' Smit said. 'Everything is money. You are a stupid policeman who assumes everyone is a common criminal. There are others like me, who believe that we can only be strong with a change of policies. Right wing is the only future for our country. The irony was that only Russia would finance the set-up, in exchange for sole rights to the uranium and the oil and the other wealth. They even want our Blacks for their mines in the Urals. It's gone too far. Yes, I'm their man, but you will never live to prove it.'

Max took another puff on the cigarette and then spoke. 'What now, Smit? A short struggle in which Vickery s unfortunately killed by me, who also happens to die?'

'Yes. I'll do it now,' he said almost sadly.

'Oh really,' said Max, who pulled the trigger of the Browning in his pocket and shot Smit through the heart. He pulled the weapon clear of his coat and walked forward. The body was very still except for a twitch in one finger.

'Max,' said a breathless Vickery whose heart had begun beating again. 'You certainly play things close to your chest. I thought we were buggered there. I really did.'

'No problem. He would never have walked away. There's a chap called Cashton up the hall with a shotgun.'

'But we would have been dead,' Vickery said.

Max smiled. 'Trust me. We'd have been fine. My deal stands, by the way. No money, no film. It's good, worth every cent. There's another one, very high up. Smit was only number two.'

That was when Pascoe stepped from the cupboard, an Ingram in his hands. 'Not interrupting, am I?'

'Trust you?' Vickery inquired.

An hour later, a telex safely received from a Jersey banker on overtime, Max walked down the hall towards the lifts, Sarah dozing peacefully on his right shoulder. Pascoe stepped from the doors of one and approached him.

'Well, then. You'll be away.' The statement was banal, but what do you say at a moment like this?

'Yes,' said Max. 'Thanks, Ken, for coming in and getting us, and your help earlier. And I'll send for Dingaan.'

'You're welcome, laddie. Any time. If you go straight to the basement there's a car and driver there. Airport is only fifty minutes and if you move it you can make the Perth flight.'

'Not Perth. Not yet. The UK first. Got to see some people.'

Pascoe nodded. He knew who that would be. Max moved Sarah to the other shoulder and held out his hand. Pascoe took it and nodded again, shook twice and then Max walked to the lift, Sarah's hair bright and shining yellow in the light.

'You're a lucky bastard, Seager,' Pascoe called.

Max frowned in confusion as the lift doors closed behind him.

The car was by the lifts in the basement, engine running, the driver in darkness. But in the light, resting on the steering wheel was a slender hand with apricot coloured nails and a large single solitaire diamond ring on the third finger. Then he knew why Pascoe had said it.

Epilogue

Polanski died eighteen months later, one of several victims of a 38th Battalion South African Defence Force mortar bomb that hit his command vehicle in Angola. Heine Guttman disappeared from sight for a while. Intelligence analysts assumed he was recalled to Berlin to answer for his failure, but he seemed to have redeemed himself because he turned up in Singapore as the Trade Attaché of the East German Embassy in that country.

The Honourable Minister was arrested by a furious and embarrassed Zimbabwean government after Max Seager's allegations to the world press prompted an inquiry. They, of course, never admitted their findings to anyone except the Minister, and he was driven down the old Bindura Road and shot in the back of the head with a nine-millimetre handgun. It wasn't his week. The day Max's allegations hit the world's press he finally tired of his mistress and after venting his anger the usual way he invited his driver and two bodyguards to do the same. He made a mistake, however. He left the girl the key to the kitchen door and she returned while he slept, obese and drunk, and opened his face with a flick knife. It was a delicate little pearl-handled number she had been given by a grateful pimp in Marseilles. He had been driven to the trial and heard the verdict swathed in bandages and went to his death the same way.

Orpheus lies in the same mass grave along with the other victims of the monstrosity and no one will ever know who he was, after all, Conrad Hugo, the man who recruited him, died years before.

There is talk around the cooking fires of the tribespeople in the Nuanetsi area of a new spirit that walks the night. The spirit is in the form of a leopard who lives in a gap in the nearby hills and at night is said to protect those most hated of all – the rangers and scouts of the no-hunting area over the river to the north.

Even those less superstitious give the Mateke Hills a wide berth after dark lest they are caught by the spirit Pungwe. There is, however, one poacher who smiles at the story and continues to hunt where he pleases.

Richard Vickery is now the sole controller of the African desk. Rumour has it that he has offered Max Seager a job at least twice.

Max and Svea Seager now live with their adopted daughter on Magnetic Island just off the north coast of Queensland in Australia. Sarah is a happy, healthy eight-year-old who calls them Mummy and Daddy. When she is older, Max will probably tell her everything, but now she's entirely theirs. Sarah still doesn't like thunder or fast-moving water, but loves an old, battered grey climber's pack with holes in the bottom. It holds her toys and sometimes she puts her biggest teddy in it with his head poking out of the top and his feet through the holes at the bottom, and Max wonders if she remembers.

They also have a son, a three-year-old called John, who is invariably called Jannie, and who has Svea's freckles and blonde hair.

Ken Pascoe now lives with his wife in Western Australia. He and Max sometimes get together at Christmas and when the men get drunk and mellow and they start to tell silly stories to each other, the ladies just shake their heads at the foolishness and admire Sarah's latest burnt attempt at chocolate chip cookies.

Max sometimes walks up the hill behind the house, where the rocks are very like parts of Africa.

High up in the rocks overlooking the Pacific Ocean there is a brass plaque with a simple inscription. It reads:

> For Jannie and Vicki, who would have liked it here
> December 27th, 1982

Below that, countersunk into the rock is a small gold cross, that all may know.

Made in the USA
Monee, IL
22 February 2024

53957327R00163